Splitting Heirs

SPLITTING HEIRS

by
Rick Hanson

KENSINGTON BOOKS

http://www.kensingtonbooks.com

KENSINGTON BOOKS are published by

Kensington Publishing Corp.
850 Third Avenue
New York, NY 10022

Library of Congress Card Catalog Number: 96-80065
ISBN 1-57566-194-2

First Printing: August, 1997
10 9 8 7 6 5 4 3 2 1

Printed in the United States of America

For the gentle people of Toledo, Oregon
You will always possess a warm place in my heart.

Chapter
One

I know a process server when I see one, and the guy on my front porch definitely fit the genus of species. When I caught my first glimpse of him climbing out of his rusting, oxidized, mango-green Vega, probably the last one in existence, I was instinctively aware that this would not be a pleasant way to start the day.

He jabbed the doorbell twice in rapid succession, as if to emphasize the vast, important, nonsocial nature of his visit. Then he eased back slowly to lurk at the edge of the stoop, alternating glances between the front door and my perfectly restored '56 Chevy convertible in the driveway, ready to tackle me if I tried to make a fast break out the back door and dive behind the steering wheel. His uniform—a green and yellow plaid sport jacket worn over shiny brown trousers—must have been too hot for the May morning, because sweat soaked the collar of his wrinkled gray shirt. His balding skull gleamed pink with sunburn between the combed and plastered strands that attempted to impersonate a full head of hair.

I yanked open the door and glared down at him in my version of an intimidating manner. I'm not very broad, but I had at least seven inches in height on this guy.

"Adam McCleet?"

His voice was nasal and whiny. Definitely, this guy was serving me with papers or had come to repossess my car, my sofa, or my lawn.

"Who?" I demanded.

"You are Adam McCleet, aren't you?"

"Hell, no. He moved out a couple months ago. I think he's in Monaco playing polo with Princess Stephanie."

"You look like Adam McCleet." He had a photograph. It was one of those publicity pictures for an art show where my sculptures were featured. Many times, I had told my beloved Alison who owns the art gallery where my works are usually shown that using my likeness for promotion was a bad idea. I was a cop once, and I'd made a number of formidable enemies on the dark side of the law.

I glanced at the picture. "Yeah, he's my twin."

The guy narrowed his beady little eyes. "Adam McCleet doesn't have a twin brother. His only other living relative in Portland is his sister, Margot."

"That's me." I grinned, thinking how unfortunate it would be for this sleazy little man if he actually was facing my younger sister, Margot the Malevolent. She was a thousand times more fearsome than me. Margot devoured process servers for lunch and snacked on Girl Scouts peddling cookies in the afternoon. Confidently, I continued. "I'm Margot. But I recently had a sex-change operation. I always felt like Boris Karloff in a woman's body."

The plaid man wasn't buying it. He hitched up the belt of his brown trousers under his bulging belly as if displaying his flab would scare me. "Well, it's too bad you're not Adam McCleet, because I'm here to inform him that he has been mentioned in the will of Graden Porcelli."

"Will?" That sounded promising. I felt my ears perk up like a hungry cat who'd just caught a whiff of tuna.

"Yeah," the guy continued, "but you couldn't be Adam McCleet because the attorney I work for has sent him four letters in the past three weeks and has left several phone messages."

I remembered the letters. As soon as I saw that the return address was an attorney, I filed them, unopened, in a large box beside my desk labeled FRIGHTENING CORRESPONDENCE. And I recalled the phone messages, all of which I had erased, following the logic that if they can't talk to me, they can't say anything I don't want to hear.

I pulled the door closed and stepped around the bulging man on the porch. "If you'll excuse me, I was on my way out."

"Well, Ms. McCleet, if you happen to run into your brother, you might tell him that he's got some bucks coming. Reading of the will is tomorrow morning at ten o'clock in Newport."

"I'll be sure and pass that on if I see him. Bye-bye, now." I got into my car and keyed the ignition, listening for a moment with great satisfaction to the purr of the engine. In the rearview mirror I watched the process server drive away. After the smoking Vega rounded the corner at the end of my block, I raced back into the house and broke open the frightening correspondence file.

I shuffled through various windowed envelopes marked "last notice." "Beware." "Dire consequences." "Don't ignore this, deadbeat." And I found two letters with the sedate return address of a lawyer in Newport, Oregon, down the coast from Portland.

Snatching the letters, I returned to the car and headed into downtown. I was already late for lunch with Alison and some wealthy buyer who wanted to meet me, the artist, before sinking large sums of money into my sculptures. I had never understood this rationale, and I always felt like a pimp when I was pushing my own work. However, at the moment I was in need of cash and willing to perform excessive acts of sucking-up.

As I drove to the city from my home near Willamette Park, I tried to recall the name Graden Porcelli and drew a blank. Who was this guy? Had this complete stranger really named me in his will? Why?

At a stoplight on Southwest Macadam, I peeled open one of the letters and discovered that the process-server guy had been telling the truth. I was mentioned in the will. If I wanted my inheritance, I needed to show up at the reading.

I parked near Tenth and Glisan and walked the two blocks to Alison's gallery in the Pearl District. As I turned the corner I spotted Alison's assistant, Monte, pacing under the awning outside the Brooks Art Gallery. As usual, Monte's fashion sense redefined flamboyant. He looked like a punk version of Gainsborough's Blue Boy in neon-blue knickers and vest with a frilly shirt.

"Oh, my God, Adam," he trilled. "There you are." He waggled his forefinger at me. "Late, late, late."

I mumbled something about how that was no way to talk to the Porcelli heir, and Monte stiffened as if he'd been smacked by a lightning bolt. "Graden Porcelli?"

"Do you know him?"

"Color me puce if I don't! Everybody, and I do mean everybody, knows of Graden Porcelli, the salmon king."

Everybody except me. "He died recently?"

"Last week. Oh, my God, it was so tragic. He was dining alone aboard his hundred-foot yacht, the *Jonah*. He was drinking champagne, probably sitting back and admiring his collection of Picasso originals, when a fish bone lodged in his throat. He choked before any of the swarthy Italian crewmen could Heimlich him. Of course, he was in his seventies and had been in mucho failing health. Some say it was suicide."

That would have to be a first, I thought. Jamming a fish bone sideways into one's own throat was a rare, if not unheard-of method of self-inflicted demise. "So, this Porcelli was rich?"

"Does Kuwait have oil? Does Cher have tattoos? Does Midol relieve menstrual cramps?"

"Was he in oil?"

"Fish, Adam. Graden Porcelli was up to his armpits in fish. Now, you run along inside. Alison is waiting."

Inside the gallery I approached her. Even when annoyed, Alison was adorable. Her green eyes flashed me a message: You schmuck! But her incredible body spoke another language, and I was lucky enough to be the only man in her life allowed to translate the subtle flare of her hips and the perfect symmetry of her breasts. I found it difficult to look at her without imagining the silken delights hiding beneath her chic outer garments. Today she wore a simple white linen shift that contrasted beautifully with her golden tan and auburn hair. I suspected a lacy white bra and thong panties.

She leaned close to me, giving me a whiff of her jasmine perfume, and whispered, "Putz!" Aloud she said, "Adam, I'd like you to meet Desiree Leggett. She's interested in your sculpture of the satyr."

I couldn't imagine why anyone would care about that particular half-finished work which I referred to as "Goat Boy." I seldom sculpt men, because I tend to be bored halfway through, and this attempt was no exception. Only because I hadn't been able to produce much of anything lately, Alison had insisted on displaying this critter.

"Actually, Mr. McCleet, I'm very interested in you."

Desiree Leggett looked like her name—an object of desire with the legs of a *Sports Illustrated* swimsuit model. Her black blouse couldn't have been cut any lower. Her black skirt couldn't have been any tighter or shorter. Her long, straight blond hair almost touched the hem.

I accepted the hand that she held toward me. "Hi."

"I believe you knew my uncle Grady," she said.

"Your uncle Grady?" I questioned.

"Yes. Graden Porcelli." She giggled, and the effect of cool blond gorgeousness dissipated in an unfortunate snorting noise. "Tell me, Adam, how did you know him?"

"Huh?" Who was this guy? Why was I the only person who never heard of him?

"Were you golfing buddies?" She twinkled and snorted. "Did you fish together? Uncle Grady loved to fish."

"I don't really remember," I said.

Her snarfing laughter took on a note of irritation, more like honking geese. "Oh, please! Don't lie, Adam. You must have known him well."

"Must have," I agreed. "Why else would he mention me in his will?"

"Exactly." She pounced on my words. Her long legs took a step toward me, covering about six feet in one fierce stride. "Why the hell would he mention you?"

"Good karma?"

"I know about you, mister. Vietnam vet. Former cop on the Portland police force. A semisuccessful sculptor, currently in a slump. You like sailing and inherited a boat, the *Raptor*. Now you're about to inherit again. I think that's pretty damn suspicious, Mister Nobody! What did you do to deserve one penny of Uncle Grady's money?"

"I was a Duncan yo-yo champ in sixth grade." I grinned in her face, noticing that her bared fangs were perfectly capped. "I could have been a contender for the national title, but a serious injury to my yo-yo finger held me back." I displayed the middle finger of my right fist.

Alison pulled my arm down. "Desiree, could we discuss the sculpture? I thought you had some questions about the satyr."

"As if!" She glared at me, then at Alison.

"But you said you were interested," Alison persisted.

"As if I would be interested in a work that is derivative of Andy Warhol on a bad hair day." She pointed at me with a long, skinny finger. "I wanted to see him and to tell him that he had better not get in the way of my inheritance." A small globule of spit shot from between her capped teeth and nailed me in the forehead.

Monte fluttered up close to us with ceramic cups on a silver tray. "Cafe mocha?"

"Take your mocha and shove it," Desiree instructed. Her next snort was like a raging bull. "If you know what's good for you, McCleet, you won't show up at the reading."

She stalked toward the exit like a whooping crane in a footrace, slamming the door as she left.

Alison gazed at me and raised her eyebrows. "A friend of yours?"

"What did she mean, Andy Warhol on a bad hair day?" I thought every day was pretty much a bad hair day for Andy.

" 'Goat Boy' is not your best work, Adam." She took a cafe mocha from Monte and sipped delicately. "But that still doesn't explain that snorting woman's hostility. Is there something you want to tell me?"

She spoke in the tone of someone who wanted to say: What stupid thing have you done this time? But Alison was my best supporter. In her classy, sophisticated way, she was my cheerleader. And she was always ready to give me the benefit of the doubt.

I pulled out the attorney's letters and placed them in her capable hands. She was good with business details; that was how she had managed to make a success of Brooks Gallery in the overcrowded Portland art world.

When she scanned the lawyer's letter and looked back at me, her eyes glittered like greedy emeralds. "You're going to inherit from Graden Porcelli, the salmon king?"

"I didn't even know his name," I said.

"I'll explain," she said. "Monte, cancel my schedule for tomorrow. Adam and I will be attending the reading of Graden Porcelli's last will and testament. We'll be in Newport. Tomorrow at ten."

The lawyer's office was standing room only, and I was the only person not wearing black. Even Alison had decided that the proper attire for a will reading was a black sleeveless rayon dress. She didn't notice how the fabric clung to her curves, but I did. And I liked it.

I still couldn't get too excited about this unfathomable connection to a man I couldn't remember. In the back of my noggin, I kept thinking that this whole business was somebody's idea of a practical joke.

Alison was taking things more seriously. She did that when money was involved. Earlier that morning, as we followed a parade of aluminum motor homes bulging with tourists down the coast highway to Newport, she'd tried to jog my memory by reading the obituary-style newspaper article that had followed Graden Porcelli's death.

It seemed that upon returning from World War II, Graden and a partner had done a Forrest Gump, but with salmon. The fish-packing plant they established on Yaquina Bay at Newport was the first to ship internationally. Graden's true genius lay in distribution, managing to get fresh and canned salmon to a growing marketplace. As the business grew, he established more plants in California, Washington, and Alaska. He was a millionaire, many times over, survived by his widow, Amelia, and a son, Harrison, and a bunch of extended family which, I presumed, included the rude, stork-legged, snorting, spitting, stalking female Desiree Leggett.

She was there in the lawyer's office, and she pointed me out to the tall, leathery gentleman standing beside her when I entered.

Alison and I made our way to the opposite side of the office by the windows.

When the lawyer, a busy little man with a walrus mustache, bustled into the room, there was a hush. "Thank you all for coming," he said. "I apologize for the delay in the reading of the will, but Graden stipulated a waiting period of ten days following his funeral so that all of you might have a chance to be present."

He took a videotape from his briefcase and held it up. "Ready?"

He plugged the tape into the VCR beneath a large-screen television, and we all settled back to watch.

The image on the screen showed a burly man with almost no neck. He completed a successful putt across the green carpet of an office, straightened the collar on his beige polo shirt, and looked up at the camera.

"I, Graden Porcelli, being of sound mind and body, dictate these conditions to my last will. If you're watching this, I'm dead and buried. But that's okay by me, I've had a good, long life that turned out a hell of a lot better than I expected."

His statement elicited a sob from an elderly woman with pure white hair piled high on top of her head. I assumed she was the grieving widow, Amelia.

On the screen, Graden moved toward the camera so that his face was in extreme close-up. I could count the pores on his bulbous red nose and see the flecks of gold in his muddy brown eyes. "Welcome to my will," he whispered. "Some of you, I loved. Others disappointed me. Others, I hated. But I'm going to do right by all of you."

He stepped back from the camera and leaned against a carved rosewood desk. On the surface beside him was a ship in a bottle which was not just any ship. It was my guess that this was a replica of his own yacht, the _Jonah,_ with colors flying.

Graden Porcelli said, "That's right, folks. I'm going to do

right by my family and associates. That's my way. I haven't changed that much from the days, long ago, when I was just a simple fisherman."

"Bullshit!" roared a scruffy old man who stood near the door. "If that cocker is a fisherman, I'm a freakin' flounder."

The lawyer paused the tape and looked at the rest of us. "For those of you who don't know him, the gentleman who just spoke is Tiger Jorgenson."

"They know who the hell I am," Tiger said. "And this is bullshit!"

"Please, Mr. Jorgenson, wait and see. I promise that this bullshit will be worth your while."

The lawyer started the tape again.

Graden now held something in his hand. It looked like a tulip, and he placed it back in a vase on the desk before continuing. "Here's what I'm going to do. Liquidate everything. I've had a number of offers on the packing plants, so I'm going to sell the damn things. And the vacation houses and the property and every blamed one of my possessions. The whole six and seven-eighths. The whole kit and kaboodle. The whole nine yards, lock, stock, and barrel. That's the job of the lawyers, like Jimmy Caruthers here."

The lawyer nodded to all of us.

"Jimmy is my executor," Graden explained, "and he's going to be in charge of the liquidating process. He's got all this stuff written out in detail if any of you have questions."

The lawyer held up a huge sheaf of papers.

Graden continued. "Then here's what happens: All the money goes into a pot. We stir it up and, at the end of one month, the cash gets broken into seven equal parts and distributed."

The grieving widow flew from her front row seat like a gawky blackbird with a white plume. "Graden, you bastard! That's my money! How dare you!"

Again, the lawyer, Jimmy Caruthers, paused the tape. "Mrs. Porcelli, please take your seat."

"He can't do that, can he?"

"It's his money. Since he couldn't take it with him, he can disperse it in any manner he chooses."

"But I was his wife! It's mine!"

"The house is yours," the lawyer assured her. "It's in your name. However, the rest of the estate belonged to your late husband and he can do whatever he wants with it."

The tape restarted. Graden was chuckling. "Bet this pisses you off, Amelia. But you're even older than me. Truth is, I'm surprised you lived this long. You'll do just fine for the little bit of time you have left."

"Doncha know, it pisses me off," the woman said darkly.

On the tape Graden strolled over to a bookshelf and leaned against it. "Here are the big seven. My wife. And my son, of course. And Sam Leggett, my nephew who once shot eight under par. My quiet little niece, Tia. Whit Parkens, my plant manager for the past twenty-five years. Tiger Jorgenson, my partner when I was first starting out. And Adam McCleet."

"Who?" There came a chorus in the room.

Alison pressed close beside me, and I was glad to have her there. She was a sweet harbor of sanity against this tidal wave of weirdness.

The tape continued. Graden said, "Mr. McCleet, would you please step forward?"

This was the first time I'd received an order from somebody who was dead, somebody who I never even knew in life. A long time ago, I was a Marine. I obeyed a lot of orders from people who, in retrospect, I realized were dullards trying to use me for body-bag stuffing. The experience left a bitter taste in my mouth, but my lack of respect for authority did not extend to dead people, so I stood.

"Mr. McCleet," said Graden. "Your inheritance is based on

a special stipulation. I want you to take a look around Jimmy's office. The other six heirs are here. Plus their families and friends and possibly even a couple of their advisers."

By my rough estimate, there must have been twenty to thirty people in that office.

"One of them," Graden said, "is a murderer."

Instead of protests, there was an eerie silence. Glances were exchanged. Elbows nudged.

On the tape, Graden slipped into a navy-blue sport jacket with a crest above the pocket and a pin that looked like a military decoration on the lapel. "Here's how you get your money, Adam. You identify the killer before you all get together again in one month. If you fail, your money goes back into the pot to be dispersed with the other six. By the way, folks, if anybody else is eliminated from the pool . . ."

Like being killed by the murderer among them, I thought.

". . . their money goes back into the pot too."

He gave a casual salute. "You once did me a bitter favor, Adam, and I've never forgotten it."

What favor? I didn't know this guy. I had never known him.

Graden waved. "So long, folks. Sorry I can't be there with you to watch the fun. I'll catch you on the flipflop."

The tape turned to static.

Jimmy Caruthers, the lawyer, switched off the television. "I have more documentation for those of you who are interested. The worth of Graden Porcelli's estate after taxes and death duties will be well over fifteen million dollars. In dividing the capital after liquidation, you will each receive in excess of two point one million dollars."

I felt Alison's hand grasp my arm. Her fingernails dug into my skin. She whispered, "Don't do it, Adam. This is crazy."

How could I say no? Two point one million bucks would buy a lot of Froot Loops.

Chapter
Two

At lunch with Alison I began to visualize my two point one million in a stack of ten-dollar bills that would reach to twice the height of the mast on my sailboat. Then I translated the tens into shiny copper-colored pennies, enough pennies to cover a football field more than thirty times, enough pennies to fill a swimming pool. In the middle of my Scrooge McDuck fantasy, as I did the Australian crawl through my fortune, blissfully choking on the metallic stink of money, Alison interrupted.

"Adam, are you listening to me?"

I focused on her lovely, practical face. "I'm listening."

"And what were we talking about?"

"Money," I intoned in a feral growl. "Money and more money. I could retire."

"Ah," she said.

Generously, Alison did not point out that my current state of self-employment was as close to retirement as one man could get without actually lapsing into a coma. When I work, I work hard. Sculpting can be strenuous, both physically and mentally.

However—and, at the moment, this however defined my entire existence—if I'm not actively creative, I do next to nothing.

Right now I spent my days floating aimlessly on the steady currents of the Willamette River or undertaking such productive endeavors as: spending an entire afternoon moving ropes from one side of the dock to the other. Or staring into space. Or planting grass seeds in my belly-button lint.

Some artsy-type people called it block, a static blip in the creative flow during which the muse is absent. Being from a humble but earnest blue-collar background, I called it goofing off. What had started as a little vacation had become a way of life.

"Adam, this whole Porcelli setup is too bizarre. I'm worried. It seems dangerous."

I reached across the table and took her hand. "I'm going to do it."

"I really wish you wouldn't. Those people—"

"Suppose Ed McMahon was standing on my front porch with his ten-million-dollar sweepstakes check and my leg was caught in a bear trap. Would I gnaw off my own limb to answer the door? In a heartbeat. If I found the winning lottery ticket while on safari, would I limp barefoot across a Sahara of molten glass to claim my prize? Without a second thought. It's worth the risk, hon."

"I'd feel a lot better if you could remember that favor you did for Graden Porcelli."

To tell the truth, so would I. "It was probably when I was a cop. Maybe I rescued him from a mugger or caught somebody who burgled his house."

"Wouldn't you remember that?"

My path had crossed many others during my years on the police force. I could recall, with clarity, only five or six incidents, all of which involved homicides and a lot of paperwork.

When the waitress arrived at the table, I was still in the throes of potential millionairehood. "Lobster," I said.

"Sorry, we don't serve lobster for lunch. I got a nice crab salad."

That would have to do. Though I felt like ordering their finest wine which, given the lowbrow atmosphere of this little diner, was probably Ripple deluxe, I opted for coffee. In two hours I would be returning to the offices of Jimmy Caruthers, the lawyer, for more instructions, and I wanted to keep my wits about me.

Alison cocked her head and studied me. "Would you really quit sculpting if you were rich?"

"I don't know. The point is that I wouldn't have to do anything. Therefore, anything I chose to do would be fun."

"Is your life so terrible right now?"

That was a loaded question, and I took care to answer quickly. "Some parts of my life are excellent. The parts in which you are involved, for example. But this whole struggling-artist thing is highly overrated. As much as I hate to admit it, I'm feeling a little discouraged. I love sculpting, but it's hard to stay at it when I don't know where the next mortgage payment is coming from. Two point one million dollars is a lot of encouragement."

The waitress returned with our lunch at the same time a familiar person strode through the door and scanned the restaurant. He was one of the people at the reading of the will, but I wasn't sure which one.

He alleviated my curiosity by swaggering his long, lanky body over to our table and extending his hand. "Whit Parkens," he said. "I'm one of the six heirs. I guess that's seven, counting you."

I shook his hand, introduced him to Alison, and asked, "Which heir are you?"

"The plant manager. I worked thirty years for the salmon king. Started as a kid on the line and stayed there."

Apparently, the job had agreed with him. Laugh lines were deeply etched into his lean, weathered face. Though he looked uncomfortable in his black suit, his grooming was impeccable. His gray hair was neatly parted on the side. His white shirt was perfectly starched.

When I invited him to sit and share a coffee with us, he waved toward the door. A wraithlike woman who was so bland that I hadn't even noticed her wafted across the tiled floor of the diner. In her black mourning dress, she looked like a crow's feather caught on the wind.

"My wife," Whit said. "Dottie Parkens. She wears the pants in the family."

I found that hard to believe. Dottie didn't take up enough space to fill one leg of my Dockers.

I turned to Whit. "What did you think of the will?"

"Just like Graden. He sure as hell liked to stir things up. Couldn't stand it if everything was moving steady and smooth."

As Whit talked, the creases in his face deepened, and I had the idea that half of the wrinkles were from laughing and half were from wincing in pain. An interesting face, I thought. If I had been into portraiture, I might have wanted to paint him. Whit waved to the waitress and ordered two coffees.

"Oh, yeah," he said. "Graden loved change, he did."

"Was that a problem for you at the packing plant?"

"Damn right, it was. Everything on schedule, and Graden would come in and tear out half the conveyor belts to upgrade the system. My workers would be off for two days, then back on overtime and double pay for four days to catch up. Sure as shit, Graden would complain about the dip in profits."

Dottie laid her dainty white hand on his shoulder. "Don't get yourself worked up, sweetie. You know what the doctor said."

"High blood pressure," he explained. His coffee arrived and he sucked down half a cup. "I'm supposed to be taking it easy."

"I wanted Whit to retire," Dottie put in.

He made a warning noise in the back of his throat that was drowned in another gulp of coffee.

"Well, now he has to retire," Dottie said. "All the plants will be sold off."

"Not so fast," Whit said. "There might be a place for me with the new management. Don't know what I'd do with myself all day if I wasn't working. I'd miss it. Man needs to go to work every day. To bring home the bacon."

"The inheritance ought to keep you in bacon," I ventured to suggest.

"Sheep," Dottie said with a perky spark of enthusiasm. "It'll buy a lot of sheep."

"That's right." Whit explained, "We've already decided to use the money to pay for Dottie's sheep farm."

There was a strange reluctance in his voice, similar to a convicted felon accepting his life sentence. It was obvious that Whit didn't want to retire from the fish business and be home with Dottie's sheep all day.

She leaned forward in her chair. Though her voice was reedy and soft, her excitement was obvious in her glittering eyes and rapid speech. "We already own a little trailer house outside Newport. Now we can buy another thirty or forty acres, and I can build my flock."

"Of sheep?" Alison inquired.

"Right now we have only three ewes and a ram. And three baby lambies. They're wonderful animals," she said. "And smart too."

"Like hell they are," Whit muttered. He finished off his coffee and ordered another cup.

"Very, very smart," Dottie said more strongly. She seemed to expand in size when she discussed her beloved ovines. "My family is Basque, and sheep raising is in my blood."

"If they're so smart," Whit said, "how come that fat ewe

waddled up the steps and into the kitchen before giving birth? Huh? Does that sound smart to you?"

"She was cold," Dottie defended her flock. "You understand, Mr. McCleet. Don't you?"

When she looked directly into my eyes, I saw a steely will-power. Or, considering her fondness for sheep, a wool power. I understood very well. Dottie was one of those iron-butterfly kind of females who look like they're so delicate they would blow away in a stiff breeze, when it would actually take a cyclone to deter them from their plans.

"If the damned sheep are so smart," Whit said, "why do they eat the roses?"

"Because they need the roughage." Dottie continued to stare at me. "Anyway, we thought it would only be polite to introduce ourselves to you and give you our address so you could ask us any sort of question that you might have."

"I could probably do that right now," I said. "Do you have any idea what murder Graden was talking about?"

"None at all," Dottie said. "We couldn't even think of a mysterious death."

I looked toward Whit. "Was there anything at the plant? Any kind of strange accident?"

"Nope."

His second cup of coffee arrived, and he downed it with the unquenchable thirst of a true caffeine freak. I wondered what else Whit might be addicted to. Running a fish-packing plant wasn't a job for a wuss. Among his male peers, I suspected that Whit was known as a rugged son of a bitch, tough enough to maintain the respect of a factory full of fishermen and packers for the thirty years he'd worked for Graden. Hard-drinking too?

It was a possibility I needed to consider.

I made another feeble attempt at a direct frontal assault in my questions. "So, you have no idea who might be the murderer among you six people?"

"Well," Dottie said, "if you ask me, it has to be Amelia, Graden's widow."

Whit rumbled, "If the damned sheep are so smart that they know what's nutritional, why will they lap up whiskey when I put it in a pan and get drunk?"

"You haven't been doing that again, have you?"

Whit chuckled. "You should see it, McCleet. Drunk sheep. They stagger around on their stupid sheep legs and fall over, making bah noises. It's their best trick."

"Whit," she snapped, "nobody is interested in hearing about how you torture the sheep."

"It's pretty damned funny. Bah, bah, and thud, down they go on their sheep asses."

Dottie turned away from him. "Oh, and that Desiree person! She's a good murder suspect. I could tell you some tales about that young lady."

"I don't like her either," Alison said, encouraging Dottie to keep talking.

"Desiree is so selfish. Her hubby, Sam, has been wanting children for years, and she refuses to get pregnant." Dottie beamed at Alison. "Whit and I have six kids and four grandchildren."

"How nice," Alison murmured.

"After we buy our acreage," Dottie said, "I'm going to ask the children to come back home and help me take care of my flock."

Whit's comment was drowned in the last of his second cup of coffee.

"With two million dollars," Dottie said, "we can buy a couple more trailers. Some of the kids have had a rough time finding work, but I'm sure they'll settle down with the flock. They really are wonderful children."

"Dumber than the sheep," Whit concluded.

Dottie glared at him and shoved a business card across the

tabletop to me. "We need to be going now. Call us anytime, Adam, we'd love to have you visit."

Whit pushed himself away from the table, finished Dottie's coffee, and sighed. "I don't think I'm going to like retirement."

When he rose heavily to his feet, Dottie fluttered close to him and straightened his necktie. "Don't you dare say that, honey pie. This is what I've been planning for. All our lives."

Her words sounded like a threat to me, but Whit shuffled after her. He was docile as a baby lamb.

"Interesting couple," Alison said, picking up the card that Dottie had left for me. She read the curlicue script writing. "Isn't this cute? It gives their address and then says: Ewe and me, baby."

"Whit's business card probably says: Ram it down my throat."

"I wonder why they wanted to talk to you?"

"Making sure that I thought they were innocent," I said. Which immediately made me think they were guilty.

"Whit didn't seem dangerous to me," Alison said. "He might be a little grumpy, but he lets Dottie lead him around."

"Like a lamb to the slaughter?"

She groaned.

"Anyway, the murderer might be Dottie. In Graden's video, he didn't specifically say that the murderer was one of the six heirs."

"He didn't?"

I might have reminded her that I was a former cop, a trained observer when it came to picking up clues, but I didn't need to show off for Alison. "Graden said the murderer was someone in the room, and he also pointed out that the room would probably be full of heirs and friends."

"You're right," she conceded. "So, instead of focusing on six potential killers, you're looking at probably twenty or thirty."

"Exactly."

"I really don't like this, Adam."

We left the restaurant and meandered in and out of several crowded gift shops along Newport's bustling bay front, killing time until our afternoon appointment with Jimmy Caruthers, attorney for Graden Porcelli.

Unimpressed with the collection of quaint souvenirs, Alison stuck on one theme: Taking on this assignment would be hazardous to my health. "How come you're so protective all of a sudden?"

"Because I care about you?"

"If I recall correctly, there have been any number of times when you've urged me to plunge into certain death."

"Only because someone near and dear was in danger," she said. "What do you have to gain from this? Only money, Adam."

"Thanks for reminding me." Two point one million dollars!

In the reception area of Caruthers and Carmichael, Attorneys at Law, we encountered the process server who had hovered on my porch the previous day. I probably should have thanked the guy for giving me this shot at the Porcelli fortune, but he wasn't the sort who would accept gratitude gracefully. I could tell by the way he slouched on the sofa and his manner of straightening the lapels on the green and yellow plaid jacket he still wore with the brown trousers.

"Well, well," he said with a greasy smirk, "if it isn't the transvestite."

Alison glanced at me, showing little surprise at this greeting. "Is there something I should know about?"

I decided to thank the guy whether he wanted it or not. I grabbed his ears and planted a juicy kiss in the middle of his balding forehead.

"Hey!" He batted me away. "Stop that."

"Of course, my good man." I planned to call a lot of people "my good man" after I was rich.

The secretary ushered us into the inner chamber. Without all the people, Jimmy Caruthers had a spacious office with a view of the bay. Very nice, very expensive, and this tidy fellow with the helpful smile under his thick mustache seemed rich enough to suit the office.

"Please, be seated." Jimmy indicated two large, comfortable-looking chairs opposite his desk.

As we sat, he rubbed his palms together as if he were washing his hands. "Would you care for a beverage? Tea? Coffee?"

I thought of Whit Parkens. Did he also have an interview with the attorney? It seemed likely.

"First," said Caruthers, clasping his hands and looking sincere. "I must apologize for the behavior of Desiree. She weaseled information from my investigator—"

"The plaid guy?"

"Yes. His wardrobe is unfortunate. Anyway, Desiree got a few tips from him on the other heirs, and your name came up, Mr. McCleet." His grin stretched to the outskirts of his mustache. "She was, however, as surprised by the provisos of the will as any of the others."

Dipping into his desk drawer, he extracted a folder and passed it to me. This time, his hand-washing gesture had a distinctly Pontius Pilate cast to it. "This should explain everything, Mr. McCleet."

"I'm not much on legal documents," I admitted.

"So my investigator tells me."

"Could you explain this without the 'whereas' and 'heretofore' language?"

"It's really quite simple," he said. "If you are able to discover which of the people in the room is a murderer before the meeting next month, you will receive a share in the inheritance."

"So I could just walk into the room, point my finger, and say: You did it."

"Not exactly." His hands clenched. "You will need to investigate and produce evidence. Though you will not be responsible for a jury verdict, your proof should be sufficient to ensure an indictment."

This was beginning to sound like a parlor game to me, and it has been my experience that murderers were not known for playing fair. Alison might be correct in assuming that the risks in taking on this challenge outweighed the possibility of reward. "Let me get this straight. I'm supposed to wait until next month, after you've liquidated everything and everybody gets together again in this office?"

"Heavens, no! As soon as you have sufficient evidence to cause an arrest, you must take action. I'll call a special meeting. Really, McCleet, we can't allow this murderer to be roaming around free."

He was talking like he knew something, so I cleverly inquired, "Why not?"

"It's obvious, McCleet."

But he wasn't going to tell me. He tilted back in the chair and swirled his fingers around each other. "This is the single most disturbing aspect of Graden's will. Believe me, I thought long and hard about dangers involved before I agreed to arrange his affairs in the manner he so desired."

"Dangers," Alison repeated for my benefit. To Jimmy she said, "It seemed to me that finding a murderer would be extremely dangerous."

"Graden assured me that Mr. McCleet would be able to handle the difficulties of this investigation."

Obviously, I was missing something. "We are talking about a murder that has already occurred. Correct?"

"Yes," said the attorney. "But Graden refused to confide any details. It is my fondest hope that the murder never occurred. Or that it was figurative rather than literal."

I was familiar with the concept of figurative death. It was the insidious kind of murder that comes from killing a dream or destroying someone's future. This was the cruelest demise, one that could take years. Given my choice, I would take a bullet between the eyes any day.

I looked triumphantly at Alison. "In that case, the danger wouldn't be real physical danger. Would it?"

"Probably not. However, it would make your job of proving guilt far more difficult."

I could see my two point one million dollars taking wing and flying far, far away.

"It's still dangerous," Alison said.

Jimmy Caruthers smiled warmly at her. "I see you have a grasp of the situation. Each of the heirs has an equal claim on the money. The fewer people with a claim, the greater each individual share becomes. Unfortunately, if we have a real killer in our midst, we have just given that individual a million-dollar motive to kill again."

Chapter
Three

Included in the dossier that Jimmy Caruthers gave me was a legal explanation of my part in this lethal game of charades along with a listing of names and vital information for the Big Six who would inherit.

The first thing I did after returning to Portland was to contact Nick Gabreski, my cop buddy who now worked in Missing Persons. For something as potentially lucrative as this case, I figured it was worth a trip to the cop house.

Though I hadn't left the Portland PD under dishonorable circumstances, most of the guys who still remembered me in a uniform also recalled the bad attitude that kept me on the beat instead of riding behind a detective's desk in plainclothes. My mouth didn't get me into a lot of trouble on the streets, but I have always had a difficult time dealing with authority figures. My basic philosophy, something I learned in Vietnam, was different from that of my superior officers. In my opinion, my job as a cop was: A. Survival. B. Catching bad guys. C. Following orders. In that order.

Invariably, my bosses disagreed.

I particularly remembered one time when the department hired a shrink, named Dr. Namby-Pamby Clown, to enhance group interaction and communication. Apart from the fact that the therapy session was off-duty time and I wasn't getting paid to bare my soul, I did not feel compelled to share warm-fuzzies with the guys on my watch. I really didn't care if I was okay and they were okay as long as we managed to protect each other's blind sides and get the job done. We didn't have to waste time patting each other on the butt.

The whole meeting boiled down to one fatal moment when my captain looked straight at me and, under the direction of Dr. Namby-Pamby, said, "I sense a deep hostility in some of the officers. I feel that they resent my authority."

"I hear what you're saying," Dr. Namby-Pamby encouraged. "Go with it."

"Adam," my captain said, "I don't think you can see past my rank. You won't relate to me as a real person."

"Or maybe I just don't like you," I said. "I don't relate to real assholes."

He went for my throat, yelling unkind things about my parentage. I took a swing and decked the shrink.

Anyway, I wasn't Mr. Popularity at the cop station. My only friend from those days was Nick Gabreski.

It was almost five o'clock when I showed up at the station. Nick's huge shoulders were hunched over his scarred and battered desk as he pursued the main responsibility of cops: paperwork. I sneaked toward him on tippytoe, but before I could say boo, he rumbled in his gravelly voice, "Hi, Adam."

"You're no fun."

"I'm impossible to ambush," he said. "Remember, I've got a wife and eight kids, and all of them, at one time or another, have tried to steal my wallet."

"I need a favor," I said.

"What else is new?"

I handed him a copy of the list. "One of these people might be a murderer. I want to check priors. Arrests, convictions, anything. Even juvenile records."

He glanced down the page. "This is very complete, Adam. Even has their social security numbers and birth dates. Did Alison put it together for you?"

"I got it from a lawyer in Newport. Can you do it?"

"Tomorrow," he said. "And you owe me."

"No problem." I was still basking in the glow of my possible inheritance. "If this pans out, I will buy you the dinner of your life. In fact, I will send you and your lovely wife, Ramona, to the classy hotel of your choice for a weekend celebration. Plus I will pay for the necessary child care."

Nick checked his wristwatch and pushed away from his desk. "I'll settle for a beer right now."

"Done."

"And an explanation."

As we strolled across the street to Bedwetter's, Nick's favorite fern bar, he proceeded to lecture me on the insanity of private citizens, such as myself, becoming involved in crime solving that was better left to the police departments. He cited a number of my past involvements in homicides as proof that I shouldn't attempt investigating.

"But I always catch the bad guys," I said.

"Catching is only part of the process," Nick grumbled. "Those of us who have remained in law enforcement make an effort to bring the perpetrators to trial. Not to throw them out of helicopters or drive their cars off cliffs."

We took a small table at the rear of the tavern and ordered our beers. Nick dug into the complimentary bowl of peanuts in the center of the table and began to peel off the shells.

"This time," I assured him, "it's different."

"How so?"

"I'm getting paid."

"Oh, shit," said Nick, "don't tell me that you've decided to become a paid private investigator."

"How does two point one million dollars sound to you?"

I outlined the terms of Graden Porcelli's will while Nick made a stack of peanut shells. When I finished, I said, "It's a great deal."

"The salmon king sounds fishy to me." Nick washed back a mouthful of peanuts with his beer. "You don't remember this guy? You can't think of this alleged favor?"

I shook my head. "Total blank."

"But you're going to do it anyway. Aren't you?"

I nodded. Perhaps my common sense had been seduced by the offer of large sums of money, but I couldn't say no. "I figure I'm going to dig around in the past and see what I can come up with. I've already got a field of suspects."

"But no crime," Nick pointed out.

"The crime is murder."

"You be careful, Adam."

It seemed to me that the logical place to start digging up past dirt was with the widow. According to the lawyer's information, Amelia Porcelli had been married to Graden for forty-seven years. She had to know something.

Her house, perched on a lush green bluff overlooking the Pacific, a few miles south of Lincoln City, was sprawling but quaint, like a traditional English countryside cottage on steroids. Four lawn jockeys stood sentinel over the cobblestone path that led to the front door. There were plenty of trees, a thick growth of vines, climbing roses, morning glories, sweet peas, marigolds, and nasturtiums in an astonishing array of colors. All of this foliage thinned and vanished abruptly at the rear of the house. Though I couldn't tell from there, I suspected that Amelia had a magnificent view overlooking the bay.

When I rang the bell, the front door was answered by the widow herself. In spite of the warm May weather, she wore a long-sleeved beige turtleneck, plaid skirt, and golf shoes. Her soft white hair swirled on top of her head like cotton candy. She stared at me for a moment, and the multitude of wrinkles on her face took on a curious expression. "Do I know you?"

"I'm Adam McCleet," I said. "I was at the reading of the will yesterday."

Her lip curled as if she needed to spit. Her withered fingers toyed with the three strands of pearls around her neck. "You're Graden's detective."

I was about to explain that I wasn't really a sleuth, and I didn't know her husband, but I decided that it was easier to simply agree. According to her vital statistics, Amelia had been older than Graden when they married. She was in her eighties, and I was expecting a few infirmities. "Could I ask you a few questions?"

"That bastard! I should have gotten everything. I was his wife, dammit. I put up with that old curmudgeon for years, doncha know. I deserve all of it, every red cent."

I decided that Amelia Porcelli was not the standard variety of sweet little old lady. As if reading my mind, she rearranged her crinkled face into a kindly expression and grinned with remarkably straight white false teeth. "Do please come inside, Mr. McFleet."

"McCleet," I gently corrected.

The interior of the house was packed with the stuff of many decades. Every spare inch of wall space held a painting or photograph. Every horizontal surface was covered with knickknacks, figurines, and vases of fake flowers.

She pointed to a plump rocking chair in front of the fireplace, where there were four different sets of fire-tending implements. Why? I wondered how many pokers were needed to keep the blaze burning. This pattern was repeated elsewhere in her decor.

There were a half dozen radios, all of different shape and style, atop a table. Hanging next to the fireplace was a four-foot-by-six-foot wooden display case of spoons in various sizes and design. A similar case held shot glasses, all displayed in neat rows.

I pointed to the glasses. "Very nice," I said.

"There's one for each of the fifty states," she said. "Most of them, I picked up myself on vacations. But I cheated on a couple and ordered them from a catalog. Like Nebraska, doncha know. I never particularly wanted to go to Nebraska."

"Have you lived in this area all your life?"

"Hell, no. I was born and raised in Chicago." She glanced at her arm, and I noticed that she was wearing two wristwatches. "Let's get a move on, McPete, I'm going to the Spring Scramble Golf Tournament in Toledo in less than an hour."

"Do you play?"

"Not anymore, but I've got over a hundred and fifty clubs. My nephew, Sam Leggett, is using one of my sets. It belonged to Arnie Palmer, doncha know."

Finally, I figured out the reason she had duplicates and triplicates of everything. "You're a collector."

"Aren't you the clever one?" I couldn't tell if she was being sarcastic or not. "I'm a collector, all righty. That's the first thing anybody would tell you about me. That Amelia, they'd say, she collects everything."

"Did Graden approve of your hobby?"

"My collections are more than a hobby, McFoot. Some of my stuff is real valuable, and Graden liked that part. You betcha, he did. Graden always liked money. I started way back, right after Graden and I got married."

"Tell me about those days," I encouraged.

"Waste not, want not. That's what I always say. I came up in the Great Depression, doncha know. We knew the value of saving. My mother, when she died, had a ball of string that was five feet around. Well, come on, McDink, aren't you going to ask me about the murder?"

"Tell me about it."

"It was in the 1950s. Do you remember the fifties?"

"A little."

"Way back when Graden and Tiger were starting up. They were just fishermen back then. But they bought a little boat and they worked it like demons. There was another fellow who went in on the boat with them. He had some money, and he was from the South, I remember, and he had the prettiest accent and he was so polite. Always called me ma'am, even in bed."

"What?" Had she said "in bed"? Had sweet old Amelia been sleeping with one of Graden's partners?

"And he used to love my apple pie. He'd look at me with those big blue eyes and say: Ma'am, I love your pie."

"Could we back up for just a second? Were you having an affair with this man?"

"Hell, no. Why would you think such a thing?"

This was going to be harder than I thought. Amelia was flitting in and out of reality with every sentence. I made a mental note to verify all her reminiscences. "What was this fellow's name?"

"Who?" Her mouth pursed in a tiny "O."

"The other fisherman. There was Graden and Tiger and who else?"

"Big Harry, I used to call him. His name was Harold, unlike my son, who is Harrison but also goes by Harry, so he's Little Harry."

"Big Harry what?"

"Big Harry Mann with two n's."

Of course, I thought. A big, hairy man. "Are you leading me down the garden path, Amelia?"

"Maybe so. But Big Harry disappeared one day, and he never

came back. He was part Indian, doncha know. Black hair and eyes as dark as ebony."

"But you just said he had blue eyes."

"Why, maybe he did."

"Have you got a photograph of him?"

"Better than that, McTweet."

She rose from her rocking chair with a creaking of joints and beckoned for me to follow her upstairs. We went down the second floor hallway, where she had a collection of what appeared to be the world's tackiest picture postcards in small black frames on the wall. Taking a deep breath, Amelia led the way up another flight of stairs to the third floor and paused outside a closed door. "This is my most prized collection, doncha know. It's worth a small fortune."

She pushed open the door. Inside were hundreds of shiny eyeballs and painted cheeks and simpering smiles. They were everywhere. On the floor, on display shelves, in the window seats, there were hundreds of dolls of every shape, size, and color. In silent convention they filled the huge room that must have taken up half the third floor. There was an adult-sized bed, two chairs and table in the room as well as doll-sized tables and chairs. Ranged across the white chintz bedspread were seven dolls.

Amelia stood in the middle of the room, smiling with her perfect dentures. "I'd like to introduce you to all of them, but we don't have the time."

"It's a very impressive collection," I said, and I wasn't lying. There were dolls under glass cases wearing fancy costumes. Porcelain dolls. Rag dolls. China dolls.

"I always wanted a girl," she confided. "Little Harry never appreciated my dolls."

Good for Little Harry, I thought. "You were going to tell me about Big Harry," I reminded her.

She went to a corner and fussed around until she located a

boy doll wearing a kilt and a painted-on beard. Amelia held him up. "Here he is. Big Harry Mann."

"Was he Scottish?"

"Well, I suppose he was because he wore one of these tartans. Or maybe it was one of my slips."

Great, I thought. So Big Harry was either a cross-dresser or Rob Roy. I strolled over to the bed. "Tell me about the dolls you've set out here. Is there something special about them?"

"I pulled them off the shelf right after the reading of the will. You see, McCluck, this is me."

She held up a dignified, white-haired doll who actually did resemble Amelia without the wrinkles. Carefully, she set it back down and pointed to the others. "Here's the others. Sam and Tiger. Tia and Little Harry. I couldn't find the right male doll for Whit, so I used this little stuffed animal of a sheep."

The Tiger doll was a detailed replica of an old sailor that looked a bit like a marionette. And Tia, the niece, was a Barbie. Little Harry was a baby doll. I picked up another male doll who was wearing orange flowered swimming trunks and grinning like a plastic son of a bitch. "Who's this?"

"Well, it's really Malibu Ken, but I'm calling it you until I know you better."

At least I wasn't represented by a sheep. "Did you have a special doll for Graden?"

"Right here."

She pivoted and picked up another Ken-type doll wearing a tuxedo. Amelia grasped the doll's head in her hands and deftly twisted it off. "Oops, sorry, Graden. You've lost your head. Can't hurt too much though. You're already dead."

Amelia scampered back to the bed and picked up the male doll that was supposed to be Sam Leggett, the husband of Desiree. The Sam doll bore a strong resemblance to Elvis, but he was holding a golf club instead of a guitar.

"We're going to go watch Sammy play at the tournament,"

Amelia said. She took the golf club from him. "Whoops, watch out, Sammy."

She boinked the doll on the head with the golf club. Then she picked up the doll of Tia and pressed her close to Sam. "Kiss it and make it better."

I decided that we were moving beyond weird into psycho. Amelia had created her own little world here, and it was a scary place, populated by vicious dolls and half-fulfilled memories.

She picked up the Malibu Ken and stared at it. In a low voice she said, "Tiger killed him. Tiger is the murderer."

Callously, she tossed Malibu Ken back on the bed. Then she turned to me—the real me—and pulled herself into a semblance of sedateness. "I really must be going now."

I followed her down the stairs. There might have been other questions I could have asked Amelia, but it felt like I was doing a mind probe on a cartoon. When I asked directions for the golf tournament, she told me it was at the Olalla Valley Golf Course in Toledo. Just take Highway 20 from Newport to Olalla Road. You can't miss it.

That seemed as good a place as any to continue my investigation. After the encounter with Amelia, I wanted to speak with someone who had a marginal grip on reality. Sam Leggett was supposed to be playing, but I might be able to walk with him between shots. That way, I hoped, his less than charming wife, Desiree, might not be around.

As Amelia Porcelli had predicted, the Olalla Valley Golf Course was easy enough to find. It took less than ten minutes to cover the five- or six-mile drive from Newport to Toledo, a small lumber town on Yaquina Bay, nestled in the coniferous forests of the Pacific Coast Range. It seemed an unlikely place for a big golf tournament, but apparently, the Spring Scramble was the happening thing for duffers in these parts.

The parking lot outside the barnlike clubhouse was overfull. I found a wide spot on the shoulder of the road about fifty yards from the entrance and parked among knee-high weeds and grasses.

On my hike back to the first tee, I spotted Harrison (also known as Little Harry) Porcelli and jogged over to his side. He wore a pink polo shirt, beige cotton slacks, and shiny brown golf shoes. A young caddy followed in his wake.

"I've just been talking to your mother," I informed him.

"Did she show you the dolls?"

"Yeah."

"That's Mama's little creep show," he said. Harrison seemed like a pleasant enough guy. With his blond hair and blue eyes he looked more like Malibu Ken than the baby doll his mother had chosen to represent him. He was mid-forties but looked younger, one of those guys who radiates health despite a slight limp. Considering his parentage, he appeared incredibly normal.

"How long has she been collecting dolls?"

"Forever," Harry said. "She used to try to make me play with them, even got a G.I. Joe so I could play war games. But it never interested me."

I thought of Amelia and her obsession. "Does she play with the dolls herself?"

"She pretends to. I think she does it just to freak everybody out."

Suddenly, Harrison stopped walking. His face contorted and his right arm constricted in a clawlike gesture. In a loud voice, he announced, "Potty breath. Suck me."

Just as quickly, he calmed and resumed his sauntering pace. "Mama likes to shock people," he said. Once again he was the very picture of a sane young executive out for a day of relaxation on the golf course.

The fact that no one else had reacted to Harrison's outburst led me to believe that either I was hallucinating or this was not an uncommon trait of his. "Um, Harrison," I said, "you just blurted out something about, um, potty breath."

"Did I?" He shrugged.

"So, what exactly did you mean by that?"

He stopped walking again, and I braced myself. But Harrison's voice was calm. "I have an illness, Tourette's syndrome. I'm mostly fine with medication, but stress tends to exaggerate my symptoms. Needless to say, there has been a great deal of stress surrounding my father's death and his inheritance."

I had heard of Tourette's, but I'd never met someone who had been afflicted. "How does your illness work?"

"It's like a brain spasm. Generally, I yell a couple of words, then it's over. I don't like to talk about it, okay?"

"Sure." So much for normal.

"Now, what were we talking about before? My mother?"

"Right," I said. "You were telling me that she likes to freak people out."

"She likes to scare the shit out of them. For Halloween, she used to make a big production with life-sized ghosts and bloody knives and Frankenstein monsters. My dad used to pay kids to stop by the house so Mama could frighten them."

"How nice that he cared."

"He indulged her. After all, she'd done her job as a wife and produced a son, no matter how big a disappointment I was."

Before I had a chance to discuss how Harrison had failed his father, he nodded toward a foursome on the first tee. "There's Sam Leggett."

"Where?" I craned my neck.

"There." He pointed to a man wearing a money-green shirt and khaki shorts. A green visor shaded his eyes. "Just teeing up."

Sam was color-coordinated but not obnoxiously so. In my experience, golfers who wore overly fancy outfits were either so good that you wouldn't make fun of their gear or so bad that it wasn't worth the effort to smirk. "Is Sam any good?"

"He used to be outstanding, but after he married Desiree

three years ago, he fell apart. He claims it's because they have such wild sex. It saps his strength."

Sam Leggett certainly looked as if he knew his stuff as he addressed the ball. He pulled a few blades of grass from the turf and released them into the air to check the direction of the wind. Then he dug in his spikes, wiggled his butt a little, and took a healthy swing. The ball launched with a solid crack. Though the altitude and distance were good, the shot quickly faded to the right and dropped directly into the middle of a meandering creek that paralleled the fairway.

"Goddamn-fuckin'-shit," Leggett bellowed.

"Sam doesn't really have the discipline to be an athlete," Harrison said.

"He's no sportsman either," I added as I watched Sam toss his driver thirty yards up the fairway.

"He's a salesman," Harrison said. "Works out of the packing plant near Seattle."

"So, he's going to be out of a job after everything is liquidated."

"Probably not. I think he's already made arrangements with the new owners. He'd been pushing my dad to sell for years."

"Your mother said she'd loaned him a set of clubs that belonged to Arnold Palmer."

"Yeah? Mama says a lot of things. I try not to pay too much attention."

Harrison convulsed again but said nothing. The way his body twitched was somewhere between a seizure and a shiver that passed in a couple of seconds.

Sam Leggett was about a hundred yards up the fairway. Apparently, he had been unable to retrieve his ball from the creek because he dug another from his bag and dropped it over his shoulder at the edge of the ditch, where his first shot had disappeared.

Again, his form looked damned good to me as he drew back and swung.

The instant Sam hit the ball with Palmer's old wood, there was a brilliant flash of red light and the deafening whump of an explosion. If I hadn't been staring right at him, I wouldn't have believed it.

Next to me, Harrison gasped and twitched. "Bitch turds. Beach birds."

Sam Leggett, or what was left of him, lay crumpled at the edge of the fairway. Dark smoke rose from the spot where his ball had been and dissipated in the clear blue skies.

I looked at Harrison and he looked back at me.

"My God, Adam. What was that?"

"Exploding golf ball."

Chapter
Four

olf tournaments, unlike hockey or bull riding, have no
ambulance with trained paramedics standing by to rush
casualties to the nearest emergency room. While everyone
else reeled in shocked amazement, I ran toward the smoldering
heap of flesh that, a few seconds earlier, had been Sam Leggett.
I didn't know exactly what to expect or what I would do when
I reached him, but if there was any way I could help, I would try.

My eyes squinted, not because of the acrid fumes from the
blast but from a tension that immediately took hold inside my
skull. This wasn't right. A small but devastating explosion had
shattered an easygoing day in May with songbirds trilling in the
evergreen trees as warm sun dried sparkling dew from the links.
This wasn't the place for violence; it would change everything,
transform the area into someplace less innocent. Instead of fib-
bing about their scores, stunned amateur golfers would spend
the rest of their lives talking about the Spring Scramble in Toledo
when Sam Leggett blew himself up. This was the wrong place
for a bomb. All wrong.

As I ran closer to the spot where Leggett had taken his last swing, I could see charred grass in a circular pattern around a patch of brown, smoking dirt. This was ground zero. A stench of smoldering vegetation mixed with the raw odor of burnt flesh. The member of Sam's foursome who had been nearest when the ball exploded was on his knees, puking his toenails onto the fairway grass.

Leggett had taken the full force of the blast in his face and chest. His left hand was gone. The skin and flesh had been ripped from the other forearm, leaving gleaming white bone. All the hair had been singed off his head, and his face was blackened and raw, oozing blood from numerous lacerations.

The worst injury was a two-foot section of aluminum alloy shaft from Arnold Palmer's old three iron that protruded from the left side of Leggett's chest like a radio antenna. His breath came in short, irregular gulps, and each time he exhaled, a plume of blood issued from the end of the hollow tube.

"Pull it out," I heard someone yell as I knelt beside Leggett. I looked up to see Harrison Porcelli's ashen face glaring down at me in horror. In spite of his limp and Tourette's spasms, he had been only a few strides behind me.

"I don't think so," I said. "We don't know what this thing looks like on the inside. It's definitely in his lung, and it could be jagged or flared."

I'm no paramedic, but I'd had emergency first aid training in the Marines and some actual battlefield experience with sucking chest wounds in Vietnam. I knew that if I tried to remove the foreign object, I might tear him up even worse.

"Help him," Harrison pleaded.

Ordinarily, the first thing to do would have been to seal off the wound, try to make it airtight so the victim might have a chance at breathing, but the shaft complicated the matter and I wasn't sure how to handle it. I moved to step two. "Help me turn him on his side," I instructed Harrison.

Together, we gently rolled the traumatized Leggett onto his left side to prevent more blood from draining into his good lung.

To his credit, Harrison stayed on the ground beside his fallen cousin. Harrison's khakis and pink shirt were covered in blood. He looked more like a disaster victim than a corporate executive.

"I think you're supposed to talk to them," he said, glancing toward me for confirmation.

"It can't hurt," I said.

"It's okay, Sam," he said to the mutilated body. "Hang on, Sam. You're going to make it."

Harrison threw back his head in a spasm. "Hooter humpers."

He looked at me. "I don't think he's conscious."

"That's good."

As I tried to think of what procedure might help, I could hear the faint whine of a siren in the distance. The ambulance was too far away. Leggett didn't have much time, and I didn't know what to do next.

An obvious thought struck me. What better place to find a doctor on a Saturday morning than on a golf course? I scanned the faces of people who had begun to gather around us, wringing their hands and gasping and turning away.

"A doctor," I said. "Is there a doctor here?"

When no one responded, Harrison picked up the cry. "Jesus Christ! This is a golf course! There must be a doctor somewhere!"

Leggett began to convulse. Blood sprayed from the tube and soaked my face and clothes as I struggled to keep him from thrashing around.

"Someone get a fucking doctor!" Harrison bellowed with all the force in his lungs.

"I'm a doctor," said a reluctant voice.

I looked up to see a tall, tanned, athletic-looking man wearing a paisley polo shirt. He wasn't exactly charging forward to take charge, and I couldn't say that I blamed him. Sam Leggett was looking like a lost cause.

"Okay, Doc," I said. "Tell us what to do."

"Just try to keep him still," he said nervously. "The ambulance ought to be here soon. I called them on my cell phone."

"Come on, Doctor," Harrison begged. "This is my cousin. I can't sit here and let him die. Jesus, there's got to be something we can do."

"I'm sorry," the doctor said. "I don't have the proper equipment."

"But you sure as hell remembered to bring your cell phone to the golf course," Harrison screamed. "What's the matter, you fuckhead? Worried about getting sued for malpractice? Scared of getting some blood on your golf shoes?"

The doctor rested his hand on Harrison's shoulder. "There's nothing we can do, son. He's dying."

Leggett began to choke and his body went rigid. Then, just as quickly, he went limp and still as a final burst of crimson gore issued from the end of the shaft. He was dead.

"Shit!" Harrison yelled.

I entirely sympathized with his statement that came not from Tourette's but from the heart. It's a terrible thing to watch a man die, worse when it's somebody you know.

When Harrison looked up at me, I gestured for him to stand up. "It's over," I said.

"Good-bye, Sam," he whispered, then stood up.

From farther back in the crowd I heard the screams of a woman. "My husband! Let me pass. He's my husband!"

No matter how much of a bitch Desiree Leggett was, she didn't deserve this. I turned to Harrison and said, "Take care of Desiree. Don't let her see him."

"Right." He looked me in the eye. "Thanks, Adam, for trying."

"Sammy!" Desiree wailed. "Where is he? What happened?"

As Harrison faded through the crowd, another woman appeared from the rows of faces. She knelt on edge of the burnt grass surrounding the body. I couldn't see her face because she was looking down, but I had the impression that she was plain, not ugly but very average-looking with brown hair and unremarkable features.

Her manner was deliberate and calm. She reached into her shoulder bag and took out a five-by-seven-inch nylon pouch which unfolded into a rain poncho in army green. Carefully, she spread the makeshift tarp across the head and torso of Sam Leggett. Then she bowed her head for a moment.

When she looked up, rivulets of tears spilled down her cheeks, and I recognized Tia, the niece who would inherit from Porcelli. Sam Leggett was her brother.

Except for the tears, her face was a mask, unreadable. In his videotape, Graden Porcelli referred to her as "quiet little Tia." What did she think? How did she feel? I had the sense that this wasn't the first time she had confronted death. As quietly as she had appeared, she vanished back into the crowd.

When the ambulance finally arrived, along with the Toledo cops and the Lincoln County sheriff's deputies, I noticed that Whit and his wife had taken up positions on either side of Tia Leggett. They patted her rounded shoulders, offering comfort, even though she seemed to be composed. Only her eyes betrayed her grief.

I glanced over the rest of the crowd, belatedly noting the presence of suspects. I had already seen or heard from Whit, Tia, Desiree, and Harrison.

Amelia was there. I saw her in the midst of women who had, apparently, discovered that she was related to the deceased. Amelia's wrinkled face was ravaged by direct sunlight that showed every line, every crease, every care and disappointment she had suffered in her long life. But I wasn't altogether convinced that she was suffering. After our jaunt to the doll attic, I wouldn't be surprised to discover that she was responsible for the exploding golf ball.

Crowds seem to take on a certain character, and these salt-of-the-earth people seemed vaguely embarrassed by the murder that had disrupted their golf tournament. A couple of folks had come over and patted my back, but now they were moving away from me, the outsider.

As I scanned the dispersing group, I spotted Jimmy Caruthers, the attorney. His expression was glum as he stared at me, and I remembered his dire statement about the possibility that a murderer among the heirs might start killing off the others. I hadn't taken his warning seriously enough.

Jimmy was too far away to speak. He raised both hands and showed me seven fingers, then he folded one finger down and sadly shook his head. One down. How many more to go?

Among the major players, the only one unaccounted for was Tiger. The old mariner wasn't the type of guy I'd expect to find on a golf course, but neither were half of the people there. Toledo is smack in the middle of lumber country, and I expected that most of the town's population worked in the mills nearby. Mingled among the more traditionally dressed golfers were loggers wearing short-sleeved flannel shirts and red suspenders to hold up their baggy denim pants which were cut off high above the ankle so the fabric wouldn't snag on broken tree branches or get hung up in lethal sawmill machinery.

The very last person I would expect to find on a spring day in the country was the woman who came charging at me. The crowd parted to let her through. She was the epitome of outsider. She stood out like the skull and crossbones of a Jolly Roger in a room full of party balloons. She was my sister, Margot, and she was in one of her less subtle moods.

Directly in front of me, she halted with her fists on her hips and her legs braced wide. Though it was only May, Margot had a spectacular tan which she had cultivated in southern California. The last I heard, she was in La-la Land, trying to sell a screenplay of her personal experiences, entitled *Margot: The Miniseries*.

When she reached toward me, I tried not to dart away in an

unmanly flinch. But that was exactly what I should have done, because she slapped hard at my shoulder, possibly the only place on the front of my body that was not stained with Sam Leggett's blood.

"Idiot!" Margot snapped. Then she slugged me again. "Moron!"

Wearily, I asked, "What are you doing here?"

"I came down here to be with a friend who needed my help."

Could such a person exist? In the first place, it was difficult to imagine Margot having any friends. But asking her for help? If I were wrestling with a man-eating gorilla, I'd ask Margot to help the gorilla.

"She said she knew you, and you were involved in her problem. So, right off the bat, I knew she was in trouble." She whapped me again. "Dolt!"

The picture suddenly came into focus. There was only one person I could think of who'd be likely to be acquainted with or even fond of my sister. "Desiree Leggett."

The mental image of both of them, marching side by side, was daunting. Both were expensive-looking, high-maintenance women, groomed to selfish perfection. Margot was dark with black hair and perfectly made-up dark eyes. Desiree had that long mane of white-blond hair and legs that went all the way up to her armpits. They would make a striking duo.

Margot struck me again. "You've really screwed up this time, Adam. You went and got Desiree's husband killed."

"Me?"

"Weren't you supposed to be the bigshot detective on the case? Well? Weren't you?"

"Not exactly. You see, it was—"

"You should have figured it out by now," she said. "If you had, nobody would be dead now, would they?"

"Gosh, Margot, I suppose not." Sarcasm was wasted on her.

She continued. "And look at you. You're a total mess." With a long crimson fingernail she pointed toward the parking lot. "Let's go, Adam. I can see that I'm going to have to take control here, you've messed everything up."

I balked. This was an instinctive response toward self-preservation. Every time I tangled with Margot the Malevolent, I got burned. "You're not involved in this, Margot. Go back to Portland."

She lunged back at me and hissed. "So, you stooge. I understand that you stand to inherit two point one million dollars if you figure this out."

Defensively, I said, "Maybe."

Her scarlet lips curled in an evil grin. There are two major principles that rule Margot's existence: You can never have too much money. And you can never marry too many men who have money. "Two point one million," she said. "I'm involved."

Fortunately, a sheriff's deputy interrupted our uneasy conversation. "Excuse me," he said to me. "Are you Adam McCleet?"

"Yes."

"I'm Margot." She thrust herself forward. My sister has never been a shrinking violet.

"That's nice," the cop said. "Did you witness the explosion?"

"What if I did?" Margot snapped.

"Then I would have to ask you a few questions."

She thought for a moment, then said, "This wouldn't involve fingerprinting, would it? Because I just got my nails enameled."

"Did you see anything, ma'am?"

"Nothing gets past me, sonny boy."

The deputy sighed. "Did you see the explosion? Did you notice anything suspicious about any of the people around or near Sam Leggett?"

"No, but it's obvious that—"

"You're free to go, ma'am." He turned back to me. "Mr.

McCleet, would you come with me? I have to ask you some questions."

"I'd be happy to." The cop was rescuing me from Margot. I had to restrain myself from leaping into his arms and kissing him on both cheeks. I glanced back at her. "This could take a while. Don't wait."

"I'll be back, Adam." Under her breath, she muttered, "Moron."

The deputy accompanied me to my car, where we found the head of Leggett's three iron imbedded in the driver's side of the windshield. I wasn't even surprised.

While the cop unsympathetically extracted the shrapnel from my window, I opened the trunk and retrieved my overnight bag, which I had packed in anticipation of the need to spend a couple of days in Newport. I planned to use the clubhouse to wash up and change out of my bloody clothes.

Together, we returned to the impromptu cop interrogation area which was four patrol cars arranged in such a way as to block the parking lot and the road, creating a bottleneck of big-city proportions.

I slipped into the rear of a patrol car with the cop. The interior of the vehicle was dark after being out in the sunshine. It was also quiet enough that I could begin to think clearly. After the cop took down the standard information about me, he asked, "Did you actually see the explosion?"

"I was looking right at Sam Leggett. He went into his swing. As soon as the club hit the ball, it exploded."

It had been fortunate that Leggett had been relatively alone when he made the strike. Otherwise, several people would have been injured.

"Are you sure," the cop asked, "that it was the golf ball that exploded?"

I nodded.

"You didn't see any other object being thrown or shot toward the victim?"

I shook my head. "I assume the ball was loaded with an unstable explosive of some kind. Nitroglycerine maybe. I'm no expert."

The only explosives of which I had any intimate knowledge were plastique, also known as C4, and TNT. I had gained an uncomfortable familiarity with both substances during my tour in Vietnam. But they were both highly stable. You could set them on fire or hit them with a sledgehammer and nothing would happen. The only thing that would set them off was another explosion, like from a detonator.

I explained all this to the cop, who was too young to recall Vietnam, except from history book photographs, and he listened to me with the sort of youthful indulgence reserved for old warhorses. "Wish I could help you," I said. "But I don't know what kind of device was used."

"That's all right, sir. Explosive technology has come a long way in the past twenty-five years."

When he asked where I could be reached, I explained that I'd be staying in the Newport area, but I wasn't sure where. I would let him know.

Apparently, my casual interrogation was completed at the same time Tia had finished giving her statement, because we emerged from separate patrol cars simultaneously. I approached her. "I'm sorry about your brother."

"Me too. Sam was harmless."

It didn't seem right to leave her alone. Besides, I had some questions of my own and Tia was on the list of heirs and, therefore, suspects. "Can I buy you a cup of coffee or something?"

"Make it schnapps and you've got a deal."

In the men's room of the clubhouse I quickly washed and changed my shirt and trousers as she waited. We took my car, and I decided that I liked Tia Leggett when she took great pains to comfort me on the subject of the shattered windshield on my beautifully reconditioned vehicle. She called the car "cherry," and I knew we were of like minds.

As she directed me toward the nearest tavern on Toledo's Main Street, she said, "Poor Sam. He didn't have a chance. I'd say that ball was filled with nitro, wouldn't you?"

Chapter
Five

A lethal, exploding golf ball would be big news anywhere, certainly worth a mention on the Portland newscasts and maybe even on Leno and Letterman. In Small-Town, Oregon, otherwise known as Toledo, the gossip value of this event ranked up there with a declaration of war on Canada.

When Tia and I walked into the dim light of the Mallard Tavern, a burly guy whose baggy jeans were held up by red suspenders was performing a slow-motion replay for the bartender and four other patrons who had paused their game of eight ball to watch. He stood in a golf stance.

". . . and den he drew back." The big guy drew his imaginary golf club into a back swing. He looked like Paul Bunyan doing an impression of Johnny Carson. "And den he swung." The guy followed through, but stopped short at the point where his air club would have connected with the invisible ball. "And den . . . kablooey!"

He waved his big arms wildly and stumbled backward until he crashed into a pinball machine against the wall. The machine made a single *doink* noise and flashed a tilt message across its scoreboard before going completely dark.

"Hey, watch it!" the lady bartender ordered. "Break that and you'll pay." Though she sounded like she meant it, she didn't budge from her station behind the bar, and the bored expression on her face didn't change. She probably repeated those words a hundred times a day.

The big guy paid no attention to her as he recovered and hurried forward to finish the story for his pals. "Blew his fuckin' head clean off, I swear to you, it did!"

"That's not how I heard," said another. "I heard that somebody threw a grenade at him."

"Yeah," said another. "There's no such thing as an exploding golf ball. Maybe that's what it looked like, but I heard there was a sniper on the grassy knoll."

One of the pool players pointed at us with his cue stick, and heads turned. Voices fell to whispering, a low hiss like steam escaping a locomotive. The bartender, a woman who was no less burly than her patrons, came out from behind the polished oak bar and approached us. She also wore red suspenders.

"You're Amelia Porcelli's niece," she said to Tia. "Sam Leggett was your brother, huh?"

"Yes."

The woman pulled her into an embrace, fluttering her large red hand and patting Tia's shoulder. "You poor, dear thing. You poor girl. You drink for free."

"Peppermint schnapps over ice," Tia said. She looked at me. "And you, Adam?"

"Double Wild Turkey. Neat."

The woman stepped back from Tia and frowned at me. "You pay," she said. "You were supposed to be the bodyguard for Sam Leggett. Shame on you."

Tia and I took a booth near the back of the Mallard, and the other drinkers gave us a respectful distance for privacy, which was good, because, although the lady bartender was entirely wrong about my being anyone's bodyguard, I had begun to redefine my own mission. Not only did I need to start doing my job better if I was going to collect any money, I also had to be more vigilant or others would surely die. With Sam out of the picture, the inheritance shares were now approximately two point five million apiece. For each additional dead heir, the split would increase exponentially. Strong motivation for murder. I was also not oblivious of the fact that I was as likely a target as any of the others.

One of the six of us was a killer, and I was pretty sure it wasn't me. I glanced over at Tia. Could I trust her?

Her appearance didn't fit with the rest of the family. Her late brother, Sam, and Harrison were both good-looking blonds who had the healthy glow of a privileged upbringing. They looked like guys who had been to prep school, drove expensive cars, and vacationed in sunny climates, where they could work on their tans. Tia had dark brown hair, basically unstyled and hanging down to her shoulders. The strands of gray had not been retouched. Her clothes were loose-fitting over an average middle-aged female body. She wore no makeup to conceal the honest expressiveness of her large brown eyes which seemed wistful.

Tia was one of those women who seem completely comfortable with themselves. She sat quietly, not needing to fill the space between us with idle verbiage.

"Tell me about your family," I said.

"Dysfunctional," she said calmly. "My father has Alzheimer's and has been in a home for the past five years. Mother was Graden's sister. She died three years ago in a car accident where she misjudged distances and drove off a cliff. The car exploded on the second bounce." She paused. "Apparently, going out in a ball of flames is becoming a family tradition."

Our drinks came, and Tia took a long sip that made my taste

buds cringe. Peppermint schnapps has always reminded me of mouthwash—the only good thing about it is that it doesn't taste any worse coming back up. "Can you think of any reason, other than the inheritance, that somebody would want to kill Sam?"

She shook her head. "I didn't know Sam well. We weren't close. I'm only five years older than he was, but that was enough to put me in the hippie generation, while Sam fell in with the upwardly mobile yuppies."

A burst of raucous laughter erupted from the corner near the pool table. The big storyteller and one of the pool players of equal size stood about six feet apart, facing each other like gunslingers. Instead of six-shooters, each held a glass of beer, filled to the brim.

Another patron began a slow count. "One . . ."

"Don't get started, you two," the bartender ordered in her bored, monotone voice.

Tia and I watched with curious fascination.

"Two . . ."

The two gladiators arched their backs and raised their shirts to expose pale skin stretched across enormous beer bellies.

"I'm not kidding," the bartender assured. "I'll call the cops."

". . . Three!"

With beer glasses held high, the big men charged. A loud slap echoed around the room as their distended guts collided with train-wreck force. Cheers went up as the pool player stumbled backward a few steps, spilling a small amount of beer onto the floor. The big storyteller also staggered backward. An unfortunately placed chair tripped him from behind. He sat down hard, but his momentum overturned the chair and his back hit the floor with a crash and a splash as the beer transferred from the glass to his face.

"That's it," the bartender said, dialing the phone behind the bar. "I'm calling the cops."

The other men cheered and laughed as the big storyteller

scrambled to his feet. "Two outta three," he said, wiping the beer from his face with his shirt-sleeve. "I wasn't ready. Best two outta three."

Tia's lower jaw hung slack, a look of astonishment in her eyes.

"The agony of defeat," I said.

She tossed back her head and began to laugh loudly. And though I knew that more than anything else it was a release of tension from losing her brother in such a violent way, it was a warm and honest laugh coming from deep inside a woman with a genuine sense of appreciation for the absurd. And her laughter made me want to trust her.

I took a sip of whiskey and savored the expanding plume of warmth in my stomach as I waited for Tia to regain her composure.

When her laughter began to subside, Tia dabbed at her moist eyes with a bar napkin, sniffed, and said, "I'm sorry. Where were we?"

"You were a hippie?"

"Still am," she said. "But I'm not so militant anymore."

"You were a militant in the sixties?" I was recalling the SDS and the Weathermen, bombings at colleges.

"There was a time," she said, "when I would have refused to sit at the same table with you because you're a Vietnam vet. I was a long-haired, braless weirdo creep. You would have despised me on sight."

"I always liked the braless part," I volunteered.

"Free love." She grinned. Her mouth had a perpetual curve, as if she'd seen a lot and found most of it amusing. "Those were the bad ol' days. I wasn't even sure who was the father of my child."

"You have a kid?"

"She's twenty-three. You might have seen her at the reading of Uncle Graden's will. Dark hair, dark eyes, Donna Karan suit, and little white pumps. She's an accountant. I named her Gemini Isis after the goddess, but she had her name legally changed when she was nine."

"To what?" I asked.

"Jane."

Tia didn't have to say more. Her love-child daughter had undertaken her own form of rebellion. Because her mother was a free spirit, she would be buttoned-down, uptight, and conventional.

"I wasn't much of a mother," Tia said. "There seemed to be so many other things going on in the world. Important things. I had to do what I could to help."

"Saving the rain forest?"

"I was in El Salvador and Bangladesh. Even spent some time with Mother Teresa in Calcutta." She finished her schnapps. "That's why I want this money from Uncle Graden. There's so many good things that can be accomplished with two point five million dollars."

It did not escape my attention that she had already done the arithmetic, adding Sam's share to the pot and redividing. "Were you close to your uncle?"

"Graden? The capitalist pig of the century? Hardly! I always liked Amelia though. What a fruitcake!" She looked down into her empty glass. "Should I have another? I'm really not much of a drinker. Probably not."

"Probably not," I concurred, pushing my own half-full glass away. "After all, there is a murderer among us."

"And I might be next?" Her eyes showed no fear. "I was wondering, Adam, what did you do for Graden that he gave you the unenviable job of tracking down the murderer?"

"I have no idea. You might be able to help me though. When I was talking to Amelia the Fruitcake, she mentioned a third partner who started the salmon-packing business. His name was Harry, I think."

"Harold Mann," Tia said immediately, thereby saving me the embarrassment of referring to Big Harry Mann. "The whole start-up of the business took place just before I was born, but I've heard about it. Kind of a family legend, if you know what I mean."

"Tell me."

More cheers came from the men in the corner near the pool table. The beer slingers had squared off for another collision, but Tia ignored them this time. "You know how, when you're a kid, your parents are always saying: If you were only like . . . some perfect kid."

I nodded. Though my father passed away when I was nine, my mother had always made a fuss about Daryl Armstrong, who was neat, handsome, polite, got straight A's, and was quarterback of the high school football team. He was every parent's dream. It had been an unending source of satisfaction to me when I met Daryl at my twenty-fifth high school reunion and found him to be a fat, bald, loudmouth used car salesman.

"My mother was like that about Harold Mann. Every time my father screwed up—which was often—she'd say: What do I expect? You're no Harold Mann."

"I understand that Harold disappeared mysteriously."

"According to my mother, he was the Johnny Appleseed of small business. He got Graden and Tiger started, including the major contribution of using his good credit to sign for all their loans, then he moved on to another place to help someone else."

"Did you ever see him or hear from him again?"

"He never came back. That was part of the mystique for my mother. I suspect that she liked men who showed up, did their job, and then left her alone."

Tia rubbed her forefinger around the rim of her glass. "Could you give me a lift back to Newport? I car-pooled over here from the hotel with Desiree and some woman with one name, like Cher or Madonna."

"Margot," I said.

"You know her?"

"She's my sister."

Tia's eyebrows shot up so high that they were hidden in her bangs. "Wow." She nodded. "Like, wow. That is too unbeliev- able. Biological sister?"

I had wondered about that myself. It seemed to me that Margot was really an alien creature who had borrowed my moth- er's womb and appeared on this planet for the sole purpose of making my life miserable.

Diplomatically, I said, "It's hard to imagine that Margot and I were ever swimming in the same gene pool. But it's kind of like that with you too. You don't seem related to Harrison."

"I go my own way. Always have. And, by the way, don't worry too much about protecting me from the family and friends." She dug into her satchel-sized purse and showed me the butt of an automatic handgun, probably a nine-millimeter. "I'm packing heat."

"Swell." Maybe Tia wasn't as well balanced as I had pre- viously assumed.

Just then the front door swung open and one of Toledo's finest stood under the exit sign, silhouetted between the hot light of the sun outside, and the cool light of the beer signs inside.

I instructed Tia in a whisper, "Put that away."

"What seems to be the trouble here?" the cop asked in a low voice as the door swung slowly closed behind him. He projected no authority whatsoever. He was tall and scrawny, like an underfed basketball player. His hat was too large, resting on winglike ears. His uniform shirt was too big, and his dark blue trousers were too short, exposing an inch of white skin above the tops of his socks. An unfortunate scattering of zits on his sunburned face gave him the look of a fifteen-year-old boy.

"Hey, Brutus," the storyteller boomed, turning away from his belly-busting tournament. "Come on in. Let me buy you a beer."

"I'm on duty."

"Oh, to hell wit dat." The big man forced a bottle of Bud into the cop's hand and escorted him to the corner, where the others stood. "Tell us what happened out to da golf course dis morning."

"So much for the law in these parts," Tia said as she closed her purse and draped the strap over her shoulder. "Are you going to be staying down here while you investigate?"

I nodded. "Haven't found a hotel room though."

"The rest of us are staying at the Sunny Beach Celebrity Hotel in Newport. Jimmy Caruthers reserved the entire place for the funeral and will reading. I think the owner is a client of his. Anyway, I know there are rooms vacant." Though she was still smiling, her eyes held a taunt. "You'll like the place. It's highly funky."

Chapter
Six

Due to the spiderweb of cracks in my windshield, I drove slowly, sighting through a three-inch hole in the center of the driver's side, where the head of Sam Leggett's three iron had come to rest.

Approaching the western outskirt of Toledo, Tia instructed, "Turn left, just before the bowling alley."

I did as she said, but now we were headed away from Highway 20. "Is this a shortcut?"

"Actually," Tia said, "it's a long cut, but only a few minutes longer. This road follows the shoreline of the bay all the way to Newport. I'm not in a great hurry to get back, and it's a beautiful drive. If you don't mind, I could use a little more time to think."

"No problem." Thinking was just what I needed to do, hard and fast. Being a water person myself, I thought a slow drive along Yaquina Bay might help to charge my batteries and get the gears up to speed in my brain-housing group. Plus, my windshield was less of a hazard on this sparsely traveled road.

With the town of Toledo shrinking in the rearview mirror, Tia took a deep breath and exhaled in a long, audible sigh as she melted into the passenger seat then fell silent. Time to reflect.

I began to consider the three primary elements for selecting a criminal suspect: motive, method, and opportunity.

Motive was easy. Bucks. Big bucks. Millions of dollars was enough motive to drive the most stable and rational of our species to the edge of bloody murder and back again. But all of mankind did not stand to profit from Leggett's death. That narrowed the field from the population of the entire planet down to the remaining heirs of Graden Porcelli, their spouses, children, and significant others. Of course, there was always the off chance that Leggett had been blown to pieces by an outsider, for some unrelated reason, and the whole inheritance scenario was merely a subterfuge, a convenient red herring to lead investigators away from the real motive. A little too convenient, I thought. I'd come back to that one if and when all the heirs were logically eliminated from the suspect list.

Examining opportunity didn't help much. Except for Tiger Jorgenson, all the heirs were at the Olalla golf course that morning. Any one of them could have slipped the deadly Dunlap into Leggett's bag. And the fact that Tiger was absent didn't exactly eliminate him, because he could have planted the ball while the clubs were still at Amelia's. In fact, it was possible that the ball was never intended for Sam Leggett. It might have been in the bag for months, or years. The intended victim might have been Graden Porcelli, or even Arnold Palmer himself, but for the time being I would stick with the assumption that Leggett was the target.

The third element, method, seemed the most logical place to begin the elimination process. Who among the heirs had the expertise, and access to the right materials, for the manufacture of an exploding golf ball? The device must have been expertly crafted, or Leggett wouldn't have hit it. A good golfer would never use a flawed or deformed ball, especially not in a tournament.

As far as I knew, none of the heirs were demolition experts. When I heard back from my cop buddy, Nick Gabreski, I would know prior arrests, but I also needed a synopsis of job history and military service that might indicate familiarity with explosives.

I wondered how radical Tia's hippie past had actually been. In the sixties and early seventies, there was a broad and colorful array of semiorganized, bell-bottomed, left-wing extremist groups with a proclivity for blowing things up. Had Tia been aligned with the Students for a Democratic Society, or the infamous Symbianese Liberation Army, or one of a hundred other pyros-for-peace clubs that terrorized the country during the Vietnam era?

Since she was a captive audience in my cherry Chevy, I decided I'd do a little more gentle probing. "Tia," I said, still sighting through the steering aperture in my windshield.

Tia sniffled and said, "Yes." Her voice sounded small and faraway. I took my eyes off the narrow and winding two-lane long enough to see that the tip of her nose was red and her cheeks were wet with tears. Reality had caught up with her.

I decided to let her have her cry. There would be a better time for questions. "It is a beautiful drive."

Tia nodded and turned her face toward the passenger side window.

I hoped that I could eliminate Tia quickly from the suspect list. I liked her, and the idea of having her arrested and charged with the murder of her brother gave me a heavy feeling in my chest. I tried considering the other heirs as suspects again, but my thoughts kept going in frustrating circles. I didn't know enough about any of them.

The midafternoon sun had sunk low enough in the tourist-blue sky so that each time I drove out of a right-hand curve a blinding laser shaft of white light shot through the hole in my windshield and stabbed me in the eyes. I countered the problem by leaning my head out the open side window, and whenever we headed directly into the sun I transferred my gaze to the yellow centerline on the asphalt. Though I felt like a large dog with my head hanging out the window gulping thirty-mile-an-hour air, it did afford the opportunity to actually see the countryside. I noticed the transition between the small and relatively quiet town of Toledo on the backwater and the busy tourist city of Newport on the coast.

In recent years the Pacific Northwest has attained a certain underground trendiness, partially due to a national obsession with coffee. I can understand this. From the depths of my neurotransmitters, I crave caffeine, thick coffee, espresso so strong that it climbs out of the cup and slaps you awake. Personally, I am delighted that there is a Starbucks on every corner in Portland.

However, the other attractions of my home stomping grounds are more difficult for me to comprehend. As far as I can figure, Seattle—which is generally considered hipper than Portland—was the acknowledged birthplace of grunge music and Kurt Cobain, the tortured leader of the band Nirvana, who committed suicide. As a son of the sixties who thought nirvana was a state of bliss achieved during deep meditation or great sex, I knew next to nothing about the current music. Gen-X sounded like a new, improved laundry detergent. I had no idea why these oddly pierced young people with multihued hair shaved in patches and the proliferation of bands with names like Hole and Anal Probe were migrating like tattooed lemmings to the area I thought of as my part of the country. But it seemed to be happening.

In places like Toledo, the popularity of the Pacific Northwest didn't matter, except for a certain resentment toward rabid environmentalists who chained themselves to trees destined for the lumber and paper mills. These people were interested in saving things—the whales, the seals, the trees, the banana slug, and a couple dozen spotted owls. Among the indigenous citizens, environmentalists were not popular. For all their deep-thinking environmental protests and legislation, they have failed to take into account the fact that the people who have made their living from this land and its creatures for generations are also part of God's great plan.

Though I'm not in favor of total deforestation, excessive bans on tree cutting have slowed the lumber industry to a crawl and sounded the death knell for many small towns along the Oregon coast. My own father fed and clothed a family of six on the wages he brought home from a small lumber mill very much like the two mills I had noticed on the way out of town, which had been shut down and boarded up. Aside from all of that, I was pretty sure nothing ever changed much in Toledo.

In Newport, however, one of the major businesses was the tourist trade. Quaintness and coffee shops were cultivated. All of those former fishermen and lumbermen—who were put out of work by the environmentalists—turned their homes into bed and breakfasts and turned their chain saws to whittling totem poles to be sold to Californians who, of course, demanded the real thing.

The Sunny Beach Celebrity Hotel was working hard to be at the forefront of trend. It was an elderly building on the shore-front of Newport. The two-story structure with weathered gray shingles for siding had a rickety wooden balcony outside each of what looked like twelve or fifteen rooms. A magnificent natural view of the Pacific was obscured with advertising signs in garish colors. One sign promised FULL-BODIED COFFEE in the Chill Wills Cafe. The name of the hotel was written in letters that were a foot high and posted on stilts. It also claimed: CELEBRITIES IN EVERY ROOM. FAMOUS PEOPLE. LOTS OF THEM.

When Tia and I entered through a wide door in the center of the building, we were greeted by the manager. I knew he was the manager because he wore an orange bowling shirt with the word "Manager" written across the back. The name over the front pocket was "Bud."

He wore thick glasses that magnified his eyes. His mouth opened wide when he smiled, and he approached me with hand outstretched. "Hiya, hiya, welcome to the Sunny Beach Celebrity Hotel."

Tia said, "This is Adam McCleet. He's with the Porcelli party."

"Do you have a vacancy?" I asked.

"Single or double?"

On the chance that Alison might visit me for the weekend, I said, "Double."

He dove behind his desk and consulted a large book before looking up. "You're in luck, Adam, I've got two rooms left. The Crazy Guggenheim Room and the Tony Perkins Room."

"Don't ask," Tia warned.

But I was curious. "Why are the rooms named?"

"House specialty," he confided. "Ever heard of 'George Washington Slept Here'? Huh, have you?"

I nodded. His eyeballs bulged through his Coke-bottle-glasses. Bud the manager looked like a wildly enthusiastic breed of insect, one that I could only hope would be soon endangered.

"Well," he said, "it's the same thing here, at the Sunny Beach Celebrity. Every room is named for a famous person who slept here." He leaned back behind his counter and mumbled a disclaimer, "Or, at least, they answered my letter inviting them to stay here."

"I see." But I didn't. "What's the point?"

"People love it," Bud exclaimed. "You see, Adam, I decorated each of the rooms with something that reminds you of the famous person. For example—" He gestured to Tia. "Tell him about your room, the Tonto Room, which is, of course, named for Jay Silverheels."

She sighed. "There's a stuffed horse's head on the wall."

"Stuffed, as in teddy bear?" I asked.

"Stuffed, as in taxidermy."

"Not just any horse," Bud explained. "That horse is an exact genuine replica of Scout, the horse that Tonto rode." He expelled a chuckle. "Hi-ho, Silver."

"Sounds like it ought to be the Godfather room," I commented.

Bud threw back his head and laughed, then sobered and considered. Then he shrugged. "So which will it be, Adam? The Guggenheim or the Tony Perkins?"

I reasoned that a room named after Crazy Guggenheim might be loud and/or full of ukulele music. Tony Perkins, on the other hand, was most famous for his role in _Psycho,_ which was lethal, but relatively quiet. "I'll take the Perkins."

Bud dangled the key before me. "You're going to love it. The Perkins is right down the hall from the Tonya Harding Suite, right next to the Bob Packwood Room."

I accepted my key and followed Tia upstairs. "Why," I asked her, "would Jimmy Caruthers reserve rooms in this particular place?"

"Amazingly enough, there's a heliport in the back."

"So?"

"Harrison flies a chopper. It's kind of sad, really. His father— the late, great Graden—was a World War Two flying ace. Harrison is always trying to live up to his father's macho image. Still, he was smart enough to stay out of Vietnam."

"Very smart," I agreed.

Tia regarded me suspiciously. "I thought you were a Marine?"

"Which is not a measure of intelligence. After my tour in Vietnam, I spent a lot of time advising others not to go."

"That's kind of how it was with Harrison. Graden always said he was glad that his only son didn't risk his life in the armed services, but he never missed an opportunity to remind Harrison that he wasn't really a macho guy. Harrison compensates with things like bungee jumping and helicopters."

I was no psychiatrist, but it sounded like a classic prove-your-manhood-to-your-father thing.

"Jimmy also picked this hotel because Bud is a client of his," she explained. "He was a local boy who made good as a producer of B movies and was charged with something white collar, some kind of fraud. Anyway, Jimmy got him off, but Bud spent most of his nest egg on legal fees. He had just enough left over to buy this hotel and set up business."

"Exploiting his sterling contacts with such famous people as Crazy Guggenheim," I said.

"And local celebs, like Tonya and the former Senator Packwood." She gave me one last smile. "By the way, Adam, if you eat in the cafe, do not order the Hannibal Lecter fava beans."

I turned to the left and proceeded down the narrow hall to a room with a small brass placard on the door. TONY PERKINS it said.

With some trepidation, I turned the key in the lock and stepped inside. It looked like a normal hotel room, plain and bland with furniture that was stylish in the 1950s. So where was the Tony Perkins decor? I thought of the movie *Psycho*. There had to be something weird in the shower.

But the bathroom appeared to be normal. I turned on the hot water in the shower. As soon as the spray pulsed, there was a blast from a six-inch speaker mounted on the wall over the medicine cabinet. It was the ear-jarring *scree-scree-scree* music that in the movie had proceeded the attack by the knife-wielding psychotic. It went silent after five seconds. How quaint.

I wondered if there would be other surprises, like a midnight visit from Bud the Manager, dressed like his mother. That would be extra special.

When I stepped out in the hall, I glanced down the narrow corridor to the Tonya Harding Suite. Had the former Olympic figure skater actually stayed at the Sunny Beach? I wondered what kind of treats Bud had installed in there, perhaps a crowbar mounted over the bed, or thirty seconds of whining when the lights were switched on. Maybe there was a sign in the bathroom that reminded the guests: DON'T FORGET TO FLUSH THE GILOOLEY.

I headed downstairs. There were a couple of other things I needed to do today before nightfall. Fix the windshield was numero uno. Locating Tiger Jorgenson was the second. He was the only one of the heirs whom I had not seen at the golf course. Though the murder of Sam Leggett did not require the physical presence of the murderer, I kind of expected that the killer would hang around to see if his exploding golf ball broke par.

I left the Chevy at a car repair shop on the coast highway and hoofed it down the hill toward the docks. Bud the Manager had told me that Tiger lived on his trawler, which was usually moored at the Embarcadero.

It felt good to stretch my legs, and the salt smell in the air invigorated me. Following Bud's simple directions, I had no difficulty in locating the moorage at the east end of the bay front. With dozens of recreational sail and fishing boats moored beside dozens of rugged commercial trawlers, the docks of the Embarcadero marina were a forest of masts, outriggers, and radio antennas. Beyond the tar-blackened pilings of the moorage, the stern wheel of an authentic Mississippi riverboat churned its way against the steady currents of incoming tide, decks awash with enthusiastic tourists. THE BELLE OF NEWPORT was stenciled on her bow.

At the bottom of the marina's gangway I found a guy who was busy gutting and scaling a sack full of prehistoric-looking bottom fish. I asked him for directions because he executed his smelly job with such efficiency that he had to be a local. Using his bloody filleting knife as a pointer, he directed me toward the southwest corner of the marina. "Look for the _Patty Carmen_. That's Tiger's boat."

The _Patty Carmen_ was a thirty-foot steel-hulled salmon trawler, a working vessel, nothing fancy about it. Though her white paint was chipped and streaked with rust stains, she looked stout, and capable of holding her own in severe weather. In spite of the outwardly unkempt appearance, her decks were scrubbed clean without nets or clutter laying about. There was also no sign of Tiger. A rusting padlock secured the hasp on the cabin door.

The *Patty Carmen's* dock neighbor was another trawler. A shirtless and tanned teenaged boy wearing a backward baseball cap and faded jeans tucked into knee-high rubber boots was at the stern, hosing fish guts off the deck.

"Excuse me," I said.

"Yo," the kid acknowledged.

"I'm looking for Tiger Jorgenson. Do you know if he's around?"

"I don't think so," the young hoser said.

"Do you know where he might be?"

"This time of day, Tiger usually goes out there . . ." The kid pointed west with his hose, and I had to jump out of the way to keep from getting soaked. ". . . past the bridge to the end of the north jetty."

"Why?"

"He's a goofy old fart. Likes to fish while he watches the sunset."

The kid seemed to have his hose under control again, so I ventured one more question. "Did he take his boat out today?"

"Don't think so. It was here when we went out this morning, and it was still here when we came in."

"Good enough. Thanks."

I couldn't see the jetty from where I stood, but the formidable green bridge that spanned the bay from north to south was less than a half mile away. When I struck out on foot again, I had no idea the man-made finger of rocks that shielded the harbor from the Pacific Ocean's perpetual surf was more than a mile long. It only began at the base of the bridge. If I'd had my car it would have been no help, because the jetty was closed to motor vehicles.

As much as I like the water, it was kind of spooky out there. To my left were the gently rolling swells of the bay, green and glassy, deep and quiet. But to my right, colossal waves of the incoming tide crashed against the jagged basalt rocks and exploded into towering plumes of foam. It felt weird and unnatural with packed gravel instead of the deck of a boat beneath my feet.

I was severely underdressed in a short-sleeved shirt. Even under the cloudless May sky, the combination of salt spray from the waves and a steady onshore wind chilled me to the bone. I stopped walking at one point, thinking I would turn back, but when I looked behind me I realized that I had already come more than half the distance, well past the point of no return. Besides, all along the way I was passed by families who had already been to the end of the jetty and were now headed back to the beach—mothers and fathers and grandparents and kids from toddlers to teens. In spite of the fact that they were all dressed more sensibly in Windbreakers and raincoats, I decided if they could do it, I could do it.

There was still a mob of warmly dressed tourists at the extreme end of the jetty when I finally got there. Most of them had binoculars pressed against their eyeballs, and the ones who didn't begged the ones who did for a peek. Part of the jetty attraction, besides getting soaked to the skin by the spray from the crashing waves, was the proximity to coastal aquatic life. I have heard that people from Nebraska will actually autoejaculate at the mere glimpse of a gray whale's gigantic tail fluke. Much to the delight of the crowd, the seals that afternoon were particularly bold, even venturing onto the rocks not more than twenty feet away.

I found Tiger Jorgenson sitting on a little folding camp chair, smoking a pipe. He wore a black watch cap and a loose-knit fisherman's sweater under a Navy-issue pea coat. His fishing rod was disassembled and stowed under his chair along with his tackle box.

The tourists gave him a wide berth, scampering along the edge of the rocks and squealing at the adorableness of fur-covered blubber with fins. Dozens of seals barked a response.

I stood beside him. "How's the fishing?"

"Sucks," he said. "It's these damned seals."

I nodded. "Protected species."

"Fat little eating machines. They've cleared the harbor of fish. Fuck 'em. That's what I say."

"Did you hear about Sam Leggett?"

"More money for me," he said, cackling. "Too bad for that scrawny, snorting wife of his." He cackled some more. "Hell, I hope they all murder each other off before the payout."

Despite the poor fishing, environmentally protected seals, and the death of a Porcelli heir, Tiger was in a fine mood. I was standing close enough to catch a whiff of the reason why.

When he stood up and shook both legs, I thought he might burst into a sailor's jig. Yo, ho, ho, and a bottle of whatever he'd been guzzling.

"Does it worry you," I asked, "that somebody is killing off the heirs?"

"They're getting what they deserve."

"But you're an heir," I pointed out.

"So are you, m'boy, and I don't see you burying yourself in a hole like a scared clam. Damn clams. Clam damns." He squinted toward Newport. "You like chowder, McCleet?"

"Sure."

"Can't see the place from here, but it's there. You mark me. It's there."

"What place?"

"Patty's Clam Dip. Best fuckin' clam chowder in Oregon.

She's my ex-wife." He spat in the dirt. "Gets half of everything I get."

He hawked up another big one, spat again, and turned toward the horizon, where the bottom rim of the scarlet sun had just touched the edge of the sea. "We're going to see whales tonight," he predicted. "You mark me. I can smell 'em."

"Have you lived here all your life?"

"Long enough. This is my home," he said. "My sun. My moon. My tides. Beautiful, ain't it? Graden never could understand. He was always worried more about counting his change than watching the golden sunset shimmer across the waves."

This poetic interlude convinced me that Tiger wasn't nearly as drunk as he pretended to be. It was a pose, I thought. This grizzled old character had developed a regular act to keep most people at a distance. Might be a reason for that. Might be that Tiger was dangerous when you tweaked his tail.

However, as he had pointed out, I wasn't hiding in the sand. "Do you remember a guy named Harold Mann?"

"Big Harry Mann. Sure, I remember. There's nothing wrong with my brain."

"According to Amelia Porcelli, he disappeared mysteriously. Have you got any ideas about that?"

"Harry wasn't no fool. Not like me and Graden. He saw the sharks circling, and he got out of the bay." Tiger stared in my face. "Women! Harry took off before he had to marry one of 'em. Like I say, he wasn't no fool."

"The way I understand it, Harry left behind all the financing for the salmon-packing plants. That must have been a pretty frightening woman to make him give up all that."

"He didn't lose nothing. Me and Graden made the loan payments. Every damned one of 'em, on time."

"Why wouldn't Harry contact you after the plants became successful? Wouldn't he want his share?"

"Maybe he did," Tiger said ominously. "Maybe he came back

here and demanded some money. Maybe Graden killed him. Hell, maybe it was me." He cackled and wiggled his hips like a hula dancer. "Yes, sir. I'm the murderer. But you got no proof, Adam McCleet, and you never will have any proof on account of nobody ever saw or heard of Big Harry Mann again."

Tiger shuffled toward the tourists. He moved close to an attractive family of four—mother, father, daughter, and son. The boy was probably eight, towheaded and apple-cheeked.

"Hey, kid," Tiger said, "c'mere."

The boy looked up at his mother and father.

"I won't hurt ya," Tiger promised. "Lemme show you where to look so's you'll see the whales."

Though the mother pulled her little girl close to her side, the father came forward with his son. "Thank you for offering. That's very kind. What do we say, Todd?"

"Thanks," the little boy said, but he looked dubious.

"You must be a real fisherman," said the father with a keen grasp of the obvious.

"Right you are. Been a fisherman all my life."

"We're from Riverside near Los Angeles."

"I'm going to show you one of nature's miracles, kid." Tiger knelt down beside the boy. "Take a look out there in the harbor. Do you see any fishermen out there?"

"I see boats."

"Those are sissy boats. Not real fishermen like me." He wrapped his arm around the boy's skinny shoulders. "Know why there's no fishermen? Do ya, Todd?"

"Nope."

"Because there ain't no fish. And there ain't no fish because there's too many seals and there's too many seals because of some ecological bullshit about protecting the critters. Are you followin' me, Todd?"

The boy looked a little tense, but his father replied. "Now,

now, old-timer. Those environmentalists have good reasons for what they do. Right, Todd?"

"I guess so, Dad."

"And those seals are pretty damn cute," Tiger said. "Aren't they? Those protected seals. Real adorable." He pointed to a seal that was skimming the waves about twenty yards out on the ocean side of the jetty. "Like that one. Look at how fast he can swim."

"Remarkable," said the father.

Someone yelled, "Whales," and all the tourists made excited noises as they scurried to the edge of the rocks to watch.

I caught sight of a pair of black, sail-shaped fins sticking three feet out of the water, fifty yards beyond where the seal was swimming. They were killer whales, and their fins were visible for only a few seconds before they slipped beneath the ocean swells.

"Ooooh," Tiger said. "Did ya see the whales, kid?"

"Uh-uh," little Todd replied.

"That's okay," Tiger patiently advised. "Just keep your eye on Sammy the Seal, kid."

I realized what was about to happen, but before I could advise Todd's father that the next show was rated PG, one of the orcas broached directly under the happy little seal and carried him fifteen feet above the water in its gaping jaws. The injured animal's screams split the air as the whale performed a twisting half gainer and came down on its side, slamming the seal onto the ocean surface with bone-crushing force. The resulting splash of sea foam was pink with blood, and Sammy the Seal was no more.

Some of the tourists screamed hysterically and ran around in circles, while others just stood staring with jaws agape. Before any of them could regroup, another whale broached and took a nearby seal in the same manner, and the hysterics began again.

The drama was replayed twelve more times over a period of three minutes.

Todd, who I was certain would be traumatized for life, ran sobbing to his mother, who was also sobbing, and clung to her leg.

Tiger cackled. "Fuckin' adorable, if you ask me."

Chapter
Seven

Tiger Jorgenson was a jolly old salt, a crusty old tar, and a poster boy for the argument: It's never too late to join Alcoholics Anonymous. How much of Tiger's ramblings could I believe? After the incident with the tourists and the seal-a-cidal orcas, I suspected he was somebody who would go a long way for a practical joke. He was somebody who might think an exploding golf ball was an appropriate murder weapon.

Tiger had as much as admitted that he killed Big Harry Mann and challenged me to find proof, which led me to wonder if proof could still exist for a murder that had taken place some forty years earlier.

Collecting evidence had never been one of my favorite endeavors. The process was slow, painstaking, and completely lacking in spontaneity. Even when I was a full-time PPD officer, I was always the guy who strolled onto the crime scene, picked up the smoking gun in my bare hands, and said "Ah-ha!" while everybody else groaned about fingerprints and fibers. As far as sleuthing went, I counted myself among the forensically impaired.

That handicap would have to change if I wanted to collect my two point one or point five million.

I left Tiger snickering at the end of the jetty and headed for town in search of evidence that the crusty old fisherman had murdered Big Harry Mann. I knew just where to start. Figuring that there was nothing like a former spouse to fill in the negative blanks in a person's character, I planned to stop by Patty's Clam Dip and still have time to pick up my car before the repair shop closed.

I walked at a brisk pace, nearly jogging. The damp air on the jetty was turning even colder as the sun slipped behind the horizon. I passed several clusters of people who had been in attendance at the seal massacre. They seemed to have recovered from the initial shock of the event, and were chatting excitedly about what they'd seen. The snatches of conversations I overheard indicated that most of the tourists felt as I did; they were honored to have witnessed the big orcas close-up, doing what comes naturally in their own element.

But as I caught up with little Todd and his family, I heard the father say, ". . . disgraceful."

At first I thought he was talking about the old fisherman who scared the shit out of his kid, but as I passed them, I heard him say, "Decent, taxpaying citizens should not have to witness such a bloody abomination. As soon as we get back to the motel, I'm going to draft a letter to the governor of Oregon. There ought to be a law."

Perfect. Why is it that only bozos write letters? The people who felt privileged to have been there would go home and enthusiastically recount the details of the whales they'd seen feeding in Newport, and their friends would share in the excitement. But none of them would think to write a thank-you letter to the governor.

A fisherman would say, "Good riddance to the seals." A Taoist would say, "It is as it should be." Bob Hope would say, "Thanks for the memories." But a taxpaying moron who thinks that nature exists solely for its recreational value to himself and his family will say, "There ought to be a law," and quicker than you can say, "Bullshit," the U.S. Supreme Court is sitting around listening to arguments over the constitutional rights of whale food.

I thought about stopping to give Todd's father a piece of my attitude, but I realized it would have been like shouting into an empty bucket. I picked up my pace to put some distance between myself and the moron.

Patty's Clam Dip wasn't hard to find on the bay front. In the architectural tradition of the Oscar Mayer wienermobile, the Clam Dip had been painted to look like a giant clam wearing a stovepipe top hat and twirling a cane as if he were ready to burst into a suave rendition of "Puttin' on the Ritz." Completing the cartoon motif, there was a large, grinning, three-dimensional, rubber octopus draped over the doorway, looking not in the least intimidated by the sophisticated hyperthyroid mollusk.

On the inside, Patty's Clam Dip was a shade too cruddy to be considered quaint. The fishnetting, stapled haphazardly to the ceiling, was tangled with dusty plastic treasures, shells, and cobwebs. On every Formica table there was a clamshell with a candle and a plastic rose in a Budweiser longneck bottle painted gold. The background music was opera. Bizet, I thought.

The sullen patrons appeared to be mostly locals. There were only a few brave tourists. I took a seat at the counter and ordered the chowder from a jaded waitress who—despite a long, curly, raven-haired wig—looked old enough to qualify for Senior Citizen discounts.

When she delivered my chowder, the thick beige liquid slopped over the sides onto the counter. "Thanks," I said.

"You're not from around here," she said.

"Nope." I flashed a winning smile. "But I have business in the area. Is Patty around?"

"She might be." I could have sworn that she was leering around the cataracts in her dark eyes. She tossed her raven-haired tresses. "What did you have in mind?"

"Are you Patty?"

"*Sí, señor.* Patrice Carmen Jorgenson. Carmen, the Gypsy woman." As the opera on the sound system segued into the familiar "Toreador Song" from *Carmen,* the waitress plucked a plastic rose from a vase and held it between her perfectly white dentures, snapping her fingers over her head like castanets. *"Ole, baby!"*

The surprised expression on my face must have been amusing, because she spat out the rose and belly-laughed. I should have guessed that Tiger Jorgensen would not have married a shrinking violet.

"I know who you are," she said. "You're that detective fella who was at the reading of Graden Porcelli's will."

"Adam McCleet," I introduced myself.

Her grip was stronger than that of most men when she shook my hand. "I heard that Sam Leggett went and got himself blown to kingdom come. Too bad." But she obviously wasn't in mourning. "Nothing's happened to Tiger, that old fart, has it?"

"The old fart is fine," I informed her. "He's out on the jetty scaring the tourists."

"Aw, hell. He's drunk, ain't he?"

I conceded the possibility. "Is this a pattern?"

"You guessed it, McCleet." Her Spanish accent, which came and went, made her words sound "choo gist eet." She continued. "Tiger's a binge drinker. When the fishing is bad, Tiger gets a snoot full, then he comes here to the Clam Dip and makes a scene. Then he takes off in his boat, gets even more drunk, and floats around until he's sober." She shook her head, sending ripples through her wavy black hair. "I only hope the old fart lives long enough to collect his inheritance. Half that money is mine, choo know."

That was some unusual alimony settlement. "You get half of what he makes?"

"Forever and ever. That's what he promised me." She cocked a hip at me, Carmen-style. "You wouldn't think it to look at me now, but I was a regular honeybunch when Tiger and I got married."

"I believe it," I said. There was a blowsy appeal to Patty the Clam Queen that demanded attention. I wondered how I had overlooked her at the reading of the will.

"When we got unhitched, Jimmy Caruthers asked for half Tiger's income in perpetuity—that means for-fucking-ever—and Tiger, the old fart, was too cocky to think he needed an attorney, so he got stuck with paying me."

She slapped both palms down on the countertop. "You can see that I'm a woman who gets what she wants. Right, McCleet?"

"Yep."

"Right now I want you to figure out which of these Porcelli money-grubbers was the murderer. 'Cause that means more money for Patty Carmen. For me."

I decided against telling her that Tiger was my favorite pick for past murderer. Instead, I took a taste of the chowder. The flavor was remarkable, creamy but not bland. "Good stuff."

"Choo bet chour _cojones,_ it is. I got the recipe off an old Spanish sailor in Madrid. But we got more to talk about than food, McCleet. How come you're here?"

"Do you remember Harry Mann?"

"Honey, there have been a lot of hairy men in my life, but I think I know who you're talking about. He was around here way back. Amelia had a thing for him."

"And he disappeared," I prompted.

"Any man in his right mind would disappear if Amelia was on his tail."

I took another savory swallow of chowder and nodded encouragingly.

"Amelia Porcelli is the kind of woman who takes trophies," Patty said. "You know, like those tourists who catch a salmon, then stuff it? If Amelia got her claws into Harry, she would have had his testicles bronzed for a door knocker."

"Did you ever hear anything suspicious about Harry's disappearance?"

"Come right out with it, McCleet. You're asking me if I think he was murdered." She shrugged. "Could be. He left behind enough financing for Graden and Tiger to get the cannery started." She scowled darkly. "If I was looking there for a motive, I would've said Graden might have killed him. But Graden's dead. That's not going to help us."

When she snapped her fingers, I hoped she wasn't going to start the *Carmen*-and-castanets routine again. "I betcha it was Amelia who bumped him off. She's your murderer."

"Motive?" I asked directly.

"You're not as smart as you look, McCleet. There's only one reason a woman kills a man. Don't you listen to opera?" She gestured in the air, indicating the background music. "It's *amour,* McCleet. *Toujours l'amour.*"

"So Harry was in love with another woman." I looked at her. "You?"

"Likely," she said, fluffing her wig. "Most of the guys were. But, back then, I had eyes only for Tiger. I'm a passionate woman. It's the Gypsy blood in me."

"Who was Harry in love with?"

"This is a hell of a long time ago, McCleet. But I think he might have had a fling with Graden Porcelli's sister. Before she got herself pregnant and had to marry Leggett."

While Patty ran off to make a quick round of the cafe, filling coffee mugs and dropping off checks, I considered the long-ago murder. Rumors, filtered through the gauze of several intervening years, were hardly a basis for accusation.

All things considered, it seemed more logical to investigate the exploding-golf-ball incident. If I was lucky, the cops would come up with some useful forensic evidence.

Patty returned to the counter and stood across from me. "Here's what I think, McCleet. You need proof. If Amelia killed Harry, you're in luck. That woman doesn't throw anything away. Not ever. You search her stuff, and you're going to find your proof."

"Thanks for the advice, Patty."

"But you might be smarter to look at what's going on right under your nose." She reached across the counter for what she probably thought was a playful tweak of my nose. "Somebody just murdered Sam Leggett."

"Right. And all the heirs were at the golf course. Except for Tiger."

"What are you talking about, honey? Tiger's the best golfer in the county. By the time the rest of those yahoos were teeing up, Tiger had already completed the course. He usually places in the money at the Spring Scramble."

"Tiger was there?"

"Choo betcha."

I thanked Patty for her information and promised I would be back for more chowder. I suspected that most men would come back. Patty was a powerful combination of lusty passion and an ability to cook—highly attractive to most men.

I leaned across the counter. "How many times have you been married, Patty?"

"Just once. There have been a lot of men, but Tiger is the only one I truly loved. I'd do anything for the old fart."

Anything?

As I strolled through the purposely scenic Newport fishing village, heading to pick up my car so I could drive back to the purposely strange Sunny Beach Celebrity Hotel, I wondered about Patty Carmen. She'd been at the reading of the will which—technically—placed her among the people I ought to suspect. So, how did the Clam Queen rank among those "most likely to commit murder"? Fairly high, I thought. If Harry Mann had been bumped off to further the cannery careers of Graden and Tiger, Patty was tough enough to do it. Despite her hearty and charming attitude—not unlike her chowder—she was acquisitive, i.e., the alimony that equaled half of Tiger's lifetime income. A scary thought! Jimmy Caruthers must be one hell of a lawyer to come up with that kind of settlement.

Overhead, I heard the ratcheting noise of a helicopter, a sound that always whispered Vietnam to my subconscious. The fleeting illusion was completed by the sunset time of evening when the skies above the Pacific were streaked in a scarlet warning. If I were someone given to post-traumatic stress flashbacks, I might have had one at that moment. Impending disaster lay heavily on my mind. Somebody else was going to die.

Not that Newport looked anything like Vietnam . . . or that Harrison Porcelli's chopper looked anything like the camouflage-colored Hueys which I was most familiar with. Those machines were no frills. They were homely, like Yugos with rotor blades.

Harrison's flying machine was a Rolls-Royce of helicopters, painted a shiny dark blue with silver lightning bolts. It was headed for the heliport at the Celebrity Hotel, which was probably ceremonially named the Buck Rogers Landing Pad.

The heirs seemed to be gathering at the hotel, and my best bet for picking up clues was to mingle. As I strolled through the center door, I remembered that mingling meant Margot. Like a bad penny, there she was, dressed in a skin-tight red and white T-shirt and white sailor pants that flared into a wide bell at her ankles. I supposed that this attire was my sister's version of casual sailing wear. She looked ready to seduce Captain Ahab.

Margot's face contorted in an unfamiliar expression of caring as she draped her arm around Desiree Leggett's sobbing shoulders.

I tried to sidle past unnoticed, but Margot spotted me. "Adam," she snapped. "Come over here and tell Desiree that I'm right."

"I'm sure you are," I said, not breaking stride.

"Adam! Get your ass over here. You owe me. I saved your life in New Mexico."

That fact was debatable—especially since the incident to which she was referring was all her fault—but I knew better than to thwart Margot when she used that tone of voice. It was best to indulge her when she got this way.

I shuffled up beside the two women, again noticing that they appeared to be the blond and brunette faces of the same coin. It was the first time I'd seen Desiree since her husband had spurted the last of his lifeblood onto my shirt. "I'm sorry, Desiree, for your tragedy."

She glared through her running mascara and gasped a weepy snort. "It's your fault. You were supposed to be protecting him."

What the hell had given everybody the idea that Graden Porcelli had appoint me bodyguard? "Actually—"

"Shut up, Adam," Margot counseled. "Now, Desiree, darling, I know you're upset."

Understandable, I thought, for a woman who had just watched her husband explode.

"I know what you're going through," Margot continued. "I myself am a widow."

Her third husband, a renowned and brilliant psychiatrist, had leapt from the fourth-story window of his hotel room in Las Vegas. In my opinion, he took that desperate course when he realized that a quick splash on the Vegas strip would be infinitely preferable to a long and agonizing divorce from Margot the Malignant.

"Losing a husband," Margot said, drawing from her extensive experience in this matter, "is like falling off a horse. You've got to climb right back on to keep your skills intact."

I doubted that Ann Landers would ever have offered that metaphor, but Desiree Leggett nodded obediently. When she let loose with a particularly loud snuffle, Margot shoved her away. "Watch it, Desiree. You're getting snot on my Dior."

"What am I going to do?" Desiree wailed. "I was supposed to get two point one million dollars."

Margot was all business. "What about Sam's other assets?"

"Oh, that! The house, the cars, the condo in Aspen, they're all mine. Jimmy Caruthers arranged for it." Suddenly, she brightened. "I know! I can sue! Wrongful death and all that. I'll get my million."

"That's my girl," Margot said proudly.

I was less impressed by this display of avarice in mourning. I hoped that when I shuffled off this mortal coil, those I left behind would give me at least twenty-four hours of remembering before they started dividing the spoils.

Margot—ever the font of advice—continued. "You need to spruce yourself up, Desiree. Funerals are sometimes the best place to meet your next mate."

Next victim, I thought. But I said nothing and started easing toward the stairs, eager to escape to the relative safety of my room.

At that moment Harrison Porcelli came through the door.

Margot nudged Desiree. "He's not married, is he?"

"No, he's not." The recent widow swabbed at the rivulets of mascara that formed sad-clown streaks on her cheeks. "I've always thought Harrison was kind of cute."

"Cute?" Margot scoffed. "Lots of guys are cute. Adam is even kind of cute in a dissipated way. What's Harrison's Dun and Bradstreet rating?"

"Not Fortune 500," Desiree admitted, "but he's much better off than Sam."

"Go ahead and talk to him," Margot encouraged. "If nothing else, it's good practice. Remember, you've got to get right back in the saddle."

I probably should have rushed over and warned Harrison: "Run for your life, man." But I was weirdly fascinated. Watching these two women was like viewing one of those specials where a predator stalks its prey. I imagined a calm British announcer's voice saying, "Notice how the long-legged, snorting, female greed monster prepares for her assault on the hapless male."

Desiree primped her long, silver-blond hair, took two gawky steps, and flung herself into Harrison's arms. As she clung to him in full frontal contact, I again thought of the nature show. "In a pretense of helplessness, the female entraps the male. He cannot escape without seeming insensitive."

She snorted, "Hold me, Harrison. I'm so alone."

Tentatively, he patted her shoulder and made "there, there, everything's going to be all right" noises. Then he convulsed, overcome by stress and Tourette's syndrome. He blurted out, "Feather farts."

"At this point," I imagined the announcer saying, "the female prepares to neuter her unwary prey by draining him of self-esteem and financial worth."

Beside me, Margot looked extremely pleased with herself. "This girl has promise. Do you see how she's subtly rubbing against him?"

Subtle? Desiree had coiled one long leg around Harrison and was practically humping his thigh.

"I'm curious, Margot. Why are you giving all this free advice?"

"For one thing, I'm not particularly interested in any of these salmon people. Fish fortunes just aren't my thing. I prefer professional men."

Harrison shouted, "Shit, shit, curdle butt."

"What's that all about?" Margot asked.

"He has Tourette's."

"It's a good thing he's rich." She cocked her head to one side, studying Desiree's progress as if she were critiquing a work of art. Again she murmured, "I'm good at this. Maybe I should open a school. Or a therapy center where I could share my techniques."

"Sure. A kind of Betty Ford clinic for avaricious widows? Swell idea, Margot. Why don't you head back to Portland and get started?"

"Not a chance, idiot boy. There's over two million bucks at stake here, and I'm going to see that you get it."

"Why?"

"Oh, gosh," she sneered sarcastically. "Would I rather be related to Adam McCleet, busted sculptor, or *the* Adam McCleet, millionaire?"

"Please don't help me, Margot."

"God only knows why Graden Porcelli thought you were capable of finding a murderer." She glared at me. "I'm feeling generous, Adam. I want to make sure you don't screw it up."

"No favors, Margot. Please."

As Tia came clomping down the stairs in her Birkenstocks, Margot whispered to me, "If you ask me, that's the one with murder in her background. I mean, look at what she's wearing."

I hated myself for asking. "What do her clothes have to do with anything?"

"She feels guilty, idiot. That outfit is practically a hair shirt."

On either side of Tia were the Parkens, Whit and Dottie, future sheep ranchers.

"And those two," Margot said. "Keep an eye on them, Adam. They've got obvious homicidal potential. Anybody whose life dream is raising lambs has got to be off balance."

It did not escape my alert sleuthing eyeballs that three of the remaining five heirs were present: Whit, Tia, and Harrison. If

I'd been Hercule Poirot, I would have suggested retiring to the parlor, where I would dazzle them with my logical conclusions.

Unfortunately, I didn't have a clue.

Figuring that Tiger was scheduled for a drunken brawl at his ex-wife's restaurant, upping the number of heirs to four, I suggested, "Why don't we all head down to Patty's Clam Dip for dinner?"

Margot rolled her eyes. "I don't do cutsy dinner."

"Fine. You can stay here."

"I'd love to see Patty Carmen," Dottie said hopefully. "She's the salt of the earth."

"Makes great coffee," Whit chimed in.

"We should have a talk," Tia said. "Desiree, we need to discuss funeral arrangements."

"I can't!" she wailed, tightening her death grip on Harrison. "It's too hard for me. Sam was my heart. My soul. My inspiration."

Desiree glanced at Margot for approval, and my sister frowned and shook her head.

Unconcerned about her beloved Sam, Desiree refocused on Harrison. "Not that I could never love again. That's not true at all. I could. I could love again. I could make another man very, very happy."

"To the Clam Dip." I linked arms with Tia.

Our mass exodus was halted by Bud, the proprietor of the Celebrity Hotel. He flung his scrawny arms across the doorway, holding back the tide of our escape. "Your table is set and dinner has been paid for by Jimmy Caruthers. In _my_ dining room." He waved his arms in the sort of dramatic gesture that a lounge singer uses to complete the final phrase of a groovy Barry Manilow tune. "The Chill Wills Cafe!"

Dottie Parkens was so thrilled that she actually forgot about sheep for a moment. "Chill Wills? I love Chill Wills."

"Who doesn't? It's almost un-American not to love Chill Wills.

And he actually ate here. Had a BLT. I tried to save the crusts of his sandwich, but Wonder Bread isn't the best memento."

Yum, I thought. "Sorry, Bud, I feel like clam."

"I have lobster," Bud announced.

Whit and Dottie Parkens fell into step behind him, and the rest of us followed like an obedient flock.

We had circled the table, when Jimmy Caruthers breezed in, congratulated us on finding our table, and announced, "I hate to say this, folks, but it's real possible that someone here is responsible for the murder of Sam Leggett."

"What about Tiger?" asked Desiree.

"What about Amelia?" asked Dottie.

Jimmy Caruthers continued. "I'm very upset about this. Frankly, if I had thought Graden's will would result in such tragedy, I never would have gone along with it. I suggest that all of you exert extreme caution. Adam can't be expected to keep watch over everybody."

"Hold it!" I said, wanting this misconception cleared up. "I never signed on as a bodyguard."

"Not precisely," Jimmy agreed, staying true to the letter of the will.

Dottie said, "But Graden said you were a detective."

"I'm a sculptor," I said.

"But you used to be a policeman," Harrison said. "And you were in Vietnam."

"Many years ago," I reminded him.

Jimmy Caruthers glanced around the table. "I'm afraid you're elected, Adam. Who else is going to do it?"

Not Whit. He was already into his own caffeine high.

Dottie, his wife, was too preoccupied with her sheep to think about protecting anything else.

Tia had spent a lifetime avoiding her family, so it hardly seemed likely that she would start looking after them now.

Desiree couldn't see beyond her own snorting nostrils.

That left Harrison. I studied him carefully. Aside from Tourette's syndrome, which was only a minor source of embarrassment to him, there was nothing overtly screwy about Harrison Porcelli, Graden's son. Why hadn't the old man passed this responsibility to his shoulders? What was wrong with Harrison?

Chapter
Eight

Dinner with the heirs was turning out to be something less than a clue fest. Few words were wasted on speculation about the death of Sam Leggett. The heirs preferred to avoid that uncomfortable subject, choosing instead to reminisce about family and discuss plans for the future spending of their inheritance. But the murder was still there, lurking at the edge of our collective unconscious like the stink of rotten salmon.

We were all wearing our bibs, disassembling lobster claws, when I brought it up. "So, Whit, where were you when Sam hit the exploding golf ball?"

"Don't tell him," Dottie cautioned. "Listen, Adam, we've talked about this, Whit and I, and we've decided . . ."

Behind her back, Whit was shaking his head, automatically denying anything his wife had to say.

"We've decided," Dottie continued, "that you can't expect us to do your job for you, Adam. You're supposed to find the murderer. Not us."

"I'd think the identity of the murderer would be of interest to you," I pointed out. "Since Whit might be the next victim."

"That won't happen. We're leaving for home tomorrow."

I raised my eyebrows. "Why wouldn't the murderer follow?"

"My children will be there. And the sheep."

Whit sipped his coffee. "Dottie thinks the sheep are smart enough to protect us."

"Guard sheep?"

He chuckled nervously, swigging his coffee. "Attack sheep. Oh, yeah, they're vicious. They can mill around and bore you to death. Before you know what's hit you, your eyelids grow heavy, you collapse in a stupor. The sheep fall on top of you and smother you."

"Vicious," I agreed. "So, where were you?"

"Front and center," he said. "I didn't actually see the explosion. But I was right there. We all were."

"Not much of a clue," Jimmy Caruthers mentioned. His lips twitched under his mustache, and I thought he seemed pleased about how difficult it would be for me to figure out the crime. "Not to mention the fact that anyone could have placed that ball in Sam's bag at any time before the Spring Scramble."

"You think that ball could have been intended for someone else, Jimmy?" I asked.

"It's possible, I suppose"—Jimmy Caruthers stroked his mustache thoughtfully—"but I seriously doubt it. Too much of a coincidence, don't you think?"

I did think, but I didn't say so. "Arnold Palmer's clubs," I said. "Does anybody happen to know when Amelia gave them to Sam Leggett?"

"Do we have to talk about this?" Desiree groaned. "I mean, Sam would want us to get on with our lives."

I hate when people say that somebody who's dead would want them to get on, be happy, don't worry. What does a dead person care about the puny actions of the living? But two could play that game. What would Sam Leggett want? "You think, maybe, Sam would have wanted his murderer brought to justice?"

"He wasn't like that," Desiree said with her trademark snorting noise. "Not vindictive. He would want me to be happy."

Margot added, "Probably would have wanted you to remarry."

"Yes, indeed." She fluttered her lashes with gale-force wind at Harrison. "Sam understood that a woman has needs."

Harrison blurted out, "Salmon turds."

From the way he was shifting around in his chair, I guessed that Desiree was engaged in an aggressive game of kneesies under the table.

The topic then turned to funeral arrangements for poor Sam. Both Tia and Desiree were delighted to pass the buck to Jimmy Caruthers. Tia's only request was that her brother be cremated. Desiree agreed, adding that she wanted his ashes stored in a designer vase. Margot knew just the place to shop for such an item which, I thought, was predictable. Of course, my sister would have intimate knowledge of all things expensive and ghoulish.

After the lobster dinner—prepared à la Julia Child, who had never actually stayed at the Celebrity Hotel but had once sent a recipe—Jimmy Caruthers informed us that we were all invited to an early dinner at Amelia's house on the following day. "Around four o'clock for cocktails."

"Including me?" Desiree whined.

"Of course, dear," Jimmy assured her. "Though you aren't really an heir anymore, you're still part of the family."

"Maybe I am an heir," she said, rising to her feet and towering over Jimmy Caruthers. "I'm Sam's heir."

Jimmy started to explain, "I really don't think—"

"I could sue!" The realization apparently struck her happy, because her horsy lips parted and she made a noise very much like braying. "I could, couldn't I?"

"Well, I—"

"Come on, Jimmy. You're my lawyer. Don't I have a case?"

"Possibly," he conceded. "This entire will is highly irregular. If one chooses to be litigious—"

"Which I am," said Desiree proudly. "I once got free repairs to my car because Jimmy proved that the stoplights in Portland were out of sync and that caused me to speed. Oh, and I won a free trip to Paris to replace a designer dress that some ass spilled red wine on."

"Brilliant!" Margot said. She turned to Jimmy. "You handled those cases?"

"Yes, but those were out-of-court settlements and—"

"I want to sue somebody!" Margot announced. She was also standing. The thrill of possible money for nothing had driven her to her feet.

Harrison twitched and shouted, "Jailbait."

Jimmy Caruthers frowned under his mustache. "Really, now. This isn't the way we decide—"

"But there are lots of people who have pissed me off," Margot said with enthusiastic relish—more than relish. She was so enthused that she spoke with all the condiments. "I want to sue them. I could be on Court TV."

Or, at least, on Wapner.

"I want to sue . . . everybody!"

"It's great fun," Desiree assured her. "I have an entire go-to-court wardrobe."

Margot linked arms with her. They were like blood sisters, twin vampires in designer togs.

While they were tossing around ideas about who would feel the first bite of their litigious lash, the dinner party broke up. I took the opportunity to get Harrison alone. I was hoping that he might be able to get me access to his mother's crap collection so I could search for clues to the long-ago disappearance and possible murder of Big Harry Mann.

In the moonlight I strolled, and Harrison limped beside me. We were behind the Celebrity Hotel, walking toward the heliport, which turned out to be nothing more than a pair of empty lots with weeds mowed short, and a wind sock mounted on the roof of the hotel. He paused once, did his Tourette's shudder, and blurted out, "Foreskin."

Tactfully ignoring the outburst, I inquired, "Why a helicopter?"

"Seemed practical," he said. "Most of the salmon-packing plants are located in places that don't have landing fields. Commercial air travel is limited, and driving takes forever. A chopper seemed like the most efficient way to get from one place to another. My job, if you could call it a job, was to travel from one plant to another."

"Sales work?" This seemed an unlikely vocation for a man with Tourette's. Though we are living in an enlightened and politically correct era, most customers wouldn't be convinced to buy from a guy who occasionally yelled semi-obscenities in their face.

"Not sales. Operations. You know, I'd check the books and make sure everything was running smooth. My duties also included handing out certificates of appreciation to employees of the month. Mostly, my visits were a free lunch for cannery execs. Once I almost got involved with a Teamster negotiation before my father got wind of the fact that the work might be important and pulled me out of there."

"Graden didn't have much faith in you," I commented.

"He was supportive in his way." He shrugged, seemingly at peace with his dismally low self-esteem. "But I wasn't him. Hell, I couldn't be the great Graden Porcelli who fought his way up from nothing to become the salmon king. I couldn't be a self-made man because I already had it made. Know what I mean?"

I nodded. Though Harrison Porcelli was born with a silver spoon in his mouth, the taste was bitter.

Harrison said, "There's no such thing as a second-string hero."

Very true. In the classic black and white war movies that I never grow weary of watching, there's an obvious hero, and then there's a sidekick who, generally, gets greased by the Krauts or the Japs. The function of the sidekick is to point out how heroic the hero is by saying, "Wow, I couldn't have done that."

With or without his disability, Harrison was forever relegated to the role of sidekick. He was the guy who flew from cannery to cannery, buying lunches and wishing he could do something to make a real difference. "It must have been tough to have a self-made man for a father."

Harrison nodded. "What about you, Adam? What was your father like?"

My brain instantly flashed an image of a strong, broad-shouldered man surrounded with brilliant light. "To the best of my recollection, he was proud and honest. He worked like a dog. I don't think he ever took a sick day until the big C knocked him off his feet. He died when I was nine."

"Sorry."

"Me too. He was flat on his back for about a year. The whole time I kept thinking that when he got better, we'd do things together, go fishing, play catch, those kinds of things. But he never got better. The last thing he said to me, on his deathbed, was that I should take care of my sister."

"Margot?" Harrison asked with obvious surprise, emphasized by a shudder and a blurt that was mostly unintelligible, but sounded a lot like "cock-a-doodle-doo." He shook his head. "She doesn't seem to need much protection."

"Dad didn't know she was going to turn into a Gorgon."

Thinking back, my father might have said: Watch out for Margot. That statement had far different implications than care-taking.

As we stood at the edge of the bluff overlooking the sea, I

gazed up at the sky. When I was a kid, I used to imagine my father was up there, sitting on a star, keeping track of me, judging my performance and maybe offering a glimmer of celestial guidance. Over the years, his presence had faded like vapors in the night.

It had been a long time since I thought of my father in a direct way, but there were always little blips of regret. When I played well in a high school football game, when I received my Purple Heart, when I sold my first sculpture for enough money that I could quit my day job, I had wished that he'd been there to pat me on the head with his big calloused hand and say, "I'm proud of you, son." I really wanted him to be proud of me.

I cleared my throat, swallowing the sentimental lump that had begun to form, and looked at Harrison. He had probably wanted the same thing from Graden.

Neither of us ever got that fatherly pat on the head. The only real difference between me and Harrison was that his father had been there, alive, and didn't compliment him. A sad story, I thought, but the tragedy of Harrison Porcelli wasn't going to solve any murders for me.

"When you were growing up," I asked, "did you have much to do with Tiger?"

"He was off limits after he and my dad split, which was okay by me because I never really liked the old fart." As soon as he said "old fart," he grinned. "I always had a soft spot for Patty Carmen though. She was a major babe when she was younger."

Ah-ha! "Did you and Patty Carmen have a thing?"

"Hell, no. I appreciated her hooters, but she was old enough to be my mother."

Since this was the general direction I was headed—toward Amelia and her collections, I asked, "What about your mother? Has she always been a collector?"

"Always." He chuckled indulgently and blurted out, "Penis freckle."

I decided to level with Harrison. "I think there might be some clues hidden in Amelia's collections."

"Clues to what?"

"The only possible murder in the past that I've come up with involves the disappearance of Harry Mann. I was thinking that your mother might have saved something that has relevance."

"What makes you so sure there was a murder in the past? Sam was killed this morning, and that, sure as hell, was no accident."

"Definitely not. But your father didn't know anything about that when he made his will. He said that someone at the reading was a murderer. Graden had knowledge of a murder in the past. It's possible the old killer and the new killer are the same person. That's probably too broad an assumption to make at this point, but I've got to start somewhere. Maybe there's something in your mom's collections that can point me in the right direction."

Harrison nodded. "That's possible. She saves just about everything. Are you thinking of a diary or something?"

"Something," I said. "Is there any chance I could get a peek at some of her stuff."

Harrison laughed. "Not likely. That stuff is her pride and joy. Nobody gets a look unless it's a guided tour."

Another trip to the lunatic fringe, I thought, still gazing up into the starry night. I wondered if there was a constellation that went by that name: the Lunatic Fringe.

Harrison turned away from the bluff. "Speaking of guided tours, do you know anything about—" He trembled and sputtered, "Monkey tits." Giving his head a quick shake, he finished the original sentence, "helicopters?"

"A little. I rode in a lot of them in Vietnam. Always thought they were pretty neat, so I took some lessons when I got out of the service. About four flights cleaned out my life savings and I started looking for cheaper ways to get my jollies.

"What do you think of *Blue Thunder?*" Harrison asked as

we walked toward the dark blue chopper with silver lightning bolts on the side.

"Pretty slick," I said. "Which came first, the paint job or the name?"

"The name. I always loved that movie, *Blue Thunder,* about the chopper-flying cops. I've watched it about a thousand times. Never get tired of it."

I was familiar with the film, macho cops flying heavily armed extensions of their penises. More than the time-saving practicalities of flying, Harrison was into the studliness of being a chopper pilot. "It's a Jet Ranger, isn't it?"

"Bat crotch," he said, sliding back the door on the starboard side. "Close. It's a Bell, Long Ranger. A few feet longer and more torque than a Jet Ranger." He reached across the instrument panel and punched the battery switch, then clicked on the cabin lights. "I've upgraded just about everything."

The instruments were all the latest in digital technology, including a global positioning satellite receiver and two different radar scopes. The two pilot seats and four passenger seats were covered with rich gray leather, as were the bulkheads and head-liner. An expensive pair of noise-canceling headsets rested on the back of each seat. Further aft, there was ample space for cargo. "This is great. Maybe you can take me for a little spin along the beach."

Harrison's entire body tensed and shuddered as his head snapped back. "Rim cheese," he barked. "Sure. How 'bout tomorrow?"

What the hell was I thinking of? Helicopters are tricky machines. One of those Tourette's jerks on the cyclic pitch stick during takeoff or landing and I could be transformed into the gooey liquid center of a molten ball of crumpled aluminum. "Tomorrow probably wouldn't be good," I backpedaled. "I've got a lot to do, and not much time to do it in. You know, the investigation and everything."

"In the afternoon," he said, oblivious of my sudden reluctance. "I'll give you a ride to my mother's when we go for dinner."

"Great," I said, forcing an eager smile. "I'll look forward to it." I knew I'd think of some way to get out of it before then. At the very worst, I could think of a hundred quicker and less painful ways to kill myself.

Harrison clicked off the lights and the battery switch. As he locked the door he said, "If you want to know about Tiger Jorgenson, you should talk to Patty Carmen." He pointed toward the lights of the bay front. "She's got this funky little place called the Clam Dip."

"I was there this afternoon."

"Great chowder."

We strolled along the bluff toward the hotel. Our companionable silence was broken by Harrison's occasional growls and barks which kind of harmonized with the noise of the seabirds, waves breaking on the beach below and the clangs, dongs, and whistles of the navigational buoys.

The sights and sounds and smells of the ocean always made me pensive. My father had once told me that the sea was the mother, giver of life, and should be treated with respect. All women should be handled with reverence. My meandering thoughts turned to Alison, the most remarkable creature I had ever known. I ought to go back to my room and telephone her. But I knew she wouldn't approve of my sleuthing—especially not since there had been a murder.

"Hot baby, hot baby," Harrison muttered.

I asked, "Have you ever been married?"

"Four times."

Wow, he tied Margot's record. "You must be paying a fortune in alimony."

"A couple of hundred a month to the first one. After that,

Jimmy Caruthers drew up a killer prenuptial agreement. No payoff unless there were kids—which there weren't."

"How come?" I asked. As the designated snoop, it was my job to be nosy. "Not about the kids, but the wives."

"Seemed like the right thing to do at the time."

I was certain that there was more to it than that. "And?"

"Isn't that enough explanation?"

"Not really," I said. "Having lunch is something you do because it seems like the right thing at the time. Getting married repeatedly is a tad more complex."

"Fuck you," he blurted out.

I wasn't sure if his comment was due to Tourette's or a more direct curse.

"I'm not good at casual sex," Harrison muttered. "The medication I take makes it hard for me to get it up. Is that enough explanation for you? Do you want a graphic demonstration?"

"Not necessary." I felt like a limp dick for pushing the guy. Nobody likes to talk about the Big I. We all go through it from time to time, but impotence is no man's favorite topic of conversation.

He gave a strangled bark like a Great Dane in great pain.

"Sorry," I said. "Guess my investigating skills could use a little more finesse."

"I'm not a Bluebeard with dead wives in my closet," he said a little huffily. "I'm not an idiot either. Just horny."

"Let me get this straight," I said. "If you're not married, you're not getting any nooky?"

"Not usually. Most women aren't too pleased when I start making weird noises in the middle of foreplay."

"Funny," I said. "Most women I know like noises."

He glared at me in the moonlight. "At least, I've been married. I've had a wife or four. How come you never did?"

Alison had often asked the same question, and I never did come up with a satisfactory answer. I was saved from even trying by several loud booms from the town. It sounded like World War II. A Roman candle arced over Patty's Clam Dip in a shower of fireworks.

I was immediately alert, on my feet and blurting out—not unlike Harrison with his Tourette's—"What the hell?"

My buddy remained calm. "You saw Tiger today?"

"That's right."

"Was he drunk?"

I nodded.

Harrison explained. "The fireworks are from him. Usually, after he gets loaded, he goes to the Clam Dip and causes a disturbance."

Another rocket lit up a piece of sky, silhouetting the bay bridge against an orange glow.

Harrison concluded, "Tiger likes fireworks."

"And exploding golf balls?"

"It could have been Tiger," Harrison conceded. "But I don't really think so."

Neither did I. Whoever had murdered Sam Leggett was motivated by greed, and Tiger wasn't the acquisitive sort. Though he was bitter about not having the Porcelli fortune, he seemed fairly content with the life of a fisherman.

If Tiger committed murder, his motive would be more earthy. I settled back to watch the glittering fireworks display of red, white, blue, and gold. Even after a divorce, a killer alimony, and all these years, he still cared enough about Patty Carmen to shoot off rockets in her honor.

If Tiger committed a murder, it would be motivated by love.

I decided against going into Newport to investigate Tiger's drunken display of affection. What I really wanted, at this point, was a good night's sleep.

Avoiding direct confrontation with heirs, I crept back into the hotel and up the stairway. Figuring that the last person I wanted to run into was Margot in her newly litigious mood, I approached my room with great caution.

I caught sight of her down the hall. She was exiting a corner room, labeled the Bob Packwood, in the company of Bud, the proprietor of the hotel.

Sometimes, cowardice is the better part of valor. I flattened myself against the wall, hiding behind a huge plastic fern.

For once, it seemed, Margot the Malicious was not on the prowl for a man. Clearly, she wanted something else from the proprietor. "Bob Packwood is old news," she said. "I mean, I know he was a senator from Oregon, but he's just an old pervert. In a few years, who'll remember him?"

Bud took off his Coke-bottle-bottom glasses and nervously rubbed at the thick lenses. "Maybe you're right."

"I'm always right," she intoned.

"I hate to give it up," he said. "I have an actual girlie magazine that was in his Washington office."

"Unsavory," Margot pronounced. She aimed a long fingernail at the tag on the door to her own room. "And this? The Tonya Harding Suite? Apart from ice skates hung over the door, what can you do with this?"

The proprietor seemed to shrivel beneath her criticism. "Some people like to pretend they're figure skaters. You know, in bed."

"Hmmm." Margot mused for about three and a half seconds. Pensive was not her favorite mood. "I can see possibilities. A triple lutz into the sack. And, of course, sticking the landing."

The proprietor jumped back as she flung her arms wide, almost slapping him. "I like Tonya," he said. "Always have."

"Rename the rooms after someone worthy," she said. "In fact, you could name this whole wing after someone who had actually stayed here. Name it after me. The Margot Wing."

"How would I decorate?"

"Expensively." She flung the door wide. "Come on, I'll show you."

I took the opportunity to duck into the Anthony Perkins chamber. When I flicked the switch beside the door, nothing happened. It was dark. In front of the open window beyond the bed, white, sheer drapes undulated in the breeze like ghostly specters. In the shadows I saw the form of an old woman, like the mummified mommy in *Psycho*. Slowly, she rocked, back and forth, crooning quietly to herself. Her long white hair spread around her shoulders in thin ripples. In her lap, her gnarly fingers knitted together.

The hairs on the back of my neck prickled. This was the spookiest damn thing I'd ever seen.

Amelia Porcelli rose from the rocking chair with a creaking of knee joints. "I was always faithful to Graden," she said. "No matter what anyone tells you. I was always faithful."

Trying to pick up her wavelength, I took a stab. "What about Harry Mann?"

"Unrequited." She turned on the bedside lamp as she walked briskly past me. "See you tomorrow at four."

I locked the door behind her and went directly to the old black rotary phone beside the bed. I needed to hear the voice of someone sane. "Alison?"

"I've already talked to Margot," she said. "You're in big trouble, Adam. You said this wasn't going to be dangerous."

I thought of the old woman in the rocking chair, ethereal and washed out by moonlight. By contrast, I remembered the green of the golf course and the red fountain of Sam Leggett's blood. "I was wrong," I said.

"Oh, Adam. I'm worried about you. There's some kind of homicidal maniac roving around and exploding the other members of their own family."

She inhaled deeply, and I imagined her perfect breasts rising. It would have been nice to have her there with me, lying beside me in the Anthony Perkins room. Better yet, we could swap rooms with Margot and practice our lutzes and sit spins. "How do you feel about figure skating?" I asked.

"I like those tight pants the men wear."

"Do you have any really short little skirts? With sequins?"

"I don't suppose it would do any good to ask you to come back to Portland," she said.

"Probably not."

"Then I'm coming down there. Tomorrow night. You be prepared, Adam. First I'm going to seduce you and ask you nicely to come back to Portland with me. If that doesn't work," she purred into the telephone, "I'll have to get tough with you."

"I love it when you get tough." I hesitated, not wanting to make things sound any worse than she already imagined. "Would you mind picking up something at my house before you come down here?"

"Sure. What?"

"I'll be needing my gun."

Chapter Nine

I was in the shower when I heard a banging on the door. Apparently the Do Not Disturb sign that I had hung out before I went to bed meant little or nothing to the early morning intruder. Planning to give whoever it was a demonstration of my pre-coffee crankiness, I wrapped a towel around my waist and yanked open the door.

Patty Carmen lounged against the door frame like a sultry antique. Except for the disheveled black wig, she reminded me of the classic Mae West. "I need your help," she said.

"Do you mind if I get dressed first?"

She barged into the room. "Choo got nothing I haven't seen before, Adam."

"How the hell do you know that? I just might have a giant carbuncle shaped like Elvis growing on my ass."

"Do you?" Her eyes lighted with sudden curiosity.

"I might."

"I should be so lucky." She sashayed across the floor to my unmade bed and settled among the covers, warm and cozy. If

I squinted, I could almost see Patty Carmen in her youth. It wasn't difficult to understand why Tiger was still willing to set off fireworks in honor of this voluptuous chowder chef.

"I'm worried about the old fart," she said.

"Tiger?"

"He came over to the diner and made a mess last night. When I went out and yelled at him, he grabbed me, kissed me." Her tongue darted between her lips. "The old fart always was a hell of a good kisser."

"Does he usually kiss you after setting off fireworks?"

"Of course. That's the point."

"So, what's the problem."

"He said he was sorry for anything and everything he might ever have done to make me unhappy." She muttered something in pidgin Spanish that might be Gypsy and might be affectation. "He said we might never see each other again. It was like he was really saying good-bye."

She snuggled in my sheets. It was a sexy, catlike reflex action that indicated a certain expertise in heating up bed linens. She continued. "He took off without making love to me. I worried about it all night. This morning I went down to the Embarcadero and checked. His boat is gone."

"Didn't you tell me that he usually takes off when he gets loaded? Makes a disturbance at your place, then puts out to sea to sober up?"

"That's right."

"So?"

"Something's wrong. Call it woman's intuition, but I know something's wrong."

She shrugged vigorously, setting her breasts to jostling. Patty Carmen had to be the sultriest senior citizen I had ever met. I made a mental note to introduce Alison to her. They had very similar styles and I thought they would probably enjoy each other.

"McCleet? Choo listening to me?"

"Yep."

"I figured I ought to tell you about Tiger. On account of you're supposed to be watching the heirs to make sure nothing happens to them."

"Wrong," I said. "I wasn't hired as a bodyguard. All I'm supposed to do is—"

"I'm giving you a lead, McCleet. You're supposed to be a detective, right?"

No, I thought, I'm supposed to be a sculptor, but I nodded.

"The least you can do is follow up. Get your carbuncled ass into some pants and go find Tiger."

Though I consider myself to be a fairly good sailor, I had neither boat nor any idea of Tiger's uncharted course. What the hell did she expect me to do? Yesterday, during my foot search for Tiger, I had seen a U.S. Coast Guard station on the bluff overlooking the mouth of Yaquina Bay. "Have you called the Coast Guard?"

"I talked to them about an hour ago."

"What did they say?"

"They said they'd keep an eye out for him." She shook her head from side to side. "That means they're not taking this seriously enough. They don't know Tiger like I do. They didn't see the look in his eyes when he said adios."

I pushed aside the window sheers for a look at the weather. In the dim light of dawn, the ocean view from my room offered about a quarter mile of visibility through a translucent veil of coastal fog. "How do you propose I find Tiger?"

She raised one hand over her head and rotated the palm. "Get it?"

Cleverly, I said, "No."

"The helicopter." Patty Carmen pushed herself off the bed and stood right in front of me. She was almost tall enough to look me straight in the eye. "You and Harrison go look for him. Please, McCleet."

I shuddered. It seemed like only yesterday that I had promised myself that I would, at all costs, avoid climbing into a helicopter with Harrison at the stick. "Maybe you haven't noticed, but Harrison has this condition. Have you ever flown with him?"

She braced her hands on her hips. "Now, don't tell me a big strong man like you is scared of a little twitch. He's been zippin' around in that chopper for ten years and he hasn't killed anybody yet."

"I believe 'yet' is the operative word in that sentence."

"Please," she repeated softly. "If anything happened to the old fart, it'd break my heart."

"When you last saw him, what time was it."

"About ten-thirty."

If Tiger had headed straight from Patty's to his boat, I doubted that he could have gotten out of the marina before eleven. I checked the clock on the dresser, six-fifteen. I knew the hull speed of a boat with the length and displacement of Tiger's trawler was about six knots. Performing some rough time and distance calculations in my head, I figured that even at maximum speed in a straight line, which was unlikely if he was drunk, he'd still be within forty nautical miles of Newport. Assuming the fog would burn off, it was not unreasonable to expect that we could locate him.

Patty sniffed, and I could see puddles of tears forming at the bottoms of her aging eyes.

I've always been a sucker for a woman's tears. Like a knight errant in a cheap motel towel, I hoisted my metaphorical lance and mounted my metaphorical steed and said, "I'll find him."

"I knew you would." She punched my arm. "You're a good man, McCleet. If I were a few years younger . . ."

"We'd both be in trouble."

In ten minutes I had dressed and gone in search of Harrison.

He wasn't hard to locate. From the general direction of the dining room, I heard an outburst: "Hump, hump, humpback. Quack."

In the Chill Wills dining room, the aroma of sausage and eggs slimed the air like greasy perfume. I wished that I had time for cholesterol and coffee before setting out on the quest for Tiger.

"Harrison, I need to ask a favor."

"You need me to help you catch a murderer? No thanks." Between his thumb and forefinger he held a sausage link. He bit down hard on the link, viciously chomping it in two. "And fuck you very much."

"It's not for me," I said. "It's for Patty Carmen. She wants us to use your helicopter to search for Tiger. She's worried about him."

"I'd be flying the chopper," he said.

"Obviously," I replied. Though I was familiar with helicopters, I was no pilot.

"I'd be in charge," he said, swiping his toast across the last yellow remains of fried egg.

"That's right."

Harrison Porcelli barked, then said, "I'm in."

The sun worked at full wattage to burn off the streaky fog, but the western horizon had taken on the ominous look of an impending storm. A freshening wind blew from the north.

A chopper at dawn—in this case, at seven hundred hours— was a great dramatic image, like _Apocalypse Now_ in miniature. I felt a sudden surge of adrenaline as we walked from the hotel to Harrison Porcelli's beloved _Blue Thunder_. I was at once energized by the prospect of adventure and scared silly about climbing into a complex aircraft with a pilot whose sudden and unpredictable spasmodic fits of Tourette's could easily auger us into the face of a cliff. I was also keenly aware that over the years, my adventures have frequently proven to be hazardous to my health.

While Harrison performed a visual preflight check of his chopper, I strapped myself into the copilot's seat and tried to make myself useful. Rummaging through his map case, I located an aeronautical chart of the Oregon coastline and began to formulate a search plan.

Harrison climbed in and quickly ran through the steps of a lengthy checklist. There were so many extras, the instrument panel looked like it had been designed by NASA. Harrison was definitely into the macho-pilot image with his khaki-colored trousers bloused above the ankles of his canvas-topped jungle boots and aviator sunglasses masking his eyes.

As he ran up the engine, Harrison gestured for me to put on my headset so we could communicate over the noise of the rotor. As soon as I slipped on the headset, I regretted it. The microphone smelled as if someone had blown tuna chunks on it. The combined stench of vomit and fish brought tears to my eyes. "Aw, shit."

"What's wrong?" Harrison inquired.

"It stinks like fish in here."

"I often carry salmon product," he said defensively. "And when I take employees of the month up for a flight, we have lunch, usually sandwiches and slaw, on the helicopter."

"How about that! A deli-copter."

"Very funny, McCleet."

As the engine warmed up, I took the opportunity to fill Harrison in on what I knew. Holding out the chart so we could both look at it, I explained. "The maximum time that Tiger has been under way is seven hours. That means he's still within forty nautical miles of Yaquina Bay. The farthest away he could be is Cape Lookout to the north or Florence to the south."

"Or anywhere in between," Harrison added.

"That's right," I acknowledged. "I figure we've got about four miles visibility in this weather, wouldn't you say?"

He nodded.

"Okay. We'll head straight west until we're about four miles offshore, then fly north toward Cape Lookout. If we haven't spotted him by then, we'll swing a forty-mile arc over the ocean, using Newport as the center." Tracing a semicircle on the chart with my finger, I continued. "When we get to Florence, we'll shorten the radius of the arc by eight miles, maybe more if the visibility improves, and head north again."

Harrison tensed for an instant and blurted out, "Snake shit. Spank me." I couldn't see his eyes behind the mirrored sunglasses, but there was a perturbed expression on his lips. "I thought you said I was in charge."

"That's right."

"Then how come you get to decide the search pattern?"

Touchy. "I'm open for suggestions. Have you got a better plan?"

"Yeah. We'll go south first."

I didn't bother to argue, or even ask why. Since neither of us had any idea of Tiger's heading, it didn't matter which direction we went first. I snapped a left-handed salute and said, "You're the skipper."

"Cinch that seat belt good and tight. We're gonna punch a hole in the sky."

He didn't have to tell me twice. As Harrison opened the throttle, I pulled on the loose end of my lap belt until I felt the buckle dig painfully into my pelvis. This was the moment of truth. If the faulty circuitry in Harrison's neurotransmitters was going to have a negative effect on his piloting skills, the greatest potential for disaster was during takeoff and landing.

With his left hand, Harrison eased back on the collective pitch stick and the deli-copter rose on its own cushion of air. A few feet off the ground, he manipulated the antitorque pedal with his right foot, and the body of the aircraft slowly rotated forty-five degrees around the rotor shaft. When the nose faced into the wind, he pressed the cyclic pitch stick forward with his right hand while his left hand continued to pull back on the collective stick. The chopper climbed and surged forward at the same time. Thirty feet above the ground, Harrison stiffened and blurted out, "Sphincter grease."

"Almost," I mumbled, acknowledging the queasy feeling in my lower viscera.

The expensive, albeit smelly headset microphone had transmitted my remark. "What?" Harrison asked.

"I said, almost perfect takeoff." With the exception of the minor fit, which caused only a slight swooping motion up and to the left. Realizing I'd been holding my breath, I relaxed a little and started to breathe more normally.

"I suppose a man of action like yourself would have done it better." He muttered a small barking noise. "You heroic types make me sick."

His hostility was totally unwarranted. Long ago, I had made a vow that if the choice came down to being a hero and being alive, I would always opt for the latter. "Get some self-esteem, Harrison."

"What a nineties thing to say," Harrison mocked as he swung *Blue Thunder* to the west.

"You've got money. You could buy confidence," I said, swiveling my head from side to side, looking for likely small craft on the ocean surface.

Harrison also rotated his head from side to side, like a human radar scanner. "Why? So I could be just like you?"

Me? Confident? Where did he get the idea that I was G.I. Joe, Chuck Norris, and Arnold all rolled into one? There were strange undertones to this conversation. If I had been stoked with my usual morning caffeine, I might have made sense of what he was saying. I might have found a clue. But that would have been too easy. I sighed. "In real life, there are no heroes."

"Spare me the philosophy."

"Or else everybody's a hero. Like all the guys who drag

themselves out of bed every day to work at jobs they hate so their kids can have the things that they never had. And the student in night school who's trying to make something of himself. And the kids who remember Mom on Mother's Day. And the mothers. And the senior citizens who made it to retirement age through sixty-five years of triumph and tragedy." I was definitely getting out of hand with this stuff. I shook my head. "We're all fucking heroes, okay?"

"Cockcicles," he slurred, directing the flying machine in a descending swoop like a drunken albatross.

Riding low across the increasingly choppy waves, about two miles out, we passed over a craft that was the right size and color, but the name on the bow was not _Patty Carmen._

The turbulent sea was a mixed blessing. There were fewer boats than I would have expected in calmer conditions, mostly commercial fishing vessels, and not many of them, so it wasn't too difficult to fly over every boat we saw. But the same wind that stirred the waves and kept the sportfishermen inside the harbor made for a nauseatingly bumpy helicopter ride. Harrison fought a constant battle with the controls to keep the deli-copter right side up. The wind had also blown away what was left of the fog to reveal low, dark clouds overhead that began to spit rain on our first leg to the south.

By the time we reached Florence, a half hour into the flight, we had passed over or near a dozen boats, all headed for safe harbor at full speed. I was beginning to wish that we would do the same. The rain had increased and was falling horizontally in a thirty-knot wind. From what little I knew about flight safety, this weather seemed marginal at best.

"It's getting pretty rough out here," I said. "You think we should head in?"

Harrison had a smug expression on his face when he said, "Scared?"

Petrified would have been a more accurate description. "No.

It just seems a little unsafe. Your chopper is taking a beating."
And my bladder is full. And there's a whirlpool of acid in my
stomach.

"You don't get medals for being safe," Harrison said.

I wasn't interested in winning any medals. My desires leaned
more in the direction of seeing another forty or fifty years worth
of sunrises, making love to Alison again, and breathing. I tried
to maintain a calm tone. "They say discretion is the better part
of valor."

"Toe jam," he sputtered, the slight jerk on the controls barely
discernible in the constant buffeting from the turbulence. "I don't
have any death wish, Adam. We're doing fine so far. I don't
think it's going to get any worse than this, but if it does, we'll
head straight for shore. Okay?"

It didn't much matter if it was okay with me or not. Harrison
had the controls and he swung the helicopter west, out to sea,
before I could further protest.

Except to point out the occasional fishing boat, we barely
spoke as Harrison navigated the search pattern back to the north.
At forty miles out, there were no more boats, and we didn't
speak at all. He'd been right about the weather, it hadn't gotten
any worse. Unfortunately, it hadn't gotten any better either. I
kept glancing at the fuel gauge, hoping it would get low enough
that Harrison would have no choice but to head back to shore.
But the deli-copter had consumed only a fourth of its full supply
and the needle seemed frozen in that position.

When our arcing course carried us to within four miles west
of Cape Lookout, forty nautical miles north of Newport, Harrison
headed due south again to cover the stretch of shoreline that
we'd missed on our first leg. The weather had still not improved,
but I felt a little better being able to see land.

We were about twenty miles south of Cape Lookout when
we spotted a fifty-foot Coast Guard vessel shepherding four
sportfishing craft toward Depoe Bay.

"Maybe they've found Tiger by now," I said.

Harrison set the digital display on one of his radios to the Coast Guard frequency and announced, "Gerbil butt." He shook his head and tried again. "Coast Guard vessel off Depoe Bay, this is Long Ranger, Bravo-Tango four-five."

A reply came quickly. "Bravo-Tango four-five, this is C-G five-two-three-one-two off Depoe Bay. Go ahead."

"Coast Guard, we're looking for thirty-foot trawler, _Patty Carmen_. Have you seen her?"

"Stand by." A minute passed before the voice came back. "Negative, Bravo-Tango four-five. We have instructions to keep an eye out for that vessel. So far, no radio reply. No visual contact."

"Fuck me," Harrison shouted.

"Say again, Bravo-Tango four-five." The Coast Guard voice did not sound amused.

"Sorry, Coast Guard. We'll call you if we make contact with _Patty Carmen_. Bravo-Tango four-five, out."

"Understand," the voice said. "C-G five-two-three-one-two, clear."

"It looks like the Coast Guard is doing a pretty good job of herding the small craft off the ocean," I said. "Maybe they haven't seen Tiger because he's already back at Newport tossing down eggs and coffee." Given a choice, that's where I would have been.

"Possible," Harrison said, nodding.

"How about if you radio the nearest airport and have them put in a call to the Clam Dip. Find out if Patty has seen the old fart."

"Good idea," Harrison agreed. "But you can make that call yourself."

I blinked dumbly, "How?"

Harrison flinched. "Pecker drool." Recovering, he explained, "There's a cell phone in the seat pocket, behind you."

As Harrison continued our southbound course, I rummaged blindly through the pouch behind my seat until I located the compact cell phone. As neither of us knew the number of Patty's Clam Dip, my first call was to directory assistance.

Armed with the correct number, I dialed the diner. Patty answered on the first ring. "Patty's Clam Dip."

"Patty, this is Adam."

"Adam." Her voice sounded hopeful. "Did you find Tiger?"

I hated having to disappoint her. "Sorry, Patty. Not yet. We were hoping you'd heard something."

"No. I just got off the phone with the Embarcadero. They haven't seen him."

That was not what I wanted to hear. "Okay," I said, trying to sound positive. "We're still looking. I'll call you back as soon as—"

Harrison jabbed me in the ribs with his elbow. He was pointing to the water, about two miles ahead and to the left.

At first I couldn't see what he was pointing at, but when he corrected our course to the direction he'd been pointing, I spotted the square cabin and the outrigger poles bobbing wildly. A white, thirty-foot fishing boat was riding low in the water.

"Adam," Patty said, "are you there?"

I didn't want to worry her unnecessarily, but I also didn't want to give her false hopes. The boat we were looking at might not be Tiger. "We've got our hands full up here, Patty. I'll call you as soon as we find him." I hung up.

By the time I got my headset back on, Harrison was on the radio with the Coast Guard again. I heard him read the last few digits of our latitude and longitude. He then added, "The vessel is adrift, one half mile due west of Whale Cove."

"Copy that," the Coast Guard voice said. "Can you hold your position until we get there?"

"Affirmative," Harrison replied. "But you better hurry. This boat is sinking."

"Understand. We'll be there in ten minutes."

Though we still couldn't be sure if the boat was Tiger's, it was obviously in distress. Each ocean swell carried the trawler a little closer to the mouth of Whale Cove, a churning cauldron of waves and rocks encircled by vertical cliffs. Once inside the jaws of the cove, the small boat would be torn apart. We had an obligation to render assistance no matter who it was.

Fifty yards from the boat, Harrison began to circle. On the first pass I saw the name, *Patty Carmen*. "It's Tiger's boat," I said.

The trawler rode bow high in the swells, its stern only a foot out of the water. The helm was unmanned, and there was no sign of life on deck.

"Tiger might have already been washed over the side," Harrison said.

"True. But he might be below deck, passed out."

The boat lurched to port as a broadside wave washed over the deck. The *Patty Carmen* bobbed up again, but now there was only a few inches of freeboard at the stern.

I checked my watch. The Coast Guard was still nine minutes away. "I don't think she can stay afloat until the Coast Guard gets here."

"Goddamn, goddamn. Whale pussy. Goddamn," Harrison barked, obviously feeling the stress. "I think you're right. Another wave like that last one and she's a goner. We've got to do something besides fly around in circles."

"You got any ideas?"

Harrison waved toward the back of the chopper. "There's a rope ladder back there. I can lower you onto the deck."

I blinked. At that moment it occurred to me that I had no sound reason not to suspect Harrison of killing Sam Leggett. This situation would provide an excellent opportunity to kill a couple of more birds with one stone. "Got any other ideas?"

"You fly the chopper and I'll go down."

I liked that suggestion even less. Scrambling around in the rear of the helicopter, I found a neatly coiled rope ladder ready for deployment.

"Shit, Adam! The boat's really low. Waves are up to the gunwale. You've got to get out there quick."

Of course, I thought. My rousing speech about every man being a hero had come back to bite me on the ass. I didn't want to risk my own precious hide by leaping onto a sinking ship. If Tiger was below deck, I would guess that he had already drowned.

"Right." Sliding open the side door to the chopper, I came face-to-face with the weather. This wasn't a full-fledged storm, but the air was wet and the wind threw the moisture in my face. I gathered up the rope ladder and stumbled to the open hatch.

"Adam, be sure you—" His words were lost in the din of the wind and rotors.

"Be sure I what?" I asked as I flung the ladder through the door.

"Tie down the ladder," he yelled.

I watched as the rope and rungs made a perfect parabola in the air and splashed into the sea. "I'm an asshole."

"Adam, the boat's going down."

"Get as low as you can." Ever the optimist, I figured that I might be able to leap onto the deck. "Lower."

The force of the rotor blades whipped the cold gray waters into a whirlpool of foamy chop. The distance to the boat was still too high and too far, but Harrison was guiding the chopper in the right direction.

I had begun to ease myself out onto the strut so I'd be ready to jump as soon as we got close enough. "Lower," I shouted.

I heard a dangerous bark from Harrison. In a strangled voice he yelled, "Stuck pig. Bite me. Bite me hard."

The chopper jolted and pitched to starboard. Suddenly I was flying solo.

The whack as I hit the water resounded and echoed through my body from my toenails to my eyebrows. I had just performed the grandfather of all belly flops from thirty feet in the air. My gut cramped in wrenching pain that I had no time to comprehend because I had plummeted beneath the murky depths. It makes no sense to scream underwater, but I gave it a try anyway.

With a complete lack of finesse, I flailed my arms, hoping that I was propelling myself toward the surface. I broke into the light and noise of wind and rain. Not unlike Harrison, I yelled, "Shit! Fuck! Shit!"

Tiger's boat was about twelve feet to my left. From overhead I heard the chopper. Fortunately, Harrison had been considerate enough to ascend so as not to drown me in the rotor wash.

I clawed my way through the frigid water and pulled myself onto the deck of the _Patty Carmen_. "Tiger!" I yelled. My throat was hoarse from gulping saltwater. "Where the hell are you?"

I yanked open the door to the cabin. Water gushed out with such force that I was knocked off my feet. The boat was definitely sinking now.

Fighting my way amid floating debris, I tried to make it into the cabin, then gave up. If the old fart was in there, he had drowned by now.

Hoping for the best, I staggered around on deck, climbed up the ladder to check out the flying bridge where nets and ropes were piled in an unshipshape disarray. There was a thick smear of blood on the control console. The possibility of accidental injury was negated by the presence of a nearby boat hook stained with blood. A classic blunt instrument.

Tiger was nowhere in sight. My best guess was that the old fart had been killed, or at least rendered unconscious, and dumped overboard. Only one thing bothered me. The pile of nets on the bridge. The boat was, otherwise, completely organized and tidy. I would have expected as much. Tiger might have been a sloppy human being, but he was a sailor to his soul and he knew the importance of keeping his gear squared away.

Another wave of green water rolled across the deck. This time the stern did not resurface. The *Patty Carmen* was going under and there was nothing I could do to stop it. I had begun to search for something to keep me afloat, when I saw a faded patch of blue cloth among the jumble of netting. Thinking that I'd found a life jacket, I yanked on the material and discovered that it was wrapped around an arm.

I dropped to my knees and began to wrestle with the heavy nest of tangles. Within a few seconds I had exposed the limp body of Tiger Jorgenson, lying facedown. His gray hair was plastered against a deep red gash in the back of his skull.

I felt for a pulse.

He was still alive.

The ocean made hungry, sucking noises, ready to pull us down. I struggled to free the old sailor from the remaining tangles. These nets were heavy enough to create a fatal shroud. If the boat went down while Tiger was wrapped in the netting, he would be stuck on the ocean floor, providing a captive buffet for the bottom feeders.

The dull blade of my Swiss Army knife was useless against the nets. I struggled with the wet knots. The water was rising, dashing against the bulkhead.

I yanked Tiger free. Using a fireman's carry, I went back to the ladder. Climbing down was an exercise in futility. Even if I could keep my balance in the squall, the water was already up to the deck house. I left Tiger and raced down the ladder, praying that the old fart still had the sense to carry life vests in bulkhead wells. Of course, the compartments were locked. I kicked through. Inside, there were old, musty, wet flotation vests. I put one on myself and grabbed another for Tiger.

I scrambled back up to the bridge and wrestled Tiger into a vest. As soon as I had it snugly fastened around him, I picked him up and tossed him over the side, then jumped in behind him, banging my hip painfully against the listing hull as I hit the water.

It's hard to describe swimming with a limp, but that's exactly what I was doing when I grabbed Tiger by the collar and paddled frantically, dragging the unconscious old fart along. I needed to get us far enough away from the boat so as not to be sucked under by the vortex that would be created when the *Patty Carmen* finally sank.

We were thirty yards away from the foundering trawler when I heard the deafening blast of a foghorn. I looked over my shoulder and saw the bow of a Coast Guard rescue ship bearing down on us at full speed.

Chapter
Ten

I flailed my arms in the air, but the fifty-foot Coast Guard craft was busting waves at thirty knots, and the crew was obviously transfixed on the sinking trawler. In our faded blue life jackets, Tiger and I were all but invisible among the whitecaps on the surface of the gray-green water. Gritting my teeth as I waited for the bow of the sleek vessel to make ultimate contact with my melon, I wished that I had taken the time to make a mean-spirited, videotaped will like that of Graden Porcelli.

To my sister, Margot the Malignant, I leave nothing except a single pair of saltwater-logged Jockey shorts with a distinctive skidmark in the back. To my beloved Alison Brooks, I leave everything else.

Though the Oregon coast was less than a mile to the east, it might as well have been a hundred miles. I bobbed helplessly in the freezing waters of the Pacific. Alone, I might have been able to swim clear of the speeding boat. But Tiger was only unconscious, not dead. I couldn't leave him, and I couldn't make significant headway pulling him along while doing a one-armed sidestroke.

The light squall attained hurricane status in my mind. I didn't want to die from stupidity in the summer rain. And from greed. That was the true motive that flung me into the seas. Greed. I wanted the millions, and I had stood ready to risk everything to get it.

The rescue boat was close enough that I could read the alphanumeric ID on the bow. C.G. five-two-three-one-two was about to punch our ticket. Suddenly the deli-copter lowered from the drizzling sky and hovered ten feet above our heads.

The Coast Guard boat had no choice but to alter its course, missing us by less than ten yards. Our salvation came at a cost, however. The rotorblades of the chopper churned the gray liquid like an Osterizer on puree speed.

The chopper jerked upward. Either Harrison was having one of his trademark fits or the unpredictable coastal winds had caught him in an updraft. I breathed a sigh of relief when he ascended safely. Not only did he not kill me, which restored some faith in my own intuition, but he had proven himself to be a genuine hero.

The Coast Guard boat slowed and came about. Above me, at the stern pulpit, I heard sailor talk. They cleverly identified Tiger's boat and acknowledged the fact that the *Patty Carmen* was, in fact, sinking.

I made a number of gurgling, coughing, strangled pleas for assistance before a face appeared over the rail. A young female seaman or, to be more politically correct, seaperson finally saw us splashing around and pronounced, "Holy shit. Two survivors in the water!"

The crew hauled us aboard with a practiced efficiency, then pretty much ignored me as they worked feverishly on Tiger, who was, apparently, standing at the threshold of death's door.

After they had done what they could for him, they pointed

me toward the cabin. Inside, I found warm blankets, relative calm, and the caffeine elixir I had been craving.

We were zipping toward Newport when the captain, who was actually a lieutenant junior grade, came and sat beside me. "What happened?"

I used to be a cop. I was accustomed to giving quick summaries of disasters. "Tiger's ex-wife, Patty Carmen, came to me, early this morning, and said she was worried about Tiger. She asked me to search for him."

"Why you?" the captain interrupted.

I really didn't want to tell this story fifteen times with embellishments, so I continued without answering. "Harrison Porcelli and I went out in his deli-copter—"

"His what?"

"We located the boat and contacted you. The boat was going down. I jumped out of the chopper, found Tiger tangled in his netting. He had been struck on the head, probably with a boat hook I saw on the flying bridge."

I made eye contact with the young officer. "This is an attempted homicide arranged to look like an accident. Tiger was so tangled in the nets that his body never would have surfaced. He would have been counted lost at sea."

The captain nodded, apparently satisfied. "It's a police matter."

"Right." I sipped the coffee. "Thanks for your quick response. Except for the part where you almost ran over me, you guys did great."

"It's our job."

Back on terra firma, I thanked the rest of the crew of the fifty-footer whose name, I had learned, was _Victory_. Tiger was loaded into a waiting ambulance, and I caught a ride in a Coast Guard jeep back to the Sunny Beach Celebrity Hotel, where I slogged directly to my room. _Psycho_ screams issued from the speaker on the bathroom wall as I turned the shower to steaming hot and peeled off my soggy clothes. My attempts to rescue the heirs was wreaking havoc on the limited wardrobe I'd brought with me to Newport. Yesterday Sam had bled to death on my shirt. Today my shirt and Levis were salt-encrusted by the dip in the Pacific.

I also seemed to be spending an unusual amount of time in the shower. Was it the Anthony Perkins ambiance that drew me to the claw-footed tub and the translucent shower curtain?

No sooner had I stepped under the spray than I heard a hammering on the door.

"Give me a minute," I yelled.

"Adam! Open up!" If I had any doubt about the identity of my visitor, it vanished with the next woof and loud blurt, "Pull my f-f-finger."

"Hold on, Harrison."

I stood under the shower spray, washing off the smell and itch of ocean water.

There was more hammering and another voice. "Adam, it's me, Tia. Hurry up."

I lathered up with the soap. The bruise on my hip where I'd crashed into the hull on my dive from the bridge of Tiger's boat had already darkened. By tomorrow it would be an interesting greenish-purple.

"Adam!" The clarion voice of Margot shattered my eardrums. "Open this fucking door or I'll kick it down."

I glanced toward the narrow window, ready to escape buck naked rather than face my sister.

"I mean it, Adam. I'm counting to three."

I turned off the shower. No way was I vaulting across the bathroom to fling open the door for the much-married Margot monster. I hoped she would break her toe when she kicked the door. I yelled back at her. "I'll count for you." I pulled on a pair of navy-blue sweat pants. "One. Two. Three."

Never call Margot's bluff. The door crashed open and my

sister strolled through like a ninja queen, calmly smoothing her artfully plucked eyebrows. "Now, look what you've done to Bud's door. He might have to redecorate in here too."

I raised one leg in the classic karate stork pose. "Don't come any closer."

"Shut up, Adam." She sat on the bed, spreading her skirts and crossing her feet at the ankle.

Over the years, I have learned to gauge Margot's goals by her style of clothing. Today, her costume was a surprisingly demure sundress, white with sprigs of flowers, probably deadly hemlock. Whom was she trying to convince that she was an innocent? She reached down and tightened the laces on her steel-toed sandals.

Behind her were Tia and Harrison. They spilled into my room, and Tia tried to close the door which hung drunkenly on its hinges.

Margot said, "The paramedics told me that Tiger was in a coma. Did he tell you who sabotaged the boat before he passed out?"

"Maybe he did and maybe he didn't." It might be to my advantage to pretend that Tiger had managed to whisper the name of the murderer before he succumbed to unconsciousness. "Why do you want to know?"

"Isn't it obvious, moron? As soon as we have a name, Desiree will know who to sue. I like the whole idea of suing people. Jimmy Caruthers seems to be very good at this, and I want to see him in action."

"And is Jimmy married?" I inquired, knowing that my sister was currently *sans* spouse.

"Please, Adam. I'm not interested in him that way."

"So, he is married."

"Yes," she admitted.

"Excuse me," Tia said. "Adam, could you tell us what happened with Tiger."

"There's something I need to say first." I rose from the bed and went to stand in front of Harrison. I stuck out my hand. "Thanks, man. You saved my life. Tiger's too."

His mouth quivered into a smile as he shook my hand. "I did, didn't I."

"You're a hero," I said. "A goddamned bona fide hero, and I'll go to blows with anyone who says otherwise." I sincerely meant every word.

Tia stepped up beside us. "Would you both mind explaining what's going on?"

I told her the story of Harrison Porcelli, the devilish deli-copter, our search for Tiger, and what happened in the few minutes after we spotted the *Patty Carmen* sinking.

"Wait a minute," Tia interrupted. "You threw the ladder out of the chopper, then you intended to leap onto the deck? What kind of Rambo fantasy is that?"

"You're not one to talk," Harrison said. "Didn't you play Sheena the Jungle Queen for a year in El Salvador?"

"Jungle Queen? That was hardly playtime, Harrison. I was trying to rescue orphans and homeless children, working with the Sisters of Poverty."

"Who?" Margot demanded. "The Sisters of Puberty?"

"Poverty," Tia spat out.

"I like it my way better," Margot said.

"You would," Tia said calmly. "I don't know you well, Mar-got, but from what I've seen, you are possibly the most shallow, inconsiderate, selfish bitch on the face of the earth. I wouldn't expect you to understand the work of the Sisters of Poverty or any other person who had dedicated their life to making the planet a better place."

"You go, Tia." I almost applauded.

Margot's eyes had narrowed to slits. I had the distinct feeling that Tia would live to regret her words.

For right now, Tia turned back toward me. "I'm sorry, Adam.

I shouldn't have made fun of you and Harrison. You were trying to rescue an old man. Please continue."

I skimmed over my part in the adventure, which was easy because the events were already fading in my memory, sliding into the closed mental file marked: DANGEROUS, DON'T TRY THIS AGAIN. But I pulled out all the stops in describing Harrison's descent to detour the rescue ship. The invasion of Normandy was nothing compared to the deli-copter playing chicken with the Coast Guard.

Tia patted her cousin's arm. "I'm proud of you, Harrison. You saved Tiger's life."

"He's in a coma," Margot muttered. "The man is a zucchini. I hardly think that's cause for celebration."

"But he has a fairly good chance for recovery," Tia said. She gazed steadily at me. "I know it's not your job to protect us, Adam. But I'd like some advice."

"You're asking him for advice?" Margot questioned.

Tia ignored her. "It seems to me that Tiger is in extreme danger from whoever scuttled his boat. When he wakes up, he'll be able to give us a name."

"If he saw his attacker," I said. "He was hit on the back of the head. And, from what Patty Carmen says, he was blind drunk when he left her place."

"I'd like to station a guard outside the door to Tiger's hospital room," Tia said.

"Aren't you the little planner," Margot said.

"Yes. As a matter of fact, I am." She didn't raise her voice, but her will was strong enough to disarm Margot. "Yesterday, my brother was murdered. Although I'm not a person who is given to great displays of mourning, I want to know who killed him. I think it's safe to assume that the same person tried to kill Tiger Jorgenson." She turned back toward me. "Wouldn't you say so, Adam?"

I nodded.

"I know someone here in town who could guard Tiger," Tia said. "I could make the arrangements to have him stationed in the hospital immediately."

Harrison barked his agreement, and so did I. Even Margot assented on behalf of Desiree.

Tia continued. "Someone ought to talk to Patty Carmen if the police haven't already."

"I'll do it," Harrison volunteered. "She might need a ride to the hospital."

They both left my room, leaving me alone with my sister. She eyeballed me like a chunk of meat. A brisket? A pork butt? "Maybe," she said, "we should hire a bodyguard for you too."

"Why?"

"Because, idiot, you're in danger. You're an heir too."

"Not if I don't find a murderer," I reminded her.

"Come on, Adam. How hard could it be?"

Far more difficult if Margot stayed around. "Thanks a heap for your concern, but I'll be fine."

"My brother, the millionaire." She threw back her head and brayed. "I can't leave, Adam. You'll never figure this out without my help. And if you don't find the murderer, who is Desiree going to sue? God, you're both a couple of babes in the woods."

She stalked toward the door, which was sprung on its hinges and would no longer close all the way. "I'd get this fixed if I were you."

As soon as she was gone, I called down to the front desk, ordered a heavy room service lunch and a new door. Then I placed a call to Nick Gabreski at the Portland police station.

Nick was at his desk. His gravelly voice was even more unintelligible because he was, apparently, eating lunch.

"Doughnuts?" I queried.

"I wish," he said. "Listen to this."

Obediently, I held the phone to my ear, paying careful attention to the sound of crunching mastication. "An apple?"

"Celery," he said mournfully. "Ramona put me on a fat-free diet. Tell me this, Adam, what's the point of living until you're a hundred if you have to eat rabbit food every day?"

I sympathized heartily. Nick and I were trapped in the curse of the middle-aged baby boomer, which seemed clearly defined by our womenfolk as a matter of diet or die. Talk about a chance for heroics! I envisioned all of us, standing in a _Braveheart_ line of defense with our pot bellies protruding over our kilts, demanding the same meat and potatoes that killed our fathers and their fathers before them. We were men, dammit. Not rabbits.

"So, Nick, did you find out anything interesting about the list of people I gave you?"

"Here's what I've got. Tiger Jorgenson has been arrested several times on drunk and disorderly charges. Amelia Porcelli has been picked up a couple of times for shoplifting. Whit Parkens had a long list of drunk-driving charges that came to a halt about ten years ago."

The pattern was not unusual for an alcoholic. I assumed that Whit was a drinker who no longer imbibed. That was good to know. "Anything else?"

"Tia Leggett was deported from El Salvador as an undesirable. The rest of them have the usual assortment of traffic violations. Sorry, Adam, they're pretty much average citizens."

I had an idea. "I want you to trace somebody else for me, Nick. This one's going to be tough."

"As if my life could get worse," he grumbled.

"Big Harry Mann."

"Come again," Nick said.

"The guy's name is Harold or Harrison Mann with two n's. He disappeared about forty years ago from Newport. I'd like to know if he resurfaced anywhere else."

"Harry Mann?" Nick chuckled. "I wouldn't be surprised if the poor bastard changed his name."

"I hope that's all."

I wished my pal good luck with the produce diet and rang off in time to see Bud push my door open. His hands were full with a tray that I hoped would be my room service lunch. His beady eyes behind the thick glasses scanned the door up and down and up and down. "What did you do?"

"It's broke," I said, not wanting to bother with an explanation. I reached for the tray, but Bud wouldn't let go. "I can't have you stay in here with the door all screwed up. Grab your stuff and meet me down the hall to your right."

The only clothing I had left was the navy-blue sweat pants I had on. I pitched the rest of my bloodstained and sea-drenched clothes in my gym bag, grabbed my wet shoes, and stepped into the hallway.

Bud was standing outside the last door on the end of the hall, flapping his skinny arms like a crow in a bowling shirt. "Down here, Adam."

I padded down the hallway, wondering which celebrity room Bud had selected for me.

"All I have left is a deluxe," he said. "It's a little more expensive, but—"

"Who's the celebrity?" I asked.

"Guy Williams," he announced with a flourish. "Frish, frish, frish." Bud drew a large Z in the air with his finger. "The man who played Zorro on TV."

That didn't sound too dangerous, except for the swords. I stepped inside a more ornately furnished bedroom with heavy velvet drapes on the canopy bed. The style was circa 1950s, heavy-looking Spanish. On a coat rack in the corner there was a black hat, a cape, and a mask. Someone, probably Bud, had slashed the sign of the Z on the bathroom door. "I'll take it."

He beamed. "Pretty cool, huh? I always liked the Zee-man."

"Cool," I agreed.

"Enjoy your lunch." He swept a bow toward the table at the

window where he had set a silver-covered plate. "It's Aunt Bea's special Mayberry meat loaf. Can I get you anything else?"

I dug into my water-soaked wallet, looking for a tip, and peeled off a soggy five-dollar bill. "Give me a wake-up call at three."

"In the morning?"

"No, this afternoon." I wanted to be ready in time for Amelia Porcelli's little afternoon get-together.

As soon as Bud left, I wasted no time in digging into the meat loaf sandwich. The thick slab of gray meat was heavy and delightful, probably packed with a plethora of saturated, monosodium-glutamated fats.

Stuffed, I staggered to the bed, threw back the covers, and collapsed onto clean white sheets. The mattress was surprisingly comfortable, but I was wide awake. Lying down with my eyes closed, I replayed my near drowning. The attempt on Tiger was far different from the exploding golf ball. In the case of Tiger, the murderer had gone to some trouble to make the death appear accidental.

Why bother? Sam's murder had been blatant, outright. Why go to all the trouble of sinking the boat and tangling Tiger in the nets so he would never bob to the surface? Was there some reason the murderer didn't want the corpse to be found?

If I were of a legal turn of mind, I might have a better idea. Without a corpse, Tiger would not be declared officially dead for seven years. Obviously that would thwart the claims of his heir, namely Patty Carmen.

It didn't make sense. The two attacks were vastly different, almost as if they had been done by two different killers. The Unabomber and a sly master criminal worthy of Sherlock Holmes. I shuddered beneath the sheets. Two killers? I didn't even want to consider the possibility.

As I drifted toward sleep, I imagined the waves crashing over me, tossing me like a bit of flotsam until I sank, unconscious, into dreamland.

The next sound I heard was a sweet female voice lightly summoning me to wakefulness. I kept my eyes closed. Was it Margot, disguising her usual snarl? Was it Tia? Desiree?

"Señor Adam, wake up."

Señor? "Patty Carmen?"

I opened my eyes.

Alison!

She stood at the foot of the bed, wrapped in the black satin cape I'd seen hanging by the door. The broad-rimmed black hat rested atop her shoulder-length auburn hair. And she was wearing the Zorro mask.

"You're beautiful," I said.

"I'll bet you say that to all the banditos."

"Just you, baby." I held out my arms, beckoning her closer.

"Who is Patty Carmen?"

"You'd like her. She's a Gypsy woman who owns the Clam Dip and was married to Tiger."

Alison nodded, disbelieving. I guess when I put it all together like that, Patty Carmen sounded unlikely. I added, "She's hot stuff, that Patty Carmen. Last night Tiger set off a fireworks display in her honor."

"Really?"

"And she's old enough to be my mother." I waved to Alison, again. "C'mere."

"Sí, señor."

She swirled the cape as she stepped around the bed and struck a pose, just beyond my grasp. With the finesse of a stripper, she removed her hat and tossed it aside. Her hair was like rich russet silk, but my eyeballs were focused lower on her anatomy. From the swirling of the black satin, I had guessed that Alison wasn't wearing anything under her cape.

She turned sideways and peered over her shoulder at me. "Didn't Señor Zorro have a whip?"

"Gosh, no. I don't think so." I'm as into game playing as the next pervert, but Alison and I try to draw the line at actual bloodletting.

"Too bad," she said. "A nice dramatic cracking of a whip might be fun."

"I guess you'll just have to improvise."

She turned her back to me and untied her cape. Slowly, she allowed the black satin to slide down her back until her creamy shoulders were exposed.

I was almost reduced to slobbering in anticipation.

Turning slightly, she poked one perfect leg outside the cape. "What do you say, señor? More?"

"Hubba, hubba." She was a sleek female Zorro. I was Crazy Guggenheim.

The cape dipped lower on her backbone, showing her slender waist. In a quick peek-a-boo, she dropped the cape to her knees. Her buttocks were perfect, round and firm but not hard. She was wearing black thong panties.

Whirling around, she tossed the cape aside with a flourish. Beautifully nude, she pounced on me like a predatory feline. In my chest hairs, she traced the sign of the Z with her fingernail.

"Now you're mine," she said.

"All yours." I reached for the mask, and she pulled away.

"The mask stays."

"But how will I know it's you?"

"Oh, you'll know."

Chapter
Eleven

My wake-up call came right after Alison had put me through the physical equivalent of a brisk sprint to the summit of K-2 followed by a bungee-jump descent. I was sprawled in the center of the bed with a broad grin on my face when the phone rang.

"What?" I said into the receiver.

A prerecorded message in a very bad Jimmy Cagney impression said: "You dirty rat! You— You— You dirty rat! Wake up."

I hung up the phone and turned to Alison. "There's such a thing as too cute."

"Absolutely," she agreed.

"Did you bring me clothes?"

"Of course. I suspected that you'd underpacked. As usual."

Alison knew my penchant for traveling light. On numerous trips together, she had observed me, still three days from home, digging through the laundry bag in search of my cleanest pair of dirty socks. The fact that she had not only become familiar with my quirks, but that she cared enough to anticipate and compensate, made me feel all warm and mushy inside.

"And my gun?"

"Yes. I packed your stupid gun too. But I would still like to register my opinion that you shouldn't be here."

She was probably right. I had not made any significant headway in the investigation, and it was humiliating to have heirs bumped off right and left while half the town thought I was supposed to be protecting them.

Nonetheless, I was determined to stay. "I like these people," I said. "Some of them. And I don't feel like I can just walk away unless I want to learn how to shave without a mirror."

While she lay on her stomach, observing me with her perceptive green eyes, I rummaged through the suitcase she'd packed for me and ran through a brief character history on Tia and Harrison. "And now," I said, "I'm invited to a dinner with the heirs at Amelia Porcelli's house."

"Amelia is the widow?"

"And a one-hundred-percent-whacked-out old broad." I picked a white rayon shirt and a pair of double-pleated beige slacks from the suitcase.

With feline grace Alison uncoiled from her position on the bed and opened the closet door. "What does one wear to dinner with a wacko?"

Alison had settled in for the duration. In the closet, she had three complete mix and match outfits, carefully arranged, using up all the hangers. My beige linen sport jacket hung on a hook. I peeked in the top drawer of the dresser. It was full of silky stuff that I knew wasn't mine.

"I'm staying," she said firmly. "If it's as safe as you keep saying, there should be no problem."

I didn't recall saying that Newport was safe, but I got the point. I wouldn't try to change her mind until after the dinner at Amelia's. All the heirs would be together in one place. How dangerous could it be? Just in case, I tucked my 9mm automatic into the waistband of my trousers at the back and deposited an extra clip in the inside pocket of my linen jacket.

On our way to the house where Amelia lived with her talking dolls, Alison snuggled back in the passenger seat of the Chevy. She looked good. A beautiful woman in a '56 Chevy. What more could one man want?

"I was thinking," she said, "about the case."

Why not? I would rather take pointers from Alison than anybody else. "Yes, my love," I said. "And what were you thinking?"

"The video of the reading of the will. That was an absolutely magnificent desk that Graden Porcelli was standing in front of."

Because she owned an art gallery, appreciated art, and had impeccable taste, Alison noticed visual details with more acuity than most people. I knew there was something more she wanted to talk about than Graden's desk. "And what else?"

"Don't you remember, Adam?"

I had pretty much forgotten about the will itself. In the course of daring deli-copter rescues, exploding golf balls, and getting up close and personal with the Porcelli loons, my brain power had been occupied by survival. "What am I trying to remember?"

"Graden handled several items. He started off by putting with a golf ball. There was a ship in a bottle on his desk. He did something with a flower, and he put on a jacket with a crest and a medal. I wonder if there's a connection to finding the murderer."

"I should take another look at the tape," I said.

"It sounds just too Agatha Christie, doesn't it?"

"Nothing about this mess would surprise me."

We must have been among the last to arrive at Amelia's sprawling cottage by the sea, because her front driveway looked like a parking lot. Mentally, I matched up vehicles with the people I assumed must be their owners. The shiny black pickup truck with vanity plates that said "EWE 2" had to belong to the

Parkenses, Whit and Dottie. The flashy lavender Miata looked like Desiree. A solid black BMW probably belonged to Jimmy Caruthers. Toward the rear of the house, I caught sight of a van with the words "Patty's Clam Dip" stenciled on the side next to the dancing-clam-in-top-hat logo. There was another, unidentified BMW in tasteful gray. As we strolled up to it, I noticed a car phone and a fine sound system that wouldn't have lasted eight seconds on the streets of any major American city.

"How odd," Alison said as we shuffled up the cobblestone path to the front door. "She has four lawn jockeys."

"She has four, or twenty-four, of everything. Amelia is a collector. Her doll collection puts F.A.O. Schwartz to shame."

"Oh, Adam. You're exaggerating."

I wasn't, of course, as Alison discovered when Harrison opened the door, took one look at us, and blurted out, "Slug poop."

"Nice to meet you," Alison said. I had already warned her about the Tourette's. She took his hand and smiled with enough warmth to melt the polar ice cap. "Thank you, Harrison, for saving Adam's life."

As soon as she stepped inside, her artistic sensibilities went into clutter shock. Her pretty green eyes widened, trying to take it all in. "Look at this."

"Mother collects things," Harrison explained.

While Alison was still reeling, Tia introduced us to the two people who had to be the owners of the gray Beamer with the car phone. "This is my daughter, Jane, and her husband, Josh."

I remembered Tia mentioning that Jane was twenty-three, but she had already taken on the ageless look of a professional woman who preferred neat, chic suits and practical but stylish haircuts. She was an attractive young woman with Tia's sharp intelligence shining from her brown eyes, but she had none of her mother's wit and charm. Her husband, though wearing a casual Oxford shirt with button-down collar, had the precise grooming of a military man.

Tia continued, further defining her love-child offspring. "Jane is in accounting."

I shook her hand, then turned to match grips with her husband. "What branch of the service are you in?"

"Navy," he said without smiling. "SEAL."

"Career man?"

"So far."

Tia regarded me suspiciously. "How did you know that? Is there some kind of secret macho handshake? I've heard that you guys have all kinds of rituals, like standing in a circle, holding your balls, and grunting."

That exercise was called "checking your package," and I wasn't particularly proud to know about it. "It's a guy thing," I explained. "If we were dogs, we'd sniff each other's butts. We just know."

Josh further proved my point by looking me straight in the eye and saying, "Marine?"

"Hoo-rah," I confirmed.

Beside me, Alison was still bedazzled with Amelia's collections. "This is more kitsch than I have ever seen in one place."

Jane looked her directly in the eye and asked, "So, Alison, what do you do?" Apparently, it was important for her to tag everyone.

Alison took no offense. One of her best attributes is mingling. "I own the Brooks Art Gallery in Portland, and my favorite sculptor is Adam."

"You're Adam McCleet?" Josh seemed impressed. "You did that Vietnam memorial statue in Noble Heights."

"Mortal Remains," I said. It was one of my best works, part gladiator and part forces of war.

Jane was actively fawning over Alison now that she knew Ms. Brooks was the owner of the hippest, coolest gallery in a town full of hip and cool. I took the opportunity to further question young Josh. Navy SEALS are among the elite of military, known for being experts in underwater demolition.

"The exploding golf ball," I said. "How do you think it was rigged?"

"Goddamned amazing," he said. "It would take a hell of a technician to put together an explosive that was stable enough not to explode when it was jostled around in the golf bag and still detonate on impact with the club. My guess is that it was detonated by remote."

"So, you think somebody waited until Sam Leggett took his swing, then set off the bomb?"

"That's my theory," he said. "But I'm not an expert in assembling explosives. We should ask the other guy here who was a SEAL back when they first started that branch."

Somebody else here? "Who might that be?"

Josh pointed through the milling crowd toward the tall, lanky man who was sucking down coffee. "Whit Parkens. He's a DUDE."

"DUDE?"

"Deadly Underwater Demolitions Expert."

Sheep man was a SEAL?

Amelia raised her scrawny arms above her head and called for attention. "I'm so pleased that you all could make it. We're going to move into the sun room now. And you should all get ready for a beautiful sunset, doncha know. Help yourselves to cocktails. The punch bowl on the left is Fuzzy Navels and the punch bowl on the right is Sex on the Beach."

Oh, yum. I was glad that I'd had the smarts to fortify myself with the meat loaf sandwich at the hotel.

Amelia continued. "And you're in for a treat later. Patty Carmen is catering, but we're not having any clam. She's making my favorite: Fried Spam, French fries, and Jell-O."

When she flung open the double doors to a room at the rear

of the house, sunlight poured through. We funneled into a room that was twice the size of the parlor and had obviously been added on to the house. It was all windows on three sides with an incredible view overlooking the Pacific.

The promised Fuzzy Navels and Sex on the Beach were set out on a table covered with a lace cloth. There was also coffee and tea and some kind of munchies in a crystal bowl which Alison, who had rejoined me, said was Waterford.

"I can't believe this place," she said. "Amelia has some really fine, expensive pieces but they're intermixed with flea-market junk. It's like opening a Cracker Jack box and finding the Hope diamond."

In the larger room, we were less crowded. I was leading Alison in the direction of Whit and Dottie Parkens, when Patty Carmen rushed by carrying a large bowl of cheese puffs. She wore a white apron with the happy-clam logo silk-screened on the front, her wig of raven locks jauntily tilted to one side.

"Hold it right there, buster," she said, depositing the munchies on the hospitality table. "I've got something for you." Throwing her arms around my neck, she planted a big carmine-red kiss on my lips. "Harrison told me all about what you did. Thanks for saving the old fart."

"How's Tiger doing?" I asked modestly.

A bothered look replaced her smile. "He was still unconscious when I left the hospital. The doctor says he might not come out of it"—her brave smile came back—"but he doesn't know Tiger like I do. He'll come out of it just to make the doctor look stupid."

"I'll bet he will."

Patty eyed Alison. "Are you the reason I can't get this big hunk to give me a tumble."

"I hope so," Alison said, offering her hand. "I'm Alison Brooks."

Patty ignored Alison's hand, instead giving her a friendly

hug. "Does he really have a carbuncle shaped like Elvis on his butt?"

Alison laughed. "I've always thought it looks more like Jerry Garcia."

The two women laughed together, bonding at my expense.

"While you ladies make fun of my afflictions, I'm going to say hi to Whit and Dottie." I wanted to hear more about Whit's explosives expertise.

I had moved about four steps in that direction, when Margot rushed up and grabbed me by the arm. "It's a good thing I'm here," she said in a hushed voice.

"I'll be the judge of that."

"I've already figured out how the next murder is going to happen." She dragged me toward the corner of the room. "Out there," she said.

In the corner, the windows transformed to sliding glass doors that opened onto a wide observation platform. The wooden deck seemed to serve as the backyard. Cantilevered from the rear wall of the house, it extended well beyond the edge of a vertical drop to the beach. Arranged at the railing were four viewing binoculars in metal stands that swiveled. It was the sort of equipment I would expect to find atop the Empire State Building, where you put in a quarter to see a magnified view of the skyline. Actually, I thought it was pretty cool.

I turned to Margot. "It's a viewing deck. What about it?"

"On a sheer cliff," she said ominously "The drop is seventy feet or more onto jagged rocks."

"What are you suggesting, Margot? You think the killer is going to carry the heirs out one at a time and throw them off the deck? Or maybe everybody will just line up single file and hurl themselves over the rail, like lemmings."

"You're an idiot! I can't believe we're related."

Neither could I.

She hissed, "See the bolts fastening the deck to the wall of the house?"

When I leaned toward the glass doors to take a gander, she yanked me backward and snarled, "Don't be so obvious."

"What about the bolts?"

"They're loosened, hanging by a thread. As soon as somebody steps onto that viewing platform, it's going to fall apart."

I had reason to doubt the accuracy of her observation. Margot's ignorance of such a practical skill as carpentry was surpassed only by her total inability to comprehend the workings of an automobile. When her cars—which she routinely drove at the speed of light—developed a problem, she'd simply trade them in.

Since she wouldn't actually allow me to see the bolts, I asked, "How did you figure this out?"

"Desiree and I got here early. Now that her husband is dead, it's important for her to kiss up to the elderly rich relatives, like Amelia, who is—pardon the expression—older than dirt. I mean, she must be, oh, about a hundred and seven."

"Only in her seventies," I said.

"She's decrepit. So Desiree needs to remind her of what a darling she is, so Amelia can remember her in the will."

"Charming," I said.

"Anyway, I had Desiree give me a guided tour, so I could point out the objects of value that she could mention to Amelia that she really wanted. We made a written inventory so the old bat could remember. And when we were in here, we discovered the loose bolts." Darkly, she concluded, "And that spells murder to me."

"Check your dictionary," I advised. "Loose bolts spell poor maintenance."

"Duh, Adam! Don't you get it? The murderer is going to lure his next victim onto the viewing platform, and it's going to fall off the wall, looking like an accident."

The only reason that I paid her the slightest bit of attention was that this scheme was so complicated that it sounded like the sort of thing Margot herself would come up with. "All right," I said. "Good work, Margot. So, we point out to everybody that the bolts are loose and nobody gets killed."

"Wrong! This is an opportunity. Whoever sabotaged the viewing deck is your murderer. They'll know the bolts are loose, so they'll make sure they don't go out there."

I still wasn't following her reasoning. "In case you haven't noticed, no one is going out there."

"Watch me," she said.

Margot sidled toward Tia, who was standing alone, staring at the ice cubes melting in her Fuzzy Navel. She looked up when Margot appeared at her elbow. The expression on Tia's face was one of undisguised annoyance.

"Oh, look!" Margot said, pointing toward the viewing deck. "Whales! There are whales out there, hundreds of them."

"Fluke you," Tia said, turning her back.

Margot bounced triumphantly back to me. "See! She's obviously the murderer. Anybody else would have run out onto the deck to watch. But Tia didn't. Because she *knew* it was sabotaged."

"Check me if I'm wrong here, Margot. Following your logic, if Tia had rushed out onto the platform, she'd be innocent."

"Right," she said proudly.

I gritted my teeth. "But she'd also be dead."

"True. That's a complication I'm still working on."

I used my most matter-of-fact, no-bullshit, I'm-not-kidding-anymore tone of voice. "Stop fucking around!"

This was, arguably, the dumbest thing my sister had ever come up with. She was trying to catch a murderer by default. At the same time—if the bolts were really loosened—she was playing a game with deadly consequences.

Margot opened her mouth to rebut, but I raised my hand.

"Enough nonsense." I pulled back the sliding door and leaned out. Nothing looked wrong, but when I placed one foot on the wooden platform, the steel flanges sprang away from the wall. Amazingly, Margot's diagnosis was correct. The viewing deck was hanging by a couple of metal threads, and it looked like sabotage.

I turned back to the room and raised my voice, "Everybody, listen up. There seems to be a construction problem on the deck, and I would advise that no one—"

"Oh, look!" Margot bellowed, drowning me out. She waved her arms as a distraction and pointed to the west. "Look! Whales!"

The heirs and associates stood in stunned silence, observing our brother-sister duet.

I continued. "No one go out on the deck. It looks like it's ready to fall off the wall."

"Gray whales!" Margot yelled at the same time. "Dozens of them. Just out there"—she pointed excitedly—"you can see them from the deck."

"Don't go out there," I concluded, closing the sliding glass door and walking back toward the center of the room toward Whit and Dottie. It would probably be best if I located Amelia and got a key to lock that door, just in case.

Whit shook his head. "It's peeling off the wall, huh?"

"Looks like it."

"Sloppy carpentry," he scoffed. "I told Graden when he hired the lowest bidder to build this addition that you get what you pay for."

Amelia flitted into the room. She seemed a bit wobbly, probably from a head start on the Fuzzy Navels. Weaving a path among us, she said, "Did someone say whales? What are we all waiting for?"

For such an elderly, drunken person, she moved fast. By the time I realized what she intended, she was already at the sliding glass doors.

"Amelia, no!"

I dove toward her, but it was already too late. She flung open the doors and staggered outside. "I just love those big grays, doncha know."

Amelia was tiny. Though the viewing deck lurched, it remained attached to the wall. I stood at the door, holding out my hand to her. If I went out there, even one step, I could cause the whole piece of overhanging construction to plummet. "Amelia, come back inside. Take my hand."

Staring out to sea, she craned her wrinkled neck. "Where are the whales? I want to see them."

When she stamped her foot, it was just enough pressure to dislodge the flanges. With a grinding squeal, it peeled away from the house.

Amelia threw back her head and laughed all the way down, seventy feet, to the jagged rocks below.

Chapter
Twelve

melia Porcelli never had a chance, but I couldn't make Brutus, a local cop who had responded to our 911 call, understand me. Brutus and I were sitting in the unmatched rocking chairs in Amelia's kitsch-filled parlor.

"She was murdered," I said.

"Huh?" Brutus looked down at the little spiral notebook where he was supposedly taking notes.

"Homicide," I said.

He pushed his cap back and rubbed an angry-looking zit on his forehead, then he looked at me as if he were trying to remember where he'd seen me before. I knew when. The first time I saw Brutus was at the Mallard Tavern in Toledo with Tia when Brutus had been summoned by the bartender to break up the rowdy game of belly bumping.

I could've told him, but I didn't want to further confuse the man. The look in his eyes was duller than a Tom Snyder interview. He cleared his throat, sending his Adam's apple bobbing.

"I still don't understand how come you think this is a homicide. Are you saying Amelia was pushed?"

"No." For the tenth time, I tried to explain. "The bolts had been loosened so the deck would fall as soon as somebody stepped on it."

He scratched again and gaped at me with a slack jaw. It was not a confidence-inspiring expression. I had dragged him in there so we could be alone and I could give him a statement. My fervent hope was that I could convince him that Amelia's death had been murder, and Brutus would call some real cops to investigate. It might have been useful to have a forensics team test the deck for fingerprints and telltale fibers that would point to the person who had loosened the bolts.

"Huh?" Brutus repeated.

His attention was distracted by noise from outside Amelia's house, where a rescue unit was engaged in retrieving her body from the foot of the cliff. I didn't want to go out there because I was sure that the efforts of the professional rescuers would be hindered by the heirs and associates who felt compelled to give advice, shoot off their mouths, and generally make nuisances of themselves.

"A homicide, huh?" Brutus shook his head, and the pattern of zits on his face seemed to take on a life of their own.

"That's right. Just like Sam Leggett."

"The fella who got blown up by his golf ball?"

"That's right," I said. "And like Tiger Jorgenson."

"Hold on there, Mr. McCleet. Tiger can't be a homicide on account of he's not dead." The deputy's mouth formed a loopy grin. Finally, he'd gotten something right. "You stand corrected, sir."

"Okay." I amended, "Tiger was an attempted murder."

"Nope. Tiger was danged careless, that's what. The Coast Guard sent down some divers to take a look at his boat. Know what they found?"

"I have no idea."

"The old fart forgot to close the toilet. Probably on account of he was drunk at the time. Anyhow, instead of the toilet water going out, the sea water came in and it just kept coming in until it filled up the cabin and—"

"I know how it works." Marine plumbing can be tricky. With the valve closed, you pump the bowl full of sea water. Then you open the valve to pump the water out. If you forget to close the valve when you leave, you can siphon the ocean back into the boat through the toilet. "That doesn't explain how he got the gash on the back of his gourd."

"An accident when he got pulled out of the drink."

"I was there," I said. "It wasn't an accident. It was—"

There was no point in continuing. The noise from the rear of the house had reached a crescendo, and Brutus was obviously distracted. Instead, I suggested, "Why don't we go out there and see if we can help."

"Best idea you've had all day."

Happily, Brutus shut his spiral notebook and loped toward the front door, leaving me alone in the home of the late Amelia Porcelli. Now might be an excellent time to search, but the idea of pawing through the old lady's stuff before her corpse was even cold didn't have much appeal. Still, the opportunity might not come again.

I sprinted up the staircase to the second floor, then to the third, heading for the doll room. There might be a clue in there that Amelia in her insane ramblings was trying to pass on to me.

From the staircase, I looked down the hallway and noticed that the door to the doll room was slightly ajar. I slowed my thundering ascent to a more subtle approach. Somebody else had the same idea I did about checking the dolls. I could only hope that it was the murderer.

This time, I wasn't leaping from a helicopter without a parachute. I took my 9mm from the back of my slacks and chambered a round.

A deep, ghostly sigh issued from the room, stirring the dust motes in a shaft of sunlight that fell through the door. Before I scared myself into thinking that Amelia had not really died in her plunge from the cliff, I heard the unmistakable growl of Harrison Porcelli. "Whale sputum."

His trademark outburst was followed by another sigh, and I put away my gun. When I eased up to the partially opened door and peeked inside, I saw Harrison's back. He sat on a little three-legged stool. His shoulders slumped. His head was bowed. In his hand he held the white-haired doll that resembled Amelia.

As I watched, he rose heavily to his feet. His limp was pronounced as he walked to the window and set the doll on a ledge, taking care to smooth the folds of the skirts.

"I love you, Mom," he murmured.

His shoulders began to tremble, and I withdrew.

In the midst of all this greedy mayhem, it was easy to forget the human factor. Harrison had lost both parents, suddenly, in the course of a few weeks. It pissed me off. I was building up to a real bad mood.

The scene at the rear of Amelia's house did nothing to alleviate my feeling that nobody was taking this murder seriously. The rescue team had rigged their equipment to rappel down the face of the cliff. There were four of them, balancing precariously on the jagged rocks below while the Pacific surf crashed around them.

Everybody else was perched in a clump on the edge of the cliff, observing with concern, muttering among themselves, and shouting instructions.

I joined the crowd, stepping up beside Alison, who was farthest from the action. "What's going on?" I asked.

"You don't want to know," she said.

I could see that they had retrieved Amelia's body, wrapped

her in a protective shroud, and placed her frail remains into a sort of basket device which they were trying to fasten to a pulley and winch. Their equipment looked state-of-the-art to me. Lots of climbing rope, pitons, and carabiners.

Alison turned to me. "Can we leave?"

The rescue crew began their hoist.

Immediately, Dottie Parkens leaned over the ledge and yelled, "Be careful."

As if Amelia cared?

Whit started talking to the man operating the hoist. "You know, son, this would've been a whole lot easier if you'd come around from the sea."

"Or by helicopter," Jimmy Caruthers put in. "You could lift her gently with a chopper. Harrison has one."

The young rescuer shot them a hostile glare, but remained professional and calm. "Thank you, sir."

"Just an opinion," Whit said, fading back.

"Careful," Dottie repeated as the basket bounced against the rocky cliff.

"Incompetents!" Margot snapped. "She's going to get all banged up."

As if the seventy-foot drop hadn't provided the ultimate bruising?

Tia stood between her daughter and son-in-law. I half expected her to step forward and tell these people that they were assholes, but she seemed detached, staring off at the horizon. This was the second violent death in as many days to members of her family. Again, I had the sense that Tia was no stranger to death and disaster.

Desiree was beside one of the younger members of the rescue team. "It must take a lot of muscle," she said, "to do your work."

"Yes, ma'am."

"I'm a widow, you know."

"I'm married, ma'am."

"Well, why would I care about that?"

"Desiree," Margot snapped. The other woman trotted over to her, and I overheard Margot's advice. "Never ever bother with the young, cute ones. They have no money."

I'd had enough of Margot and her dangerous advice. I strode over to her. "Margot, we need to talk."

"We certainly do. This is all your fault, Adam."

I pulled her aside, none too gently. What I was about to say didn't need to be overheard by the assorted heirs. Jerking her along beside me, I proceeded toward the cars parked at the front of the house. "Listen to me, Margot, and don't speak or I'll knock you out."

"Don't even try to push me—"

I showed her my fist. "No more screwing around. This isn't one of your musical husbands games. Nor is it catch the brass ring and win a million bucks."

"What are you saying?" She shook off my grasp. "What's the matter with you, Adam?"

"Shut up, Margot." I continued. "You may not have noticed, but this is a tragic situation. Because of your stupid scheme for trapping a murderer, an old woman is dead. You're dangerous. I don't want your help, and I don't want you interfering in these people's lives anymore."

"But Desiree needs me."

"If Desiree has two living brain cells in her shallow head, which is doubtful, she'll get her butt out of town as soon as possible. She should go home, mourn her husband, and forget about the Porcellis."

"You'd like that, wouldn't you? More money for you if she doesn't sue."

Somehow, my direct confrontation had gotten off track and doubled back around to the question of money. But then, in life, doesn't everything? Get back to money?

"You're going to leave, Margot. This bullshit stops here."

"Don't give me orders."

"How about this? If you don't go, I will inform the police that you knew about the loosened bolts and you tricked Amelia into running onto the deck. In effect, you are responsible for her death. I believe they call that manslaughter."

"You wouldn't!"

"I would. In a New York minute. With pleasure."

It was close enough to the truth that she couldn't really deny it. This time, I thought, Margot's game had turned around and bitten her on the ass.

I concluded, "I want you to get out of Newport. Go back to Portland and inflict yourself on the people of that fine city."

"I have a mind to do just that. I might just leave you here to mess everything up all by yourself." She paused, lifted her pointy chin, and said, "I'm going, Adam. You'll never get your filthy mitts on the Porcelli millions without my advice, but I guess that's your loss, brother dear."

She stepped away from me and waved to Desiree. "Hey! I want to go now."

Desiree came scampering over. "What's wrong, Margot?"

"Let's blow this pop stand. Newport is simply too small a town. We can certainly find better fish to fry in Portland." Margot hopped into the passenger side of the Miata. "Or in Hollywood."

"Hollywood?" Desiree snorted excitedly. "Do you think I could be in movies?"

"You?" Margot laughed, unbowed by her own actions or my threats. "I might find a part for you in *Margot: The Miniseries.* Oh, my, Desiree, you have so much to learn."

As they whisked away in a swirl of dust, Harrison came out of the house and walked up beside me. I turned to him. "I'm sorry about your mother."

"Thanks." His eyes were red. "She was a fruitcake. But she was still my mother."

I thought that might make an excellent epitaph, but I said nothing.

"When I saw her at the bottom of the cliff, she looked so pathetic. Like one of her dolls that was broken. Aw, hell, she lived a long life. Maybe it's better that she go like this than sink into some deteriorating illness. Still, this is so wrong."

I agreed.

We both turned toward the mob at cliffside. Only Alison stood apart, arms crossed beneath her breasts and looking questioningly at me.

"Adam," Harrison said, "I want to help you find whoever is responsible for my mother's death, and I don't mean your sister, who was only stupid."

"If there's anything you can do, I'll let you know."

"I can help."

He reached into his pocket and showed me his handgun. Great! Now he and Tia were both armed. "Jesus Christ, Harrison, I wish you wouldn't carry that. Most of the accidents with firearms occur when—"

"I'm keeping it." He twitched and blurted out, "Blowjob."

"But, Harrison—"

"Somebody is killing off the heirs, and I don't intend to be next." He leaned back against the shiny fender of Jimmy Caruthers's BMW. "I have something I need to tell you, Adam."

"I'm all ears."

"I know why my father appointed you to the job of finding the murderer."

He had my full attention.

"It was because of me," Harrison said. "I don't expect that you'll remember this, but it was April first, 1969."

I tried to remember that time. Aside from April Fool's Day, it was the era of Vietnam, of hippies and cheap drugs. It was the dawn of disco meat markets and polyester.

Harrison continued. "I had just turned eighteen, and my birth date had come up high in the draft lottery. It was pretty certain that I was going to get the call."

"What about your Tourette's syndrome." I couldn't imagine that Harrison would be too handy on a silent night patrol in the jungle when he had this tendency to blurt out semi-obscenities every time he felt stressed.

"It wasn't so pronounced back then. The doctors hadn't diagnosed me. They thought it was just teenaged acting-out." A strange smile crossed his lips. "If they had known, my whole life would have been different."

"You wouldn't have been drafted," I said.

"No. But nobody knew. Anyway, my mom was devastated with the idea that I might have to go into the Army. I was her only child. She didn't want to lose me. And my father wasn't happy about it either. Though he was a big-time war hero in World War Two, he was politically opposed to Vietnam."

"Couldn't he have kept you out?" I asked. In my experience, there weren't many rich boys on the front lines. Somehow, they always managed to find cushy alternatives to carrying an M-16.

"He wouldn't use his influence like that. Remember, he was Graden Porcelli, self-made millionaire and war hero. If he'd gotten me out of the service, it would be like sidestepping his duty. I was his son. It was my duty to go get killed in a jungle to preserve the family name. I didn't know what to do."

Harrison looked directly at me. "Then I met you. Adam McCleet. It was in a bar in Portland."

During that time in my life, I had spent a lot of time in Portland bars. It was all kind of a haze.

"You were back from Vietnam," Harrison reminded. "But you weren't a cop yet."

For a couple of years I drifted aimlessly. During the late sixties and early seventies, it was easy to float. This was the era of red beans and rice and free love. Everybody was crashing at someone else's place.

"I told you my problem," Harrison said. "I didn't really want to go, but it didn't seem like I had a choice. My parents didn't want me to go, but they couldn't avoid it without losing face. I asked you what was the right thing to do, and you told me."

I was pretty sure that whatever advice I offered at that time was ten degrees past moronic.

Harrison continued. "You said that if you had it to do all over again, you wouldn't go into the Marines. If it came down to a choice between going to Vietnam and shooting yourself in the foot to avoid the draft, you'd take the bullet."

"Jesus Christ, Harrison, you didn't take me seriously, did you?"

"I was still pretty loaded, even after I drove back here. A couple more drinks, and I took one of my father's guns and shot off my baby toe."

"Holy shit."

"I drove myself to the hospital, thinking how clever I was to have solved my problem about being drafted. My father didn't agree. He thought I was the most cowardly asshole on the face of the earth. He didn't realize that I'd done it for him and for Mom."

Harrison shrugged. "Anyway, he asked me where I'd gotten this insane idea, and I remembered your name. After that, he followed your life. At first he'd tell me all the dumb things you had done. His point was that I was an idiot to listen to you. Then, after you became a cop, he started telling me how brave and dedicated you were. He even followed your life when you became a sculptor and got involved in a couple of crime-solving adventures."

I had a very creepy feeling about this. Graden Porcelli, whom I don't believe I ever met, had been keeping tabs on me since I was a young punk back from Vietnam. "I guess it's too late to say I'm sorry."

"Actually," Harrison said, "it's precisely the right time. I saved your life, Adam. When that happened this morning, it somehow vindicated me. I'm a hero. I have what it takes."

He sighed again, and I knew he was thinking that his heroism had come too late. Neither his father nor mother would ever know. "I'm sorry, Harrison."

"You're forgiven."

He turned away from me and limped back toward the house. It might have been my imagination, but his shoulders seemed a little straighter. Throughout our conversation, he hadn't had one outburst.

Silently, I wished him well.

Glancing over at the crowd gathered at cliffside, I saw that the rescue team had finally raised the basket containing Amelia's body. Jimmy Caruthers caught my eye. He looked sad. Even his mustache was drooping. He raised both hands, holding up seven fingers, he lowered one and then another. Two down. Five to go.

I gathered up Alison and drove away from the giant cottage on the cliff. The spring flowers in Amelia's yard were still blooming. The skies were turning pink with a magnificent sunset. Alison still looked beautiful in the car. But there was a pall on the day. None of this was turning out the way I wanted, and I felt like the world's greatest asshole for touching young Harrison's life and changing it for the worst.

"Here's what I think," Alison said.

I braced myself for more insistence that I go back to Portland and forget about the Porcelli heirs.

"I think," she continued, "that we should solve this as soon as possible and get the hell out of here."

"Solve this? That's a rather large shift in your opinion, isn't it?"

"It makes me mad that somebody is terrorizing these people. I mean, they're nice folks. They shouldn't have to be threatened by a murderer." She smiled at me. "And I believe you're the man to stop the killer, Adam. Did you ever know that you're my hero?"

"The wind beneath your wings?"

"Exactly." She leaned over and kissed my cheek. "Besides, I don't think we've fully explored the possibilities of the Zorro room."

After a quick consultation, we decided to stop by the hospital. My reasons were twofold: I wanted to see how Tiger was doing. And I wanted to check on Tia's idea of a guard. Unconscious, Tiger was a helpless target, and I was worried that Tia had sent some limp environmentalist to protect him.

The Beachfront Hospital and ICU on the outskirts of Newport seemed like a friendly little place. We were greeted at the front desk by a smiling lady in a happy yellow volunteers' uniform. When she asked if she could help us, it felt like she really meant it.

"We're looking for Tiger Jorgenson."

She checked a clipboard in front of her. Concern pulled her eyebrows into a frown. "My golly, he's not feeling very well, is he?"

"He's in a coma."

"Dear me, well, oh, dear. I'm sure he'll be fine." She looked toward Alison and whispered. "I usually work in obstetrics. Everybody there is happy with their new babies."

"Where's Tiger?" I repeated. The volunteer lady's infernal optimism caused an ache in my sweet tooth. When people are too nice, it makes me want to squash them like ladybugs.

She pointed. "West wing. He's out of ICU."

Alison was careful to thank the volunteer before we started down the polished floor to the west wing. Tiger was out of intensive care. That may be good news and maybe not. The way I understand it, intensive care is for people who require careful monitoring. They might go into crisis at any moment.

Either Tiger was on the mend. Or he was on his way to permanent coma.

It wasn't hard to find his room. Sitting outside the door was one of the meanest-looking hombres I have ever seen in my life. From the waist up, he was massive with thick, heavy shoulders. He had a long mustache that drooped over the edges of his mouth. His dark eyes were fixed in a permanent squint. This guy made Pancho Villa look like the leader of a ladies' sewing circle.

I stopped in front of him. "Hi," I said, "I'm a friend of Tia's."

"So you say."

"My name is Adam McCleet."

"Do you have some identification?"

I showed him my driver's license.

"You're okay. Tia said you might come." He rose to his feet, an act that was similar to erecting a twelve-story building. "I'm Ernesto."

The last time Alison and I were in Taos, I'd picked up a little Spanish, but I didn't think Ernesto would find it humorous if I butchered his native tongue, so I stuck to English.

"I'm curious," I said. "How do you know Tia?"

"El Salvador," he said.

Alison made the obvious inquiry, "How is Tiger doing?"

Ernesto shook his head. "The doctors disconnected the respirator, and he's breathing on his own with oxygen and an IV drip. CAT scan shows a concussion, but no permanent brain damage. He is in a light coma."

When Ernesto lapsed into silence, a tiny smile touched the corners of his mouth, knowing that his articulate medical description had been unexpected. What other surprises did Tia's friend have for us?

"Has he spoken?" I asked.

Ernesto shook his head. Negative.

Alison and I slipped into the room with Ernesto following.

Tiger looked smaller and much weaker than the robust old fart who had scared little Todd at the jetty. But his color was good. And his scrawny chest, beneath the thin cotton hospital gown, moved up and down steadily. Apart from the tubing that ran into his nostrils and the IV stuck in the back of his hand, the old man appeared to be sleeping.

It was depressing to see him so deflated, and I didn't stay long in the room. Out in the hall, I turned to Ernesto again. "Are you here twenty-four hours a day? Do you have someone to spell you?"

He nodded. "I have a friend. We'll take care of him. We'll do anything for Tia."

I started to say, "If you need help—"

"No," he corrected me. "I won't need anything. If you need me, Tia knows how to reach me."

Since there was obviously nothing else I could do there, Alison and I headed back through the hospital, passed the cheerful volunteer who implored us to "have a nice day," and went into the parking lot.

"Well, what happens next?" Alison asked.

"Nothing for tonight."

I was feeling a strong need to smash something delicate with my fist. In the course of the day, I had participated in the rescue of Tiger, watched Amelia fall from a seventy-foot cliff, and seen a cranky old man reduced to a pallid, silent form in a hospital bed. Not to mention the news that I had caused a man to shoot off his own toe. I was surrounded by vulnerability, and I was helpless to stop whoever was killing them off.

"What about tomorrow?" Alison asked.

"I made arrangements with Jimmy to view the tape again," I said. "And I want to get a look at Amelia's collections. There might be a clue somewhere in there. Her son, Harrison, said she never threw anything away."

"Well, that sounds like a plan."

Alison was being extra perky to compensate for my low mood, and I appreciated her effort. But I still didn't feel any better.

Back at my car, I opened the door for her and went around to my side. As soon as I slid behind the wheel, I saw him. A guy wearing a surgical mask and holding a gun. The barrel was aimed directly at my forehead.

Chapter
Thirteen

y reflexes aren't what they were when I was eighteen, but a little shot of adrenaline still goes a long way toward the enhancement of basic survival skills. My brain flashed the message to my body: Danger. Death imminent. Act now.

I yelled at Alison in the passenger seat, "Get down!"

In a motion that would have been fluid except that my sport jacket got in the way, I yanked my gun from the waistband of my slacks, aimed in the direction of the would-be assailant, and fired. Directly through the windshield of my car. This was the brand-new windshield, of course. The newness of it might have accounted for the spectacular spiderweb of cracks that radiated instantaneously from the 9mm hole creating tiny glass chunks, approximately the size of sugar cubes, which then began dropping into the front seat of the car like hailstones.

"Shit!" With my ears still ringing from discharging my weapon inside the closed vehicle, I leapt from the car and charged in the direction where I had seen the guy with the gun—although it wasn't necessarily a guy. I had an impression of someone wearing mirrored sunglasses and surgical scrubs, complete with mask and matching aqua-colored cap. Either I'd just been attacked by psycho-doc, or this individual was taking pains to disguise him or herself.

Attacked, I realized as I dashed across the asphalt parking lot, wasn't exactly the correct term because I fired the first, and only, shot. At the edge of the parking lot was a minimall that hadn't bothered with the tourist trappings of the rest of Newport. This was a practical, square one-story building of cinder-block construction. It housed a cafeteria, a flower shop, an appliance repair outlet, a novelty store, and two vacant retail spaces for lease. I glimpsed a flash of aqua at the far end of the building. If I caught this fucker, I would inflict great bodily pain and possible permanent disfigurement. Then, they would personally pay for my windshield.

I heard the crack of a pistol. An inch from my head, a fragment of cinder block ripped away from the wall and slammed against my cheek. I flattened myself in the doorway of the novelty store. The posted signs on the locked door read: SORRY, WE'RE CLOSED. FAKE NOSES HALF OFF.

Pressing my hand against my face, I could feel small specks of gravel under the skin. I knew the wound was superficial, but the bleeding was profuse. When I poked my head out, another shot was fired. Ducking back, I yelled, "You missed again, ass-hole."

There was virtually no place to hide in the empty parking lot, but I was not of a mood to stay put in the relative safety of the doorway. In a shootout, a safe place can become a deathtrap if you linger too long. The best defense is a strong offense. I needed to act. Hell, I wanted to act. I wanted to expel some of the excess frustration and energy that churned inside me. I wanted to shoot somebody.

This had been one of the most harrowing days of my life.

The only good thing about it was Alison and the Zorro outfit. Alison! I glanced back over my shoulder toward the car which still sat in the near-empty hospital lot with both its doors hanging open. She had taken it upon herself to find cover. Smart girl, that Alison.

In my brain I mapped a running course that would make it tough for the gunman to draw a bead on me. Then I bolted, sprinting twenty feet, then ducking into the entrance of the flower shop. I paused there for a few seconds to catch my breath and psych myself up for the next sprint. I repeated the door-to-door dash-and-duck advance five more times until I'd worked my way to the end of the minimall.

Nobody shot at me. When I poked my nose around the corner of the building, no one was there. A few feet from the spot where the shooter had been standing, a pair of brass shell casings lay on the asphalt—9mm, same size as the bullets that my guns used.

Still pumped with adrenaline, I circled the building, yelling more obscenities than Harrison in his worst Tourette's outbreak. Finding nothing, I returned to the car.

Alison waved to me from the hospital door. "Adam, get in here. I called 911."

Of course she did. When in a life-threatening situation, call for backup. That was sensible. The only reason I hadn't done it myself was my obsession to catch the bad guy and make him pay, in a most gruesome and physical way, for all the pain and grief of the past two days.

Before I could step inside the hospital and explain everything to Alison, a police cruiser pulled into the parking lot with siren blaring. I was highly disgruntled to see Brutus climb out and saunter toward us.

"I can't believe it!" I greeted him. "Aren't there any other cops working in this county?"

"How're you doing, Mr. McCleet?"

"Call the sheriff," I demanded.

"Well, he's feeling poorly and also he's real busy with the case of the exploding golf ball. That's how come I'm doing so much overtime." He grinned with idiotic affability. "What can I do for you?"

"Somebody tried to kill me," I raved.

"Dear me." Brutus chuckled. "Now, Mr. McCleet, I surely do hope this isn't another one of your phony-baloney homicides."

I pointed to my car. The glass continued to drip from the busted windshield. "Does that look like I'm making this up?" I pointed to my bleeding cheek. "How do you think I got this?"

"That's serious, all right. How did you get your windshield broke?"

"I shot through it." That didn't sound good.

"You shot it."

"That's right," I said. "I was trying to shoot a person who was aiming a gun at me."

"Did this person shoot at you?"

"Not until I chased him behind the minimall. He was wearing a surgical mask and scrubs. Actually, I couldn't even tell if the person was male or female."

Brutus cleared his throat. "Are you meaning to tell me that the person with a gun was a doctor?"

"Of course not. It was a disguise."

"Did you catch 'em?"

"What do you think?" I flapped my arms. "If I had caught the person, I'd have him with me now, wouldn't I?"

"I suppose so." Brutus turned to Alison. "And did you see this person who was dressed up like a doctor?"

She cast an apologetic look in my direction. "No. Adam told me to get down, and I did."

"Was this before or after he shot out the windshield of his own car?"

"Kind of at the same time," she said. "But I know Adam's telling the truth. Why would he invent a story like that?"

Brutus wrinkled his brow. He started scratching his head again, then moved to scratching his chin, followed by his armpit, and finally his butt. "Are you a drinking man, Mr. McCleet?"

I didn't dignify his question with a response. "Just file your report on this, Brutus." I marched toward the car. "And forget it. I'll handle it myself."

"Sure will, Mr. McCleet. There's just one more thing."

"What?"

"I'm goin' to have to write you a citation for discharging a firearm inside the city limits."

I turned on my heel and charged toward him. "Why, you little son of a—" I checked myself, feeling that I had no time to waste sitting in jail. I wanted to beat him mercilessly, but I said, through clenched teeth, "With all due respect, could you write it fast? I'm trying to catch a fucking killer!"

"You bet," Brutus said. "I always aim to please."

I scribbled my signature on the ticket and, as Brutus drove away, I crumpled the yellow copy in my fist and pitched it at his cop car.

As we brushed the bits of glass from the front seat, Alison said, "We should go back into the hospital and have someone look at your face."

"I can look at my own face," I snapped. Instantly feeling like a two-hundred-pound sack of dog whip for barking at my only ally, I added, in a gentler tone, "Really, hon. It looks worse than it is. We'll stop at a grocery store and pick up some disinfectant. You can be my nurse."

As I drove, Alison was wise enough not to speak. For one thing, she could see that I was on the brink of losing control of everything, up to and including my bodily functions. For another, it would have been highly difficult to carry on an intelligible conversation with the fresh, salt-scented wind roaring in our ears through the empty space where my windshield had been.

En route to the Sunny Beach hotel, I pulled into the parking lot of a Safeway store on the coast highway. So as not to frighten the shoppers with my battered appearance and surly disposition, I waited in the car while Alison did a quick shop for medical supplies and something to snack on—Amelia had taken her plunge before Patty Carmen could get around to serving the fried Spam and Jell-O.

When we were back in the Zorro room, Alison settled on the bed with her legs crossed, yoga-style, while she administered to my wound. Plucking a piece of gravel from my cheek with an eyebrow tweezer, she issued a one-word directive. "Talk."

"Ouch!" The treatment was more painful than the injury. "Okay. I'll talk. Just don't hurt me anymore."

"Want something to bite on?"

"Don't mind if I do." I poured wine into a pair of hotel water glasses and unwrapped the smoked salmon that Alison had purchased at the store.

"Where to start?" I bit off a large chunk of the salty fish and washed it back with a gulp of wine. "You were there for the debacle with Margot causing Amelia to take the plunge."

"Yes," she said. "That wasn't your fault, Adam."

"Then, how about this: The reason Graden Porcelli named me as the detective in his will is because, more than twenty-five years ago, I told Harrison to shoot off his own toe. You have noticed his limp?"

She nodded.

"I caused that." I told her the whole story, not bothering to make myself look better or braver or smarter than I had been at the time. "I feel like shit about it. Who knew he would take me so literally?"

"Who could know," she echoed, digging the tweezer into my face for another small chunk of cement.

"So?" I looked at her for the first time in my long recitation. Her hair was adorably mussed from the ride in the windshieldless car. "Am I still your hero?"

"You're a good man, Adam. You always have been, and you always will be." She shrugged. On Alison, even that simple gesture looked graceful. "That doesn't mean you don't make the occasional mistake."

"Like completely screwing up Harrison's life?"

She doused a cotton ball with peroxide and dabbed my cheek. "All finished. I think you'll live." She uncrossed her legs and curled them beneath her, then leaned close to whisper in my ear, "I love you."

Somehow, that simple assurance made everything a lot better. "I love you too."

I fell asleep in her arms and woke the next morning feeling somewhat renewed, despite the severe bruising on my hip from the Tiger rescue and the lacerations on my face from the shootout and the contusions on my ego from learning what a jerk I'd been twenty-five years ago.

"Today," Alison assured me, "we'll get some of this mess figured out."

"I'm game."

Our first job in the morning was to get the window fixed, then we would head over to Jimmy Caruthers's office. Yesterday, at Amelia's, he promised to make a duplicate of the taped will so I could study it for clues. Then, I figured, Alison and I would visit Whit and Dottie at the sheep ranch.

The guy at the window glass repair place gave me a questioning look when I pulled in. "Don't ask," I advised, and he didn't.

"Let's check out the Clam Dip," I suggested.

"Chowder for breakfast?" Alison made a face. She was picky about what she put into her body, very aware of fat and cholesterol content. "Don't get me wrong, Adam, I like Patty Carmen, but clam is not the breakfast of champions."

"A nice clam omelette?" I suggested.

"May I just say: Yuck?"

"Coffee?"

"Okay, as long as it isn't clam flavored."

Patty Carmen greeted us at the door. The past few days had been hard on her too. Her wig was even further askew than usual. Before we could order, she had the coffee poured and was leaning across the counter. "Have you heard anything new about Tiger?"

"We saw him last night," Alison said. "For someone in a coma, he looks well."

Patty Carmen nodded. "The old fart is going to pull through. We've got a pool going here on the day he'll wake up. Nobody is betting on more than two days from now. In case of a tie, the closest to the actual time of day wins. You want in?"

"Put me down for midnight tonight." I fished a five out of my wallet and handed it to Patty. "What did you think of Ernesto?"

"*Muy* macho." She wiggled her eyebrows, and a spark of her former bawdiness returned. "He's a lot of man. I'm glad he's there. Nobody is going to get Tiger with Ernesto standing guard."

"He said he was from El Salvador," I said.

She nodded. "A friend of Tia's. He told me that our quiet little Tia single-handedly rescued his three little sisters from the Sisters of Poverty mission when the war got too close."

Quiet little Tia was beginning to worry me a bit. From what people said about her, she was capable of thwarting a revolution, plus she had a radical background that indicated some familiarity with explosives. And whoever shot at me last night had taken pains to be disguised. I didn't want to believe that she was the murderer, but she did have a gun—same caliber as mine.

The other person I knew was armed was Harrison. Though he had every reason to fire a bullet into my cranium, or at least blow off one of my baby toes, I didn't believe it was him either. If he'd wanted me dead, he could have let the Coast Guard boat grind Tiger and me into plankton.

While I ruminated, Patty Carmen and Alison chatted amiably. I had known these two would hit it off. Though I try not to stereotype the female of the species, I have discovered that sooner or later the conversation would revolve around clothes, makeup, cooking, and ultimately men.

I tuned in for just a second as Patty Carmen told Alison about the first time she posed for Picasso.

I liked Patty Carmen. Unfortunately, I was finding more friends than suspects in this investigation. I started thinking about the methods used in the chain of assaults. First, an exploding golf ball. Then, an unchecked toilet that almost flushed Tiger down the tubes. Loosened bolts on the landing outside Amelia's house was the strangest form of attack. Anybody, any one of us, could have stepped onto that porch. Of course, virtually everyone in attendance had been an heir or an associate of an heir. Still, the wholesale-murder aspect seemed disorganized, and the other two attacks had taken a certain amount of planning. Was the stress affecting the murderer?

I listened for a second to Alison and Patty Carmen. Their conversation had progressed to music. Specifically, to opera. I heard Alison say, "There's nothing better than Pavarotti, a nice merlot, and a loving man."

Patty Carmen acknowledged with a sophisticated wink.

Now, I thought, they would move to a discussion of men and their foibles.

But Patty Carmen said, "Alison, the next time I visit Seville, you come with me. In the Gypsy caves, the flamenco is superb."

"Are you really part Gypsy?"

"*Sí.*" Patty Carmen grinned widely. "But I'm not sure which part."

Alison and Patty Carmen talked nonstop for twenty minutes

and never got around to the topic of what morons their menfolk are. Unusual women, I thought. Fascinating women. I was lucky to know both of them.

At a minor break in their dialogue, I was able to slip three words in edgewise, "We should go."

It took a few more minutes for summations, but we ultimately took our leave, picked up my newly repaired car, and headed to Jimmy Caruthers's offices. He wasn't in, but the secretary gave us a copy of the tape.

On the way out we bumped into the sweaty little process server on the way in. The flesh around his left eye was swollen and colored in dark, iridescent shades of purple, blue, and plum. The colors around his eye blended fashionably with his jacket— a plaid of polyester, incorporating the same yellow and green with a touch of gold to bring out the flecks in his beady eyes.

Alison stepped around him with a simple "Excuse me."

When I tried to do the same, he said, "Kill any heirs lately, Ms. McCleet?"

"That's a beautiful shiner you have there. Did the toilet seat hit you in the eye while you were gettin' a drink?"

Lightly, he touched his puffy cheekbone with his fingertips. "Not everybody in this business is as happy to see me as you."

I sensed that this hadn't been the first time the process server had been dismissed with a fist in the eye. "How could anybody not like you?"

He was done bantering. He stepped around me and moved toward the receptionist. "Any messages?"

"Yes, Mr. Wiley. You have three," I heard the receptionist say as I closed the outer door.

On the way to Whit and Dottie's house, driving along the less-traveled backroads of the Coast Range, the sky looked particularly blue and the air smelled extra fresh and the road felt less bumpy with Alison beside me. I knew we'd found the right place when I saw the sheep-shaped mailbox. I climbed out of the car to open the gate, drove through, and closed the gate behind my car. The trailer where Whit and Dottie lived was only about a hundred yards away. A cute little place.

As we approached through the wooded area, I realized that— like Amelia's cottage by the sea—the amount of usable living space was deceptive. While Amelia's house had been added on to a number of times, the Parkenses had expanded by pulling up other trailers. Behind the main, double-wide mobile home were two other single-wide sixty-footers. All of the structures were vinyl sided and impeccably clean.

I parked beside Whit's pickup and glanced over at Alison. "Ready?"

"Lead on, sheep master."

I peered out the window. "I don't see the sheep. From Whit's remarks, I expected to be greeted by a bleating horde of woolly creatures."

"Maybe they're sleeping," Alison said. "Livestock isn't my strong suit. What do sheep do during the day?"

"I think they just flock around, mostly."

As soon as we stepped out of the car, the missing sheep appeared. They popped out from behind bushes and bounced around the end of the trailer. There were three little ones, and three older who were making weird nasal noises. They were all nudging at us, obviously looking for a handout.

"Pungent," Alison muttered. "This crew needs a bath."

There was a loud bleating sound, almost like a trumpet blast announcing the arrival of the king. The lesser sheep paused in their nudging and turned. A massive ball of wool appeared behind us. He was the biggest ram I'd ever seen, with curling horns on either side of his nasty black face. He was, obviously, the master of the flock. As he swaggered toward us, the ewes and lambs scattered.

The big ram walked over to my car, took one look, and tossed his head as if to say: Is that the best you can do?

179

"Yeah?" I said to him. "And what do you drive?"

He edged around to the front bumper, sneered at me again, and knocked his head against the chrome. The way my luck had been running, I half expected him to leap onto the hood and butt out the windshield.

He was prevented from inflicting further damage by Whit Parkens, who stepped onto the small square porch attached to the main trailer. Whit bellowed, "Move it, you dumb sheep."

Apparently, these two alpha males—Whit and the ram—had an understanding, because the big sheep rolled his bulging eyes at me, then waddled up to the porch where Whit stood.

From inside I heard Dottie yell, "Whit Parkens, don't you hurt Gibby."

Whit came down the porch steps, grabbed the sheep, Gibby, by the horn, and tried to fling him out of the way, but the ram stood firm and stubborn.

"Fuck you, Gibby," Whit said, stepping around the ram to approach us. "Good to see you, both of you. Nice to talk with humans who aren't sheep obsessed."

"How's the retirement going?" I asked, carefully keeping the smirk from my voice.

"I wish to hell I'd never been named in that fucking will of Graden's. I mean, I appreciate the sentiment, but a man like me needs to work for a living, not have it handed to him. I've got to get a job."

The sheep had closed ranks around us, poking with their sheep noses, looking for food.

Whit regarded them with total disgust. "Stupidest creatures on earth. Come with me, you two. I have a place where the sheep can't get in."

He led the way to a white, no-frills trailer behind the main house. "This is my workshop," he said. "The only place where nobody is allowed unless I invite 'em."

Ignoring the door in the front, he led us to the end, where

he walked up a ramp and pulled up a wide door that swung up, like a garage door. As soon as we were inside, he closed it. But not fast enough.

The big sheep, Gibby, was inside with us. He plopped down on the linoleum floor and looked at Whit as if to say: I dare you to move my big sheep ass.

Whit folded his long, spindly frame in half and got right in the sheep's face. "You're mutton, buster. Remember that. Guys like me eat guys like you."

Rising, he shook his head. "I'm talking to a sheep. I've been out of a job only a couple of weeks, and I'm talking to a damned sheep."

I had to agree. It didn't look good.

His workshop, on the other hand, was the dream hideout of every American male. In addition to the long workbenches with every power tool known to man, he had a wide-screen television mounted on the wall, and a refrigerator in the corner. I spotted the coffeemaker on the counter by the sink. There were several tall stools and one big, fat, overstuffed chair facing the television. The room was neat but not tidy—a comfortable guy kind of messiness that told me Whit was a man who could live with clutter but always kept his equipment oiled and operational.

Several repair and furniture building projects, in varying states of completion, lay scattered on the benches. "I like it," I said.

"Me too."

He sank into the chair, slouching down in a posture that Dottie probably wouldn't tolerate in the main trailer house. I slung one leg over a stool. Alison perched on another stool with her knees together and her fingers laced. This room was so masculine, she probably felt like an intruder.

"So, Adam"—Whit looked up at me—"go ahead and look

around. I've got the necessary equipment to manufacture a golf ball that would detonate on impact, except for the explosives."

"I figured you would," I said, "being a former underwater demolition expert for the Navy SEALS."

"Man, there's a real job," he said. "Every mission was dangerous as hell, but the payoff was better than any special effects you'll see at Universal City."

"Why'd you leave the service?"

"Playing the odds. You can dance with the devil only just so many times. After three tours, I figured I was lucky to still have all my parts attached. I wanted to keep it that way." He shifted his butt in the chair. "Wanted a wife and kids. And a home. Dottie was my high school sweetheart."

"And she waited for you to come back?"

"Hell, no. She was engaged to some other guy when I came back. But as soon as she saw me in my uniform, she dumped that guy faster than I can measure a time fuse."

"You started working for Graden?"

"That's right." He opened a drawer in a table beside his chair and pulled out an ashtray with a fat cigar butt resting on the rim. He picked up the brown chunk of tobacco and eyed it lovingly. Glancing at Alison, he asked, "Do you mind?"

"Not at all," she said, even though I knew she did.

Gibby the ram had noticed that Whit had something in his hand that might be food. He pushed his woolly body upright onto his spindly legs and swaggered over to the chair which he rhythmically butted with his flat forehead.

Ignoring the bumps, Whit measured what was left of the cigar with his thumb and frowned. "Too short. I promised Dottie I wouldn't smoke them down below four inches."

He took out a fresh cigar for himself and offered one to me.

"No, thanks," I said.

"Okay." Striking a kitchen match with his thumbnail, he fired up his own smoke, then lit the butt and plugged it into Gibby's mouth. The sheep seemed content. It looked at me, then at Alison, then swaggered toward the door, puffing on the cigar.

"Damn sheep," Whit muttered.

"Give me the benefit of your expertise," I said. "How did somebody rig the golf ball."

"Well, sir. Talked it over with Tia's son-in-law. He's a SEAL too."

"I know."

"We both think it was detonated by remote. It's the only thing that makes sense."

Therefore, the killer had to be at the golf course. Unfortunately, all the heirs were there.

Whit sucked on his cigar. "I could have done it. The hardest part would be making the golf ball look as if it hadn't been tampered with. Sam Leggett was mostly a fool, but he knew his balls."

That description would fit a lot of people I knew.

"And how about Tiger," Whit said. "I could've done that one too. Scuttling his boat would be nothing for a SEAL. Hop in a Zodiac rubber boat and track the old fart down. Board him, whack him, and open the toilet."

"Do you have a Zodiac?"

Whit shook his head. "But I could find one if I wanted."

"Why wouldn't you think the killer just boarded him before he left harbor."

"How would he make his getaway?"

"Swim," I suggested. "Tiger's boat wasn't all that far from shore. A good swimmer could have made it, easy."

"Too much pain in the ass," Whit said. "If you bring your own craft, you can take it anywhere on the shore and leave Tiger drifting."

"Don't you think Tiger would have noticed another boat approaching."

Whit considered for a moment, then frowned. "Well, you'd

cut the engine, of course. But that might be risky. If Tiger noticed you coming up on him, he would be ready and waiting with a club in his hand. Unless . . ."

"Unless it was somebody he was expecting." That would explain his farewell scene with Patty Carmen. Tiger might have known he was floating into danger.

Whit climbed out of his comfortable chair and shuffled over to the corner fridge. "Want a beer?"

"Sure." That surprised me. According to the arrest record I'd gotten from Nick Gabreski, Whit Parkens had a bunch of DUIs, but they ended ten years ago. I had assumed he didn't drink.

If Whit was, in fact, the killer, he might have been driven to drink again by the pressure of his atrocities. I liked that theory, which also played into the reason each of the murder attempts were sloppier and sloppier.

Whit placed an ice-cold nonalcoholic beer into my hand. Our eyes met, and he grinned. "Fooled you, didn't I?"

I hadn't been aware that he was playing games with me. But he was. I was going to have to stop underestimating these people and start treating them like master criminals. "Okay, Whit," I said, "supposing you committed these crimes, what's your motive? You're not greedy enough to kill for more money."

"Sheep don't look like much of a future to you?" he said, crossing the workshop to Gibby and pulling the stub of cigar from the animal's lips before it burned. "To tell the truth, sheep don't look like a future to me either. But it's better than nothing." Which is what he would have if he was the murderer. Nothing. Except a prison cell.

Chapter
Fourteen

"I don't think you killed anybody," I said to Whit. "Except as an act of war, and that doesn't count."

"Right on target, my boy. Not as dumb as you look." He took a long sip of his nonalcoholic beer. "What makes you so sure?"

"Greed is the only motive that makes sense," I said. "The only reason for killing off the heirs is the Big M. Money."

"You think?" Whit raised his eyebrows, making his lengthy face even longer.

"Yep."

"But what about the murder Graden wanted you to solve?"

"It can't be done." Though I hadn't realized it before, I was pretty clear on this point. Feeling smug and incredibly dull-witted at the same time, I said, "A murder in the past is all but impossible to prove. Whatever evidence may have existed is long gone."

As a former cop, I should have recognized the futility sooner. Every homicide division in every police department in the country adds a stack of unsolved crimes to their mounting backlog every year. Unless they have the perpetrator identified and it's only a case of the killer skipping town, the ratio of eventual solution is just about zilch point shit.

I said, "This isn't about a murder in the past."

The reason Graden Porcelli got me involved wasn't really to catch a killer. He wanted to force a meeting between me and Harrison, causing me to confront my stupidity and Harrison to deal with the mistakes he'd made in his life. Though I couldn't remember ever meeting the salmon king face-to-face, or even gill to gill, I assumed that he was a manipulative son of a bitch. Even after his death he was pulling strings, making his friends and family dance to his tune.

"Adam," Whit said thoughtfully, "are you giving up?"

"Are you?" Alison echoed from her dainty perch on the stool beside Whit's workbench.

"When it comes to figuring out some kind of lunatic murder that may or may not have occurred forty years ago—"

"What murder?" Whit demanded.

"I'm talking about the disappearance of Big Harry Mann."

"He's kind of a legend," Whit said. "I wouldn't even believe he existed if he hadn't signed the loan papers to get the salmon factory going. You think he was murdered?"

"Something happened," I said. "Something dramatic. But it was a long time ago, and I'm not Sherlock Holmes. Truth be told, I wasn't even a very good cop."

And the goddamned salmon king knew that. What a bastard! He'd taken the trouble to follow my checkered career, and he knew I was more prone to screw up than the average flatfoot. "I'm not a sleuth."

"Of course not." Alison cleared her throat. "Adam, you're a sculptor."

"That's the rumor," I said. Lately, I hadn't been doing much in the way of sculpting either. "How am I going to find evidence of a crime that happened forty years ago? Short of a notarized confession or digging up the decomposed corpse in somebody's backyard, it's impossible."

Helpfully, Whit pointed out, "Might be that you're looking for a more recent crime."

"That's right." And that was why I wasn't going to quit. "I'm looking for the person who killed Sam Leggett, who tried to kill Tiger. The person who loosened the bolts and caused Amelia's death. I'm looking for the asshole who took a potshot at me last night." I was on a roll. "And that person is motivated by greed."

That logic eliminated Whit Parkens from my list of suspects. He didn't even want the money he had coming to him. Whit was one of those guys who needed to work. Without a job, he'd be stranded here, surrounded by sheep, bonding with Gibby the ram.

There was a vigorous banging on the door of Whit's workshop. Dottie's reedy voice called out, "Whit Parkens! I know you're in there."

His eyes flicked left and right as if he were looking for somewhere to hide. Gibby the sheep responded to his mistress's voice and bleated loudly.

"Whit? What are you doing to Gibby?"

Disgruntled, Whit responded, "What do you want, Dottie?"

"Tia just called. It seems that Tiger is waking up from his coma. I'd like to pick some flowers and pay him a visit."

"Hot damn!" Whit turned to me. "Looks like we're going to find out how Tiger got dry gulched."

And maybe we'd find the murderer.

While Alison and I drove back to the hospital at a fast scoot, I told her about my reasoning concerning Graden Porcelli, the slimeball salmon king. In the most intelligent voice I could muster, I concluded, "Therefore, I daresay we can eliminate Whit Parkens from the list of potential perpetrators."

"Except for one thing," she brightly pointed out. "Dottie."

I didn't like having my deductions questioned. "What do you mean? What about Dottie?"

"Dottie could be motivated by greed. The more sheep, the better. And Whit will do anything she says."

"Hadn't thought of that," I said.

"There's another thing you haven't thought of," she said.

"Please, Alison. Don't help me too much. My ego can't take it."

"If Graden Porcelli studied your career, he would have noticed the most important thing about you, Adam."

"My rapier wit? My classic profile?"

"Graden Porcelli might have been smart enough to notice that you are, above all, a decent human being. He might have known that his friends and loved ones would be in danger, and he wanted you there to help them."

I liked that explanation a whole lot better than the idea that Graden had manipulated me into this web because he wanted to humiliate me.

Alison continued. "Look what you've done for Harrison."

"Gotten his mother killed in a particularly gruesome manner?"

"No, you big lug. You've made Harrison Porcelli into a hero."

Though it was debatable that putting myself into mortal danger to enhance Harrison's self-esteem had been a purposeful act, the result was as Alison had pointed out. Harrison got to play the role of Mighty Mouse in a deli-copter and save the day.

Fondly, I gazed at the pretty woman beside me and growled, "I like the way you think."

I also liked the way she looked, and the way she felt when her curvaceous body was pressed up against mine. I hoped the heirs would stop killing each other long enough for me to show Alison how much I liked her.

In the hospital parking lot I recognized the Beamer belonging to Tia's daughter, and Jimmy Caruthers's car. Whit and Dottie were behind us. The occasion of Tiger's wakening seemed to be another chance to gather all the heirs, and I hoped it might be the final chapter. Tiger could point to the killer, and everybody would be safe.

We gathered in the hallway outside Tiger's room: Tia and her daughter, Jimmy Caruthers, Whit and Dottie, Alison and me. Ernesto stood in front of the closed door, blocking our way like an implacable El Salvadorean barricade. While he maintained vigilant silence, Tia explained to the rest of us that Tiger had begun to rouse, then Ernesto contacted her. Right now the doctors were inside with the old fart.

The tall, tanned doctor whom I recognized from the golf course stepped into the hall and closed the door behind him, keeping Tiger in seclusion. "I'm sorry, folks. It's not a good idea for all of you to visit at once."

"How's Tiger?" Tia asked.

The doctor blessed us with a benevolent smile. "He's going to be all right. He has regained consciousness."

"Then why can't we see him?" Dottie questioned. "I would think he'd like to have his friends around."

I rolled my eyeballs. Was she talking about Tiger Jorgenson, the crusty old seaman who liked to scare little kids? I seriously doubted that he gave a damn about seeing any of us.

"The excitement," the doctor said, "might be difficult for him to process. Let me explain a few aspects of this sort of severe concussive brain trauma. Frequently, there is loss of memory, especially short-term memory surrounding the events immediately preceding the, um, the concussive, um—"

"Bonk on the noggin?" I supplied the medical terminology.

"Exactly."

"Like amnesia?" Dottie asked in a squeak.

"That is correct," the doctor says. "Also, on occasion, there are personality quirks. Quite often, after such an injury, the patient might exhibit slightly more hostility than normal."

More hostility? Obviously, this doc didn't know Tiger. If he got more hostile, he would have to be subdued with a tranquilizer gun. But that wasn't the medical opinion that bothered me. I was far more concerned about the possibility of short-term memory loss. It wasn't going to help me figure out who whacked him if Tiger couldn't recall.

The doc was making shooing motions with his hands. "I'll have to ask all of you to leave. Maybe tomorrow Mr. Jorgenson can see one or two people at a time."

A clarion voice resonated down the hospital corridor. "Is my sweet Tiger awake? I've come to see him."

It was, of course, Patty Carmen, charging toward us—bosom first—with curly black wig hair flying. She marched up to the doctor. "Move aside, sonny."

Harrison followed behind her, carrying a bower of forty long-stemmed roses.

The doctor frowned at both of them. "I'm sorry, Mrs. Jorgenson, but Tiger isn't able to have any visitors just yet."

"I'll believe that when I hear Tiger tell me to leave. Now, Doctor, please step aside."

Ernesto had already responded to Patty Carmen by twisting the knob and opening the door to Tiger's room. But the doctor stood firm. "No," he said. "I would be negligent in my duties if I allowed you to disturb Mr. Jorgenson at this juncture."

Harrison twitched and blurted out, "Naval lint. Belch wad."

"Doctor," I said, "Mrs. Jorgenson is next of kin. She has a right. And, more important, she has her lawyer with her."

I motioned for Jimmy Caruthers to step forward.

The doctor blanched as white as his lab coat. "I suppose it's all right," he said. "Mrs. Jorgenson, will you take full responsibility?"

"Yes, yes, yes."

From inside the room we heard a low voice, "Patty Carmen? Baby, is that you?"

She plunged into the room. "I'm coming, Tiger."

With absolutely no concern for the tender reunion between Tiger and his ex-wife, the rest of us shuffled in Patty Carmen's wake, surrounding the bed while Patty Carmen planted a big wet kiss on Tiger's lips.

Harrison was standing beside me. "It's not fair, is it? That old fart hasn't ever done anything to deserve a wonderful woman like Patty Carmen."

The old fart looked damn good for somebody who had been unconscious for two days. I was astonished when he grinned at all of us and waved his skinny arm. "Nice to see, folks." He squinted at us one at a time as if to refresh his memory of who was who. "Looks like everybody who's anybody came down." He checked all the faces again. "I'm surprised Amelia ain't here."

"Amelia's dead, honey," Patty Carmen said.

Tiger frowned. "Oh, I'm sorry to hear that. What happened?"

"It was a terrible accident," Jimmy Caruthers said.

"Bullshit," Whit injected.

"Don't upset yourself with it right now, Tiger," Patty Carmen said. "I'll tell you all about it when you're feeling stronger." She pointed to Harrison, who was still holding the huge bouquet of roses. "Look what I brought you," Patty Carmen said.

"Flowers. They're very lovely." Tiger gently took her hand. "But not as pretty as you."

Her eyes narrowed. "What are you up to, Tiger?"

"Nothing." Behind his gruff features and stubble, his eyes looked innocent. "I've always thought you were the most fragrant, lovely flower in the garden."

Patty Carmen reached into the container that held the roses and pulled out a pint bottle of Seagram's. "Look what else I brought you."

"I couldn't," Tiger said. "But thanks for thinking of me."

"You couldn't?" Patty Carmen looked shocked.

"Well, it's really not good for me, and everyone at the hospital has been so kind."

"Oh, my God! What have they done to you?" Patty Carmen burst into tears. "Tiger, you're so . . . nice."

He smiled blandly. "There, there, sweetheart. I'm sorry. I didn't mean to be nice."

Sobbing, Patty flung herself into Alison's arms. "What's wrong with him?"

Alison attempted to explain. "The doctor said there might be some changes in his personality."

"But this?" She wept even harder. "He's just like everybody else."

Casting me a hurry-up-and-help-me look, Alison ushered Patty Carmen into the hallway.

"The doc said he'd be more hostile," Whit commented. "But I guess Tiger was as cranky as he could get, so's he had to go back the other way."

I stepped up beside him. "Tiger, could I ask you a couple of quick questions?"

"Certainly, young man." Completely without guile, he asked, "And who are you?"

"Adam. Adam McCleet."

"Oh, yes. You're the detective."

That remained to be seen. "Tiger, can you—"

"Excuse me, just one minute, Adam. Could you do me a small favor? I would prefer to be called by my given name. Theodore."

"Okay, Theodore. Do you remember anything about when you were attacked?"

His forehead wrinkled. "It was at night. I was on my boat."

He seemed to be concentrating hard, trying to see the picture on the back of his eyelids.

Helpfully, Whit suggested, "I bet you heard an outboard. Saw a boat coming toward you."

"Hush," said Jimmy Caruthers. "That's leading the witness."

"This ain't a courtroom," Whit said.

"Let him come up with his own words."

"I don't know," Tiger said. "There was a fight. I remember that. Seems like somebody hit me on the head, then I got in a couple of punches, then everything went blank."

"Did you recognize the person who attacked you?"

He squinched his face in concentration, then said, "Sorry. It was real dark. I don't know how I got out of there."

"Harrison rescued you in his helicopter," I said.

Tiger beamed at the young man who stood at the end of the bed. "You're a good boy, Little Harry. I always said you were. Smart kid, and tougher than your dad gave you credit for."

"Thanks," Harrison replied humbly.

Hopefully, Tiger looked up at me. "How's my boat? The _Patty Carmen,_ she's okay?"

"Sorry, Tiger. I mean, Theodore. She's scuttled."

"Sunk?"

"Buried in the briny."

There was a flash of the old fire in his eyes. "Goddamn son of a bitch. When I get my shit hooks on the asshole who—"

Just as quickly, it faded.

"Maybe we should leave," I said.

"Not yet," he said. "I'm not remembering too good about what happened a few days ago, but I can see stuff that happened a long time ago as clear as dawn on a cloudless horizon."

"Like what?" I prompted.

"There's something I have to say." He glanced around the bed at the faces surrounding him. "Thank you for coming to see me. I hope you'll forgive me if I ask you all to leave. Everybody except Adam. And Tia, you stay."

The others shuffled out into the hallway, and I closed the door behind them.

"It was more than forty years ago," he said. "Graden, Big Harry, and I had just gotten started, and we were working like beavers patching a dam in a tide pool. Those were nervous times, excitin' times. I never in my whole life felt so alive."

"Tell me about Big Harry," I said.

"Hold your horses, Adam. I'm getting there. It was the beginning of spring. Maybe April. The time of year when a young man's fancy turns to you-know-what."

Tia was clearly fascinated. She sat on the edge of his bed and gently held his hand, careful not to disturb the IV tubing.

"I hadn't met Patty Carmen yet, and I kind of had an eye for Graden's sister, Pam."

"My mother?" Tia sounded surprised, but not shocked.

"That's right, Tia. Your mother. Graden didn't like that at all. He told me to keep away from his sister, but Amelia kept encouraging me, so I thought I had a chance. Then I found out the real reason Amelia wanted to fix me up with Pammy."

"Why was that?" Tia asked.

"Well, Amelia was having herself a fling with Big Harry Mann."

"An affair?"

"You bet." His eyes went hazy. "I remember this like it happened yesterday. I heard them going at in the garden outside her house. I thought it was Graden and Amelia, so I thought I might sneak up on them and play a joke. When I saw them, I ran away quick."

"Is that why Big Harry disappeared?" I asked. "Because Graden found out about the affair?"

"I don't rightly know if he ever did. You see, I talked to Big Harry afterward and told him he'd better learn to keep his dinghy on its davits. And he told me that he wanted to break it off with Amelia because he was in love with Pam. Seriously in love. He wanted to marry your mom. That's why Amelia was so anxious for me to sweep Pammy off her feet. To win her away from Harry." Tiger paused. "But I never really had a chance. She was already pregnant, Tia. With you."

Tia recoiled as if she'd been punched in the chest. "Big Harry Mann is my real father?"

"I wished there was an easy way to tell you, but there isn't."

Tia's rich, full laughter bubbled up in her throat and spilled from her. The sound of it wasn't hysteria, more like relief. "That explains so much."

Her laughing faded but the smile remained. "That's why I never fit in with the rest of the family. Unbelievable! I was a love child, and I didn't even know it."

"Are you all right?" I asked.

"I'm terrific! I'm still a square peg in a round hole, but at least I know why." She leaned forward and kissed Tiger in the middle of his forehead. "Thank you. I wish somebody had told me this a long time ago."

"Your mother never did?" I asked.

"Not a word."

I turned back to Tiger. "So, what happened to Harry?"

Tiger rolled his head from side to side. "Graden went out of town for a week to set up some contracts, and Harry went over to Amelia's house to break the bad news. I never saw him again."

"Do you think Amelia killed him?"

"I'm pretty sure of it. I've kept this a secret all these years to protect Amelia. Now that she's gone, well, I guess there's no one else to hurt."

"What makes you so sure it was Amelia?" Tia asked.

"Have you ever seen her collection of knives?" He shook his head. "That Amelia could be a frightening woman. And she could've gotten rid of his body by pushing him off the cliff and letting the tides do their work."

But there was no evidence. As I had realized that morning, lack of proof was the major problem in definitively solving old murders. Forty years ago. Body washed out to sea. There was nothing but conjecture and the ramblings of Tiger, who was, in his normal state, a raving alcoholic. In his current mood, he was brain damaged.

The other players—Graden, Tia's mother, and Amelia—were dead.

Still, I had to ask, "I don't suppose you've got any proof that Amelia killed Big Harry."

A sly expression slid across his stubble-covered face. "Amelia never threw away anything, but she sometimes made donations to local churches and to the schools. A few years back, she gave the biology teacher at the high school her collection of sea mollusks and a tattered old tray of mounted butterflies that Harrison started and never kept up with. And something else."

"What was that, Tiger?"

"It's still in the high school biology department, if you care to take a look."

"What?"

"A human heart in a jar of formaldehyde."

Chapter
Fifteen

Alison snuggled under the bedcovers in the Zorro room, listening as I recapped Tiger/Theodore's memories.

"In a jar?" Alison made a gagging noise. "She kept his heart in a jar? I thought that sort of thing went out with the Aztecs."

"Too literal for me," I said.

"What do you mean?"

"Your heart will never belong to another."

"But now it does," she said, pushing her auburn hair back on her forehead. "It belongs to the high school biology department. I'm beginning to have second thoughts about protecting the Porcelli heirs. These people are very, very strange."

"Ah-ha!" I said. "But now we're back to greed. My greed."

"Come again?"

"A human heart in formaldehyde is not only creepy, it's also evidence. This could be proof that dear old Amelia bumped off Big Harry. Therefore, I have solved Graden's puzzle. Therefore,

I win my"—I ran some division in my head—"three million dollars."

While Alison headed for the shower, I sat on the bed and dialed long distance to Nick Gabreski's home phone. One of his eight children picked up, groaned when she heard it was for her father, then bellowed like one of Dottie's sheep: Dad! Dad! Dad!

Nick came on. "If you're selling something, let's save ourselves both a lot of time and energy. I've got eight kids. Even if I wanted to buy anything, I can't afford a rubber band. Okay?"

"It's Adam," I explained.

I heard the pitter-patter of little Gabreski feet surrounding Nick while he was on the phone. He snarled, "Get away from me, you sand crabs. Can't you see I'm busy?"

There was a slam and relative silence on Nick's end of the line. I assumed that Nick had stretched the phone cord to its max and locked himself in the bathroom.

"Okay," he said, "about that Harry Mann thing that you wanted me to check. I found three of them in the greater Portland area, which indicates to me that people named Mann are either real dumb or have sick senses of humor when it comes to naming their children. My point, Adam, is that if you want specifics, you're going to have to give me a social security number or a driver's license."

"Forget it," I said. "Big Harry died forty years ago."

"Thanks for sending me on a wild-goose chase," he said. "As you know, I have nothing else to do with my time. It's just one long couch trip after another."

"A little cranky today?"

"It's becoming a permanent state," Nick said. "You had the right idea, Adam. Get out of police work before you're certifiably insane."

Thinking of Whit Parkens, I said, "What would you do if you were retired?"

"I'd take my lovely wife, Ramona, and move her to a secluded tropical island without a forwarding address. With any luck, the kids would never find us."

"Really," I asked. "What'll you do?"

"Probably what my father did," he said. "Loaf around the house. Listen to baseball on the radio and build weird things in the garage."

I wondered if my father would have done that. Nick and I, and Whit for that matter, had just come from a generation of fathers who worked hard until they retired, then quickly died. It wasn't a bad life, really. They didn't have twenty years after working to sit around and experience the joys of having their organs shut down one by one. Which reminded me that I definitely needed to start an exercise program. It also brought up the thought that my work wasn't like a regular job. Did sculptors retire? Was I already retired, puttering and making weird things in the garage?

Nick asked, "So, what's your latest problem?"

"If I happened to have a human heart, preserved in formaldehyde, and gave it to the medical examiner, could he make an accurate DNA test?"

"Definitely. I'm amazed at the stuff they can use for DNA tests. Fingernail clippings. Drops of blood."

"But you would have accurate identification, right?"

"Sure, as long as you had something to match the DNA with."

"Right." What was I thinking? That everybody had their chromosomes on file at the county seat? "I'd need a comparison. The DNA wouldn't do any good unless I had something to match with it."

"Right," Nick said.

"Okay." I had to find another piece of Harry. "I know what I need to do. Thanks, Nick."

I said good-bye just as Alison came out of the shower with a towel draped around her lovely form. I remembered to tell her she was beautiful before adding, "Tomorrow we're doing a detailed search at the home of the late Amelia Porcelli."

"Goody," she said. "But don't you think that's a little crass, asking Harrison if you can pick through his dead mother's things before she's even cold."

"Crass?" The heirs of the salmon king gave new meaning to the word. "Harrison routinely screams out obscene phrases. I don't think the etiquette of the situation, or lack thereof, will bother him."

She nodded. "And tonight? What are we doing tonight?"

I grabbed the towel. "This time I wear the mask."

Several hours later, Alison slept soundly while I lay awake, savoring the pleasure of drawing a Z on her torso with my tongue and thinking with displeasure of what lay ahead.

I didn't know if my motivation to figure out the long-ago murder came from pure acquisitiveness on my part or if the reason I needed to know was more subtle. It felt like a challenge, stirring my blood and making me wakeful.

The moonlight through the window fell on the videotape we'd picked up from Jimmy Caruthers's office. I slipped out of the bed and turned on the television, leaving the sound off. Fortunately, the room came equipped with a VCR and tapes of Guy Williams's greatest flicks. Both of them.

I plugged in the cassette.

When Graden Porcelli appeared, soundlessly staring at me, I stared back. How well did this guy know me? Was he acting purely on instinct when he pulled me into this confusion?

If Graden had known that Amelia murdered Harry, he had ample opportunity to gather evidence and present it. Even if he didn't want to do that to his wife while he was still alive, he could have posthumously arranged the proof.

After Graden finished his putt, I stopped the tape and stared at his fuzzy image on the screen. *Why, Graden?* What did he hope to accomplish by throwing out this accusation?

I ran through the brief tape, making mental notes of the images.

First, there was the golf putt, obviously a reference to the late Sam Leggett. Possibly, the fact that Graden sank his putt had special reference for Sam, but that idea would be buried with Graden's late nephew.

Second, there was the ship in the bottle, which I had assumed was Graden's yacht, the *Jonah*. There was a venue I hadn't even begun to explore. Of course, Graden couldn't know that he was going to die on board, but it might be worth checking out.

Third, Graden played with a flower that looked like a tulip and placed it in a vase on his desk which had the usual desk stuff, like a pen set, a letter opener, a green banker's lamp, and a blotter.

Fourth, he wandered to the bookshelf.

Fifth, he slipped into a navy-blue sport jacket with a crest and a military decoration which I recognized as the ribbon for a Purple Heart because I had one of those myself.

Operating on the theory that Graden was taking subtle digs at each of the heirs, I pondered the references. Sam was the golf scenario. The Purple Heart was probably meant as a dig at Harrison and his avoidance of military service.

I backed up to take a close look at the ship in a bottle. Tiger had been the fisherman. A ship should be a reference to him, but not a yacht. Tiger's boat was a commercial trawler, practical and not at all sleek.

There were two interesting things about the model ship: The miniature American flag at the fantail hung upside down, the international signal for distress. On the videotape, the image wasn't clear enough to make out any of the writing on the hull or the plaque beneath the ship that identified it. But there was an obvious reference onboard. Standing at the helm, just in front of the flag, was a tiny plastic figure of a tiger.

Okay, so it could be a warning for Tiger. This was Graden's extremely subtle way of telling his estranged buddy that he was in danger.

I stared at the desk until my eyeballs went blurry. Nothing looked unusual. These were expensive but nondescript office accessories. On the tape, while he was talking, Graden touched the letter opener and the sharp end was pointed at the yacht in a bottle, but it looked like he was just fiddling around.

I was beginning to despise the salmon king. If he had really wanted me to protect these idiots and solve a murder, why hadn't he written it out for me? He could have given me a sealed envelope, to be delivered posthumously.

I turned up the sound on the tape to a whisper so I wouldn't wake Alison. While Graden fiddled around at the desk, he talked about how his assets would be sold off. And he moved the letter opener to point at the ship which was flying the distress signal.

Was there something dangerous about selling off his assets? That didn't seem likely.

The important thing that happened at the desk was Graden playing with the tulip. The only flower reference that came to mind was Tiger's little story about Amelia and Big Harry making out in the garden beside her cottage. The garden was remarkable. So, I guessed, the flower was some kind of reference to Amelia.

That took care of Amelia, Sam, Tiger, and Harrison.

Only Whit and Tia were left.

When Graden stood by the bookshelf, I got the Whit Parkens reference immediately. There were two outsized books with titles written in letters large enough that I could read: *Animal Farm* stood beside *The Old Man and the Sea*. Neither one seemed like a pattern for life, but I thought Graden was pointing out to Whit that he had a choice.

That left the jacket. The only heir not referenced was Tia.

The crest on the jacket—which looked like a coat of arms with stripes of blue, white, and blue—had to mean something. But what?

I turned off the tape and thought about Tia. Of all the heirs, she had led the most interesting and active life. Her reaction to the news that her real father was Harry Mann was as unusual as she was. There had been an instant of shock, then robust laughter. Most people would have run screaming to the nearest psychiatrist if they suddenly found out that their parentage was not as they had believed all their lives. But she seemed delighted. What did that mean? A dead, absent father was preferable to a living one who disapproved of her life?

I needed to find out more about Tia and her adventurous past.

A snuffling noise from the bed drew my attention back to Alison. I wasn't sure why she was here with me in Newport, but I was glad that she had come to stand by my side in my hour of stupidity. Such loyalty was the test of a good woman. I slipped under the covers beside her and cradled her warm body next to mine.

At nine o'clock in the morning, Alison and I emerged from the Zorro room. We were dressed for searching through Amelia's junk collection. Alison made her pink T-shirt and jeans look as chic as designer couture. I wore my cotton shirt untucked so I could hide my gun in the waistband of my jeans. This wasn't the best way to carry a handgun. The jeans were too tight and I could feel the shape of the gun against the small of my back. The next time I told Alison to bring my firearm, I would also have to specify that I wanted the ankle holster that went with it.

Bud, the proprietor of the Sunny Beach Celebrity Hotel, greeted me with a beaming smile. "For breakfast this morning," he announced, "we are featuring the Gomer Omelette from a recipe sent to me by Jim Nabors himself."

"I'll take two," I said. "With lots of bacon on the side."

Alison made a disapproving noise, but I didn't change my order. She, of course, ordered a bran muffin and cantaloupe.

"All this health," I asked her as we took our seats in the cafe, "where's it supposed to get you?"

"Into my nineties with a beautiful complexion and strong bones," she replied.

Tia, who was eating with her daughter and son-in-law, came over to our table. Her mood was lighter than air. "Okay, Adam," she said, pulling over a chair. "What do you know about Big Harry Mann, my real father?"

"Not much," I admitted. "I had a friend in the PPD check out his background, but he said there wasn't anything he could do without a social security number."

She lowered her voice. "Do you think that's really his heart on display in the Newport High School biology lab?"

"I don't know."

"I could check it out," she said excitedly. "I could go over there with Ernesto this morning. He teaches at the high school."

"Ernesto?"

"He teaches Spanish. Actually, he's quite a brilliant man and his family are all intellectuals. When they fled El Salvador, the only work they could find was up here as fruit pickers."

"I don't think we should leave Tiger unguarded just yet. His memory might come clear, and that's still a threat to the murderer."

"I've got it covered," Tia said. "My son-in-law, Josh, said he would relieve Ernesto."

Alison, the mistress of understatement, said, "You seem pleased by this turn of events, Tia."

"You wouldn't believe what this has done for my relationship with my daughter. All of a sudden she's willing to understand me and make allowances. We have a bond. As I told Adam, my daughter was also a love child without a real father."

"Okay," I said. "You and Ernesto get the heart and meet us at Amelia's house. I'm hoping I can get Harrison to agree to a search of her stuff."

"I hope you haven't told Harrison that we suspect his deceased mother of being a cold-blooded murderess," Tia said. "The poor guy has been through hell. He and his mother weren't very close, and he's feeling guilty for all the things he didn't do for her while she was alive."

I nodded. My mom was still thriving, free from raising children, and traveling as much as possible. I made a mental note to track her down and send her roses. Or tulips?

"Tia, is there any kind of family connection you can think of that involves tulips?"

She bit her lower lip while thinking, then shook her head. "Nothing comes to mind."

I wanted to ask her about the crest on Graden Porcelli's jacket, but thought better of it. If the crest was meant to be a clue to Tia, she certainly wouldn't be forthcoming about it.

I heard Harrison coming before I saw him. In his familiar outburst, he yelled, "Bird feeder. Suck me."

He also joined us. His mood was morose enough that I was glad Alison and I had almost finished our breakfast.

Alison touched his arm. "How are you feeling, Harrison?"

"Like shit," he said succinctly. "I wanted to ask you something, Adam."

"Shoot."

"I want something special for my mother's grave. We have a family plot in the local cemetery, and I'd like to commission you to do a sculpture for her, for all the Porcellis, in fact."

I'd never done a gravestone before, but it seemed thoroughly appropriate. "What are you thinking of?"

"I'm not an artist. But you are, aren't you?"

His question was perceptive and acute. With all this crime solving and running around, I had lost track of my own life. "Yeh," I said, "I'm an artist."

"Will you do it?" he asked. "Cost is no object."

I had the feeling that I was being subtly manipulated for my own good, shoved back on track as a professional sculptor. There was something in Harrison's manner that reminded me of Graden. "You're more like your father than you realize, Harrison."

"Will you?"

I realized that Alison was holding her breath, watching me with a shimmer of hope. "I'll do it."

Both she and Harrison sighed, and their combined breath felt like a cool, refreshing breeze. I hadn't known that anybody gave a shit about my flagging career—nobody except the process servers in plaid jackets. It was nice to have encouragement.

I asked Harrison about searching at his mother's house, and he handed over the key. "I'm going to sell her stuff. I don't imagine the auction will be as big as Jackie O's, but there's some decent junk in there." He turned to Alison. "If you find anything of real value, will you make a list for me?"

"Certainly."

"One more thing," I said. "I've been wondering about your father's yacht, *Jonah*, there might be a clue on board about the murderer. Could you arrange with Jimmy to meet me there. Let's say around five o'clock."

Harrison nodded. "Good idea. I want to say good-bye to the *Jonah* before she's sold. Actually, I was thinking of buying her myself."

"I didn't know you were a sailor."

"I'm not," he said. "I thought I'd buy the boat and give it to Tiger and Patty Carmen. They could take a cruise for their second honeymoon."

"They're divorced," I pointed out.

"Viper hygiene," Harrison blurted out. "Clean 'em up, Mabel."

Calmly, he continued. "The new Tiger, or should I say Theodore, has been proposing marriage to Patty Carmen with every other breath. Apparently, that bump on the head knocked some sense into him."

"You must be feeling proud of yourself," Alison said. "Tiger would have died if it weren't for you."

"That's true." He was still looking bummed about his mother's death, but there was a difference in Harrison Porcelli. Definitely stronger and more confident, he was taking charge. "Good luck on your search."

I knew we'd need it. From what I understood, Amelia's house was stuffed, top to bottom. And I wasn't eagerly anticipating the thrill of digging through an old lady's antimacassar collection.

Fortunately, I was not alone.

When we arrived at the house, Alison scoped out the front parlor with a single glance, and proceeded through the rest of the floor plan quickly. She reported: "On the first floor there are two bedrooms with dressers, armoires, and closets, packed to the ceiling. There's a kitchen, pantry, utility room, dining room, bathroom, the big sun porch, and a den with another closet."

I winced. "Big."

"It would help a lot if you could give me a better idea of what we're looking for. Did Amelia mention a diary? Maybe photo albums? Or old letters?"

"I was thinking more of hair, fingernail clippings, and blood samples," I admitted. "Hey, don't some women save teeth? My mom had a little glass jar full of our baby teeth."

Dryly, Alison said, "We're looking for body parts?"

"I'd like to get a DNA match on that human heart. Of course, it would have to be from Big Harry."

She wasn't completely disparaging. "I've never heard of a woman collecting her lover's teeth. But sometimes a lady might take a lock of her true love's hair and keep it pressed in a favorite book of love poems, or a diary."

"Okay," I said. "Cool."

Alison nodded once. "I'll start going through Amelia's jewelry and personal stuff in the bedrooms, working my way to the front of the house. You start in the kitchen pantry and work toward me."

"Right."

"And, Adam," she added, "keep looking for hidden cubby-holes where she might have stashed her precious things. I have a feeling that this house is honeycombed with secret stashes."

She charged off toward the farther bedroom, and I stood in the hallway, scratching my head and feeling nearly as stupid as Brutus.

It wasn't that I couldn't imagine places where a woman might hide her special things. I didn't want to pry. Many of the female mysteries seemed dangerous. Even with a woman who was as level-headed and confident as Alison, there were secrets that I shouldn't know. I remembered once when I asked her about the necessity of a cream that she used on her elbows, and she responded with a snarling lecture about the unfairness of women having to be soft all over. It concluded with something about how nobody demanded that female elephants have touchable knees, and I decided that there were some things that I simply didn't need to know.

But the pantry seemed safe enough. I spent some time trying to discern some semblance of order among the many canned goods, finally deciding there was none. In one corner I discovered eight cans of Spam. There were dozens of boxes of candles in all colors and shapes. I fumbled around until I spilled an opened box of ziti. I wasn't going to find anything pertaining to Big Harry Mann in the kitchen, bathroom, or pantry.

Though I could have proceeded down the hall and helped Alison, I meandered into the sun room overlooking the ocean.

Yesterday, disaster struck before I had a chance to appreciate the views from the windows that surrounded this room on three sides. To the north, jagged cliffs of volcanic rock stretched as far as the eye could see, journey's end for waves formed by Pacific storms, where silver swells burst into colossal fountains of white mist and foam. To the south, more cliffs capped with lush green blankets of grass and wild rhododendrons were dotted with Monterey pine, gnarled and twisted by the relentless west wind. In the far distance, an ivory lighthouse stood alone at the edge of a high bluff, a solitary audience to the air show of the seabirds that soared and dipped over the tide pools at its feet. To the west, under endless blue skies, the largest ocean on the planet stretched beyond infinity to kiss the shores of a thousand islands. I imagined myself at the helm of a fine long schooner, disappearing over the horizon, bound for adventure.

My sailing daydream reminded me of Graden Porcelli's yacht in a bottle, and my imagination washed back onto the beach in a breaking wave of reality. The oblique subtlety of his cryptic clues had already cost the lives of his nephew and his wife and, unless I could crack the code soon, others would die. He'd made a big point of having the model boat visible during his tape. There had to be something, maybe a log or a diary, on the boat.

And what about the flower? The tulip?

I went through the house, yelling down the hallway to Alison, "I'm going to check out the garden."

After the cloistered atmosphere of Amelia's house, it felt good to be outdoors with the four lawn jockeys for companions. Her garden, like her home and her life, seemed to be without order, but as I studied the landscaping, I could tell that Amelia had planted so that something would always be blooming. Spring flowers were rampant. Showy peonies, rows of purple iris, and perky jonquils decorated the front of the house.

Moving toward the rear, I passed budding rosebushes. Just as I was trying to remember if tulips were spring flowers, I came upon the patch. The color of these flowers—an orangish-red—exactly matched the flower that Graden had played with in the videotape. There were orange and yellow nasturtiums around the border, but the center of this seven-foot-by-three-foot plot was all tulips.

The corners were perfectly square and the dimensions were suggestive. It looked like a goddamned grave. A burial mound.

I knelt down and touched the moist soil. It made perfect sense for Amelia to bury Big Harry in the garden where they had made love, marking his gravesite with tulips. Two lips.

But did it make equal sense for me to excavate? If I found a body, probably only a skeleton after all these years, I would be a genius. If not, I was a major asshole for destroying the garden.

I went in search of a shovel, figuring that I'd been an asshole before and it wasn't so bad. As I rounded the house, I caught a glimpse of movement on the far side of the garage. I froze, staring in that direction. I hadn't imagined it. My brain replayed a vision of a person dashing behind the garage to hide.

I pulled my gun and moved quickly in that direction. When I was attacked in the hospital parking lot, the bullet had come damn close, excellent marksmanship. If this was the same person, I intended to keep a respectful distance.

As I got to the garage, Alison opened the front door and yelled, "Adam! Come here! Please hurry!"

Chapter
Sixteen

The urgency in Alison's voice tightened my sphincter. It wouldn't be the first time that my attempts to solve crime and restore justice to the universe had placed her in jeopardy. I sprinted toward the porch, my gun at the ready.

When I hit the front door, I was running so hard that I would have bowled Alison over if she hadn't taken the simple expedience of stepping aside, allowing me to charge headlong into Amelia's front room and onto a throw rug that skidded out from under my feet when I hit the brakes. I performed a double twisting reverse somersault and landed with a brain-jarring thud on my back with my gun aimed straight at the ceiling.

Alison stood over me with her hands on her hips. "What are you doing?"

"Protecting you."

"That makes me feel so very safe and secure. Can I show you what I found?"

"Of course, dear. If I'm not paralyzed from the waist down, I would be delighted to see what treasures you've uncovered."

She extended her hand and helped me to my feet. I heard a lot of middle-aged grunting and groaning. It might have been me. My spine crinkled and popped as I stood, but I hobbled after her when she darted to the rear bedroom, graceful and fleet as a gazelle.

Alison stood beside a watercolor seascape. Very nicely done, but I really wasn't in the mood for an art show. "Is this why you called me?"

"I found it in the back of the closet. Take a look at the signature, Adam. It's a Wyeth. Andrew Wyeth. Can you believe it?"

"Nice."

"It's rather a good piece too. This is worth a ton of money. What do you think, Adam?"

Feebly, I offered, "I thought I saw somebody outside."

"Who?"

"Couldn't tell. But there was definitely someone there." If any harm came to Alison, I wouldn't be able to live with myself. "I'd better stick with you."

"Don't be silly. We'll get twice as much done if we split up. Besides," she said with perfect logic, "nobody would be after me because I'm not an heir."

"I don't want to leave you in here, unprotected."

"And what are you planning to do next."

"I'm going to dig a large hole in the backyard." I held out my pistol. "Take my gun."

Alison directed me to a straight-back chair with a lacy pillow on the seat and helped me sit. She placed both hands on my shoulders and looked into my eyes. "This is crazy, Adam. Who do you think is going to kill me?"

That was the question of the hour, the one I had been avoiding. The only heirs left besides Tiger, who was still in the hospital, were Tia, Whit, and Harrison. Personally, I liked all of them.

With slight paraphrasing I quoted from Graden's tape: "Take a look around Jimmy's office. The six heirs are here, plus their families, friends, and associates." I shrugged, causing a knife of pain in my lower back. "One of them is a murderer."

"Tia or her daughter? Whit or Dottie? Harrison? Maybe, it's Jimmy himself. Or one of those other people we haven't even talked to yet."

That would have been nice, I thought. The murderer might be an anonymous outsider whom I hadn't met and talked to and become friendly with. But I knew it wasn't true. "Somebody's a killer," I said. "Two people are dead. Two and a half, if you count the attack on Tiger. Plus, in case you've forgotten, somebody took a shot at us."

"It's serious," she agreed. "But I just can't imagine Tia blowing up her own brother. Or Harrison causing his mother's death. And Whit doesn't even want the money."

"I know there's a trick in Graden's tape, but I haven't figured it out yet. All I can think is that one of these nice people isn't so very nice after all."

Hopefully, Alison said, "Maybe Graden was talking about Amelia."

That was possible, but Amelia wouldn't have loosened the bolts and run out on her deck. Margot's idiot logic held true on that point. Whoever went out to see the whales wasn't the murderer. Glumly, I said, "Maybe they're all murderers. Graden made a point of dropping hints in his tape about each of their identities."

"In any case," Alison said, "I don't feel in the least bit threatened. You keep the gun, and I'll make sure I lock all the doors behind me."

It still didn't sound safe to me, but further discussion was halted by the arrival of Tia and Ernesto. Since I'd cleverly left the front door hanging wide open after my spectacular entrance, they walked right in, hollering, "Yoo-hoo, anybody here?"

Alison and I emerged from the bedroom to see Tia holding a gallon-sized mason jar with a yellow-beige organ floating in an amber-colored liquid. It looked like something from a B-grade horror movie.

"The good news," Tia said, "is that we've got it. See, there's a plaque on the side, saying that this thing was donated by Mrs. Graden Porcelli." She set it down on an end table. "The bad news is that the heart isn't human. It's a pig's heart. The biology teacher was delighted to get rid of the thing. He'd kept it around for years because he didn't want to offend Amelia."

That was very bad news, I thought. My evidence of murder was a pig's heart. "But Amelia thought it was a human heart."

"Oh, yes," Tia said. "When she presented her crap collection to the high school biology department, she clearly stated that this human heart came from a Pygmy tribe in Africa, where they had, oddly enough, discovered formaldehyde."

Like everything else about Amelia, it made virtually no sense. I had no idea how her brain worked. She seemed to jump from one bizarre fantasy to another without rational connection. And why had she planted herself in my room, like the ghost of Norman Bates's mother, to tell me that she was never unfaithful to Graden. "Tiger," I said.

Tia nodded. "Apparently, Tiger also thought it was real."

"Or he was purposely lying to cast suspicion on Amelia. Maybe it was Tiger who killed Harry Mann."

"Maybe nobody killed Harry Mann," Tia said excitedly. "Maybe he's still alive."

"Don't get your hopes up," I warned her. "Okay, here's what we're going to do. Tia, you stay in the house with Alison and help her search through Amelia's stuff. Ernesto? How do you feel about a treasure hunt?"

The massive Salvadorean raised his eyebrows and said, "An exercise in futility."

"Will you help?"

"Absolutely, I find the interplay of relationships, greed, and love to be fascinating."

Tia explained. "Ernesto is thinking about writing a book based on the Porcellis. Kind of like *Macbeth* for the nineties."

"If I remember correctly, everybody was dead at the end of that one."

"Not everyone," Ernesto said. He cracked a grin that consumed his whole face. "Amelia Porcelli would make a crackerjack Lady Macbeth."

"That she would."

Ernesto and I left the women behind and went to the garage to look for digging implements. Amelia, of course, had seven shovels—one for each of the dwarves in case they dropped by for tea. Armed with spades, Ernesto and I returned to the perfectly square plot of tulips.

After I had explained my theory, he grunted approval and we started digging. The pain in my back had settled to a dull ache. Though I hoped the physical activity of digging would help loosen the clenched muscles, I was lying to myself.

At first, we were careful not to damage the flowers, thinking that we could replace them. But it was too much hassle. Tulips and pansies went flying along with mounds of dirt. Since we were on a rocky cliff, I figured the top layer of dirt wouldn't be too deep. Maybe three feet.

I paused, panting, and looked at the stronger man. "Water?" I croaked.

"Sí," he said.

We threw down our spades and went into the house. From the upper floors, we could hear Alison and Tia discovering goodies with lighthearted, girlish giggles. Ernesto smiled at the sound of Tia's laughter, and I wondered if he might be in love with the Porcelli heiress.

While we slugged back copious amounts of liquid, I asked, "You and Tia met in El Salvador?"

"*Sí.*"

"Tell me about it."

"The revolution was a terrible time. Blood ran in the streets. Everyone was an enemy. Men, fired by the heat of battle, killed without reason. In the small village where my family had taken refuge, we thought we might be overlooked."

His expression showed that he was reexperiencing the pain. "All that we wanted was to live in peace. My father was killed early in the fighting. I was the man of the family. I was twelve."

Stories like his always reminded me of what an easy life we had in America. Never attacked. Never even threatened. Each time some crazoid American militia group committed an act of terrorism, I was appalled. Didn't they understand? There are more than a few countries where they would be executed without a trial for their radical ideology.

Ernesto continued. "Tia came to live with us. I thought she was the most remarkable woman on earth. Strong and brave. She worked with the Sisters of Poverty, trying to teach at the school and maintain sanity amid madness."

His words held passion, yet he spoke almost without expression. "My family was sympathetic with Duarte, and we had given food and shelter to rebel guerrillas many times. It was evening, dinnertime. We could hear fighting in the nearby hills. We were seated around the dinner table, except for Tia, who was standing at the kitchen stove. She and my mother were talking about how we would hide in the jungle if the fighting came too close. Suddenly the door burst open. It was a uniformed soldier with a machine gun."

From the far upstairs of the house, I heard Alison and Tia exclaiming surprise over some bizarre treasure of Amelia's.

"He ordered us to stand and raise our hands," Ernesto said. "Fearful for our lives, we did as he said. The soldier pressed the barrel of his gun against the side of my mother's head. Tia shot and killed him. Then we fled."

It took a moment for his words to sink into my brain. Ernesto had just given me an eyewitness account of a murder. Tia was a murderer. I could prove it. For evidence, I had an eyewitness.

While one might argue that it was self-defense, I had no doubt that in El Salvador the killing of a soldier of the republic would be considered murder. Maybe this wasn't the murder that Graden Porcelli had been talking about, but it had happened. I could inherit millions . . . if I were willing to betray Tia's secret.

"Ernesto, what color is El Salvador's flag?"

"It has three broad bands of blue, white, and blue."

"Powder blue?"

"Yes." Ernesto looked puzzled. "Why do you ask?"

"Just curious." These were the colors of the crest on Graden Porcelli's sport jacket. I looked into Ernesto's dark eyes, hoping he couldn't read my mind because—if he could—he might beat me to death with his spade. "You love Tia, don't you?"

"With all my heart."

"Are you married?"

"How could I be?" The hopeless smile of a true romantic touched the corners of his full lips. "I will never love another as I love her."

"Have you told her?"

"No. But someday I will." He cleared his throat. "Perhaps after she inherits, she will need a man like me to help disperse her money for the greatest good."

I slapped his huge shoulder. There was no way I could screw up their lives—not even for three million dollars. "Let's dig."

By midafternoon, Ernesto and I had peeled off our shirts and left our handguns within reach, but not pressed against our bare skin. I could feel a major sunburn developing on my shoulders, my back was killing me, and my conscience was going through all kinds of acrobatics. Maybe I could kind of tell about how Tia had performed an assassination in El Salvador. But I knew that still didn't solve the puzzle that Graden had posed. Tia wasn't the person who murdered Sam or Amelia. Or had she? Had she rationalized that their deaths would provide her with more money to do greater good?

Our hole in the tulip bed was about four feet deep. We were hitting bedrock in some places, and I was beginning to think that my theory was incorrect.

At three o'clock, Alison and Tia paraded out of the house, wearing incredibly ornate, old-fashioned hats, piled high with fake flowers and feathers.

Beautifully, Alison beamed at me. She seemed to be having as much fun as a little girl playing dress-up. "Adam, you wouldn't believe all the fabulous vintage clothes! There's a blue silk dress that I have to get Harrison to sell me."

I climbed out of the pit to stand beside her. "I don't suppose you found anything resembling a clue?"

"Nothing," she said, "but we're not half through."

Tia had knelt in the dirt beside the hole. She and Ernesto were gazing at each other with curiosity, as if they'd never really seen each other before. He whispered something in Spanish, and she touched the brim of her fancy hat and chuckled happily.

"Aren't they cute?" Alison murmured to me.

Handsome would have been a better description. Neither Tia nor Ernesto were children. They were mature adults, possibly discovering something that had been growing for a long time without nurturing.

"Anyway," Alison said, "we came out to remind you that we're supposed to meet Harrison and Jimmy at the *Jonah* in about an hour. I'm afraid you boys will have to quit playing in the sandpile."

It was then that I spotted the guy with the gun hiding in the shrubbery that bordered the garden. He was taking aim.

"Get down," I yelled, shoving Alison to the ground behind the low mound of displaced dirt.

Ernesto yanked Tia into the pit beside him.

There was a gunshot.

"Fuck you!" I screamed.

I grabbed my gun and fired back. Unless I practice, I'm not the world's finest marksman. I had a better chance of accidentally drilling a passing pelican than hitting a guy who was a good thirty yards away.

But the shooter didn't know that. He began to run.

Ignoring the pain in my back, I bolted after him. This time, the son of a bitch wouldn't get away. I wanted an end to this shit, and I wanted it now.

He ran toward the rear of the house. I knew he'd hit a dead end at the cliff, so I cut a diagonal toward the front door. Charging through a rose garden in my path, thorns stabbed and tore at my bare skin.

The guy had a lead on me, and he was running like a world-class sprinter. Though my course was calculated to intercept his, it didn't feel like I was closing the distance. I wasn't going to catch up. If he hit the road, he could run unobstructed and, eventually, would outdistance me.

At that moment, I regretted every day I hadn't worked out to stay in shape. I despised every ounce of fat that I'd put into and onto my body.

I was panting like an old dog when Patty Carmen's clam wagon pulled into the driveway. I wanted to yell to her to get out of the way, but I didn't have the breath.

As the shooter ran onto the drive, the clam wagon swerved. He dodged in the wrong direction and bounced off the front of the van. His gun went flying as he rolled across the driveway and came to rest in the grass, groaning and holding one knee.

I pounced on him. With his arms pinned under my knees, I sat on his chest and pressed the muzzle of my gun hard against his forehead. "Who are you?"

"My knee. My fuckin' knee's busted."

"That's the least of your worries, fuck-O," I said, gasping for air.

His nasty little ratlike face was completely unfamiliar. If I'd ever seen him before, I didn't recognize him. He flailed madly underneath me.

I reached back and clubbed his injured knee with my gun.

He screamed and thrashed more violently until I pushed my gun barrel against his left eyeball and commanded, "Lie still."

He stopped squirming. "But my knee! It hurts!"

If I'd thought about my next course of action, I might have been more clever. But my brain was stuck in attack mode. The frustration that had been building inside me exploded in a red, homicidal rage. I wanted to kill the son of a bitch.

I whacked the butt of my gun against his forehead. The skin split and blood began to pour from the gash. "Does that hurt?"

"Stop it," he wailed.

"Who are you?" I demanded.

"Pete Foreman. Shit, get off me."

"Not likely. Why are you shooting at us?"

He screamed again. "Somebody help me!"

"Help yourself. Just answer my questions. Did someone hire you?"

He went still, real still. It must have cost a great effort. He trembled from the pain. Blood ran into his eyes, but he looked back at me mean and hard. "I don't remember."

This guy was a pro. He wasn't going to tell me a damn thing. Even if I broke his nose, both his arms and legs, he wouldn't say a word. He knew that as long as he kept his mouth shut, the worst he could get would be an aggravated assault charge. A good lawyer would get him off with probation and public service.

Goddamn, he pissed me off. I laid the barrel of my gun along the line of his jaw with the muzzle touching his earlobe and pulled the trigger.

He screamed in agony as blood mingled with the blue smoke that clung to the powder burned place where his earlobe had been.

"Ouch," I said. "I'll bet that hurts, don't it?"

"You're crazy," he bellowed. "You're gonna kill me."

"Maybe. But first I'm going to shoot you in a whole bunch of places that'll just hurt and bleed a lot." I cocked my gun and pressed the barrel against his other earlobe. "Unless you tell me who hired you."

"Nobody. I was hunting." Furious, he had the balls to confront me. "This is assault. You shoot me again and I'll sue your ass."

"You and my sister." I shot his other earlobe.

When his screaming subsided, I said, "Man, Pete. You should see how much blood is gushing out of your head. You need a doctor pretty bad. Who hired you?"

"You fucker," he roared. Tears of rage ran from his eyes and mixed with the blood. "I'll kill you."

"I'm afraid that option is not available to you at this time." I cocked the gun again and aimed it at the palm of his hand. "Who hired you?"

Patty Carmen grabbed my shoulder. In a calm voice she said, "Adam, stop. He's not going to say anything."

"Do you know this prick?"

"Never saw him before in my life."

"Where are you from, Pete?"

"Chicago." He tried to pull his arms free, but I kept them tightly pinned under my knees. "I'm on vacation."

"Adam," Patty Carmen said, more adamant. "Don't kill him."

She was right. I looked up at her. "I want to tie this asshole up. Do you have anything in your van?"

"Sure do."

As Patty Carmen rummaged through the back of the clam wagon, Alison, Tia, and Ernesto arrived.

"Who is he?" Tia asked.

"He says his name's Pete Foreman, but that's probably a lie." I looked up. "Does he look familiar?"

Tia and Ernesto both shook their heads.

I looked back at the gunman. "I think he'll loosen up a little when he starts to hallucinate from loss of blood."

When Patty Carmen emerged from her van with a large roll of silver duct tape, Ernesto helped me bind Pete's wrists to his ankles, behind his back.

"That'll hold him," I said, wiping the blood from my hands onto the gunman's shirt.

When I stood, the three women were looking at me as if I'd just sodomized Big Bird. "He tried to kill us," I said. "Don't waste any energy feeling sorry for him."

They nodded in agreement.

I turned to Patty Carmen. "What are you doing here?"

"Uh, Tiger has something that might be proof. He wanted all of you to come to the hospital."

I asked her what it was, and when she told me, I had what could only be called an epiphany. The whole blurry picture came into sharp focus. I knew who was killing the heirs.

I inhaled a deep breath. There was still a throb in my lower back, but in the back of my brain the tumblers had fallen into place with a final click. I knew the answer. I'd figured it out.

"This is important, Patty Carmen, can you bring that piece of evidence to the *Jonah?* In about half an hour?"

"Sure thing, sweetie. I guess it means something to you, eh?"

"It means everything."

As Ernesto and I lugged Pete to where my car was parked, I asked Patty Carmen, "How's Tiger doing?"

"Health-wise, he's fine. Personality-wise, he's a wimp. Theodore. He wants to be called Theodore."

"And he wants to marry you," I said, remembering what Harrison had said that morning.

"Fat chance," she said. "I like some fire in my men. Maybe not as much fire as you've got, Adam, but a spark."

I groaned at the pain of a thousand knife blades stabbing into my lower back as Ernesto and I hefted the hog-tied shooter into the trunk of my car.

"Adam," Alison said, "are you all right?"

"I'm fine, hon." I wiped a smudge of dirt from her cheek and kissed it. "How 'bout you?"

"We found him," she said, excitement rising in her voice. "When Ernesto pulled Tia into the hole you'd been digging, they scraped away the last bit of dirt. There was a skull. Facedown."

Harry Mann. The legend was true. "Show me."

At the pit, Ernesto and Tia jumped in and began digging with their hands, like archaeologists, careful not to destroy the bones that had been interred for more than forty years. The clothing he had been wearing when he was buried clung to the dull brown bones in muddy tatters.

After only a few minutes of clawing at the black soil, Tia held up a scrap of leather. "It's his wallet. Driver's license. Identification. Harry Mann." Her voice caught in a gasp. "My father."

Alison took my arm. "Now you've got your evidence."

What I had was a corpse, a body to go along with all the rumors. But I had no proof of who had murdered him. It might have been Amelia. Might have been Tiger. Might have been Graden himself. Tiger had the real proof, and I was eager to get a look at it.

With some urging, I got everybody on the road to the marina where the _Jonah_ was moored. Pete Foreman, tied hand and foot, whimpered annoyingly in the trunk of my car. If Alison hadn't been present, I might have succumbed to the urge to pull over and finish him off. She did, however, have a civilizing effect on me.

The _Jonah_ was easy to find in the Yaquina yacht basin. The 1930s vintage commuter vessel was a hundred feet long with a pristine white hull. Everything from the gunwales up was a bright, varnished teak. All of the hardware was either bronze or brightly polished brass. Harrison and Jimmy Caruthers stood side by side at the rail, waving to us as we made our way up the gangplank to board her.

In comparison to the Bristol condition of the *Jonah,* we were a motley crew. Pete, bloody and battered, limped ahead of me with my gun at the base of his skull. Ernesto, Tia, and I were filthy, hot, and sweaty from digging. Alison had cobwebs in her hair from her search through Amelia's belongings. I felt an explanation was required. To Harrison and Jimmy, I said, "We found Harry Mann. He was buried under the tulips in Amelia's garden."

Harrison blurted out, "Cock-a-doodle-doo, fuck me."

Not too gently, I shoved Pete Foreman onto the deck. "We also found this. It was shooting at us."

"Hunting," Pete said loudly. "I was hunting and this man assaulted me."

"That's right," I said, "he's an innocent hunter, armed with a forty-five automatic in case the wildlife gets rough."

"Congratulations," Jimmy said. "Now you have evidence."

"But not proof. Now, I know a murder was committed, but I couldn't tell you who killed Harry Mann. And I know somebody hired this asshole to kill us, but he's not going to tell me who."

"So, why did you want to meet here?" Harrison asked.

"I've been studying your father's videotaped will," I explained. "He was a clever man, leaving clues in every frame. I think there must be something important hidden on the *Jonah,* because he had that ship in a bottle."

Tia rubbed her hands together. "What are we looking for?"

"A diary. Maybe a ship's log. Letters. A note." I suggested, "Let's go below and discuss strategy."

We were all settled, more or less comfortably, in the elegant salon. Tia and Ernesto snuggled, side by side, on a leather sofa.

She looked a little nervous, her purse clutched on her lap. And he mirrored her apprehension. "Okay, Adam," she said, "what should we do?"

Feeling like one of those master sleuths, I started talking, outlining all my brilliant deductions. "Graden Porcelli was a clever and manipulative man."

Harrison twitched and muttered, "Spittle foam."

I continued. "According to Harrison, Graden had followed my life story, through the years that I was a cop and into the present. Anyone who has gone to the trouble of watching me in action would realize fairly quickly that I'm not a master sleuth. My crime-solving efforts are usually a combination of bumbling and blind luck."

"Oh, Adam," Alison murmured, "you're being too modest."

"Thank you, my love." I wished that we were all drinking sherry and I was more sophisticated. "So, I wondered, why didn't Graden give me more to go on than a taped will and a dossier on each of the heirs?"

I left the question hanging while I proceeded. "In the tape, I could pretty much figure out all the references to the heirs. Except for one thing. While Graden was talking, he subtly moved a letter opener on his desk to point at his ship in a bottle. This ship. The _Jonah_. The flag at the stern hung upside down, an international signal for distress."

They watched me with rapt attention. God, I was enjoying this moment. I almost hated it to end. "I watched the tape repeatedly. I tried to figure out the subtle messages. Then I realized that Graden made the pointing motion at the precise moment he mentioned a name." I whirled around. "The name was"—everyone held their breath while I paused for dramatic effect—"Jimmy Caruthers."

"What?" The lawyer twitched his walrus mustache. "Surely, you don't suspect me. I'm not even an heir."

"You're the executor of the will. If all the heirs were dead, all the money would be yours. Graden knew that. He knew you couldn't be trusted, that you were dangerous. And you proved him right."

"This is insane." Jimmy raised his hands in appeal to the others. "You can all see that he's crazy, can't you?"

"On the day following the reading of the will," I said, "Sam Leggett was blown to bits by a fairly sophisticated bomb. It was so well disguised as a golf ball that Sam, an expert golfer, didn't suspect that anything was wrong with it."

"But I don't know anything about bombs," Jimmy said.

"And that made it a clever way to divert suspicion toward Whit Parkens, a former demolitions expert. And toward Tia, who had been involved with explosives in her radical youth."

I shrugged. "The key point here is timing, Jimmy. You had known about Graden's will for months and months. You had time to procure such a device and have it perfected."

"My God," Tia said, "I think Adam's right."

I pressed on, delighted with my own brilliance. "After Sam's death, the character of the murders changed. Sam had been attacked directly, but the attempt on Tiger was arranged to look like an accident. This came after Desiree made those threats about suing as the heir of an heir. I suspect that Jimmy's lawyer-like brain kicked into gear, figuring that he could save himself a lot of trouble if the deaths looked like accidents."

Harrison was gaping. "You figured all this out?"

"From listening to your father. He was a smart man, Harrison. Maybe tough and demanding, but smart. He wouldn't have trusted me to deduce all of this. I'll bet that he had it all written out to hand to me with the dossier that was in Jimmy's possession. If Jimmy suspected Graden's plan, he would have gone over that information before he gave it to me. He would have removed the explanation that implicated him."

"Ridiculous," Jimmy blustered. "This is all conjecture. You don't have proof."

Right on schedule, we heard footsteps on the deck overhead. Patty Carmen came down the companionway. With her, looking wan and weathered but able-bodied as he ever could be, was Tiger. In his hand he held a soggy jacket, a grotesque plaid jacket. "Hey, you sons of bitches," he roared. "Look what the Coast Guard brought me! They plucked it out of the flotsam from my boat."

I grinned at the pasty white face of the lawyer. "I think we know who that jacket belongs to. He works for you. And that, Jimmy, is what we call proof."

"That," he corrected me, "is what we call bad taste."

He was still unbowed, but flagging. I had mounted enough information and logic to sink his little ship.

"Tell me this," Jimmy said, mustache twitching wildly, "if Graden was so smart and he suspected me, why did he use me as his attorney? He could have afforded anyone. Why would he use me if he thought I was dangerous?"

"Because you knew the truth, Jimmy. You knew that Graden Porcelli murdered Big Harry Mann." It was a guess, but a good one, because Jimmy Caruthers's next words confirmed it.

"I never thought you could figure it out." Jimmy lowered his head, but not in shame. When he looked up again, he had a gun in his hand. "Too bad that the secret is going to die with you. With all of you."

Not counting Pete, there were seven people in the room. He couldn't kill all of us. My gun was in the back of my waistband. Ernesto was likewise armed. "Give it up, Jimmy. You can't get all of us."

"But I could take out two or three of you. Maybe Alison. Or Tia."

His threat made me realize that all my cleverness had been stupid. This kind of thing never happened to Hercule Poirot. The bad guy was supposed to confess and be led away to life in prison.

Jimmy ordered, "I want your gun, McCleet. Yours too, Ernesto. Place them on the table in front of me. If you try anything, Alison and Tia will die."

Ernesto and I exchanged a glance. Heavily, he rose to his feet, paced toward the table, and laid down his weapon. He was willing to die to protect Tia.

I did the same.

Harrison shuddered slightly and shouted, "Owl shit."

"Thanks for reminding me," Jimmy said. "Harrison? Put your gun on the table."

With a pained expression, he glanced toward me.

"Do it," I told him.

Harrison complied.

I asked, "So, Jimmy, what was the proof that you had on Graden?"

"This." He raised the revolver. "When the corpse of Harry Mann is excavated, investigators will find three bullets. They all came from this gun, which belonged to Graden Porcelli. I also had signed testimony to discredit his alibi about being out of town."

"What are you going to do to us?" Patty Carmen asked.

"I think we'll motor out to sea, and there will be an explosion onboard. All hands will be lost at sea. How tragic!" He gestured with the gun. "All of you, let's go. Into the master suite. I want you out of my way."

As we shuffled forward, a shot rang out. Then another.

Caruthers clutched his chest and blood oozed between his fingers. His eyes registered an instant of shock and dismay as he stared at Tia. She fired again, and Jimmy Caruthers sank to the floor. Dead.

Chapter
Seventeen

In June, Alison and I returned to the offices of Caruthers and Carmichael in Newport, Oregon. The crowd had thinned considerably since the first time we were there. Only the named heirs and significant others were present. A more calm and confident Harrison Porcelli, Whit and Dottie Parkens, Tia Leggett and Ernesto, Theodore Jorgenson and Patty Carmen all waited for Barry Carmichael—law partner of the late Jimmy Caruthers—to stop shuffling papers.

When Carmichael laced his fingers and cleared his throat, everyone leaned forward and scooted toward the edge of their seats. He then spent the next fifteen minutes apologizing for the actions of his late partner, and disavowing any knowledge thereof.

We all nodded our heads impatiently.

Finally, Theodore said, "Jumpin' Jesus, Carmichael. Yer talkin' like a man with a paper asshole on fire."

"I'm sorry, Theodore. It's just that—"

"It's just that yer scared limp that we're gonna sue ya, if you ask me. Just get on with it. And don't call me Theodore. My name is Tiger."

Patty Carmen put her arm around his shoulders and kissed his stubbled cheek. "That's the Tiger I love."

"Yes. Well." Carmichael looked over his bifocals at me. "Mr. McCleet. There is a proviso in the Porcelli will which basically states that you will share in the inheritance if you bring a murderer to justice."

"Right," I said, smiling broadly. "How much do I get?"

"I'm afraid," Carmichael said, "nothing."

My heart sank into my scrotum. "But I caught the murderer."

"Did you?" the lawyer said. "Who?"

I was on my feet. "Are you playing games with me? You know who. Your partner, dammit. Jimmy Caruthers."

Carmichael squirmed uneasily in his chair. "Yes. Well. Though it certainly does appear that Jimmy may possibly have been involved in some nefarious activities, I'm afraid you can't prove that he actually murdered, or conspired to murder, anyone."

"I have proof," I said, on the verge of foaming at the mouth. "Six of the people in this room besides me heard him confess."

"Is that true?" the lawyer asked, scanning the faces of the others.

Patty Carmen said, "I believe his exact words were 'I never thought you could figure it out.'"

"That's right," Tiger said.

Tia, Ernesto, Harrison, and even Alison nodded agreement.

"But he had a gun. He disarmed us and he was going to lock us up and—"

"As I understand it, Mr. McCleet, you had just shot the ears off a man. I think it's reasonable to assume that Jimmy Caruthers feared for his life."

I looked to Tia and Harrison. They were my friends. We had bonded. Surely they would come to my defense.

But they just sat there, mute, smiling politely. I felt like a drowning man about to go under for the third and last time, desperately waving my arms for help as my friends stood on the dry shore, happily waving back.

"His accomplices," I said, "Wiley and Foreman, we turned them over to the cops. They're the proof."

"Both men deny any complicity," Carmichael said. "As their legal counsel, I feel confident that the district attorney will eventually drop all charges for lack of evidence."

I couldn't believe my ears. "Are you shittin' me?"

"I'm quite serious. Furthermore, I am advising Mr. Foreman to sue you for the pain and suffering you inflicted upon him. So you see, even if you were entitled to a share of the inheritance, you'd lose it all in a lengthy and expensive civil trial for which you have no defense. I assure you, my client would win. I'm a very good lawyer."

The little weasel was running a game on me. Paying me would be like admitting that his clients were guilty of, at the very least, conspiracy to commit murder. He was using the additional threat of a civil suit to shut me up. I could feel the blood rising in my face. My head was pounding. My hands trembled. I was about to super-nova.

I shouted, "You little motherfu—"

Alison grabbed my arm and pulled me back into my chair. "Quit while you're ahead, Adam," she whispered. "He's holding all the cards."

It took every ounce of restraint I could muster to keep from imploding as I listened to Barry Carmichael announce that the four remaining heirs would each inherit three point eight million dollars.

I was still reeling from the shock of losing all that money as I staggered out of the law offices.

Alison tried to prop me up with words of encouragement.

"It's okay, Adam," she assured. "You'll be fine. You don't need their money. I love you."

Of course I'd be fine, especially as long as I still had Alison. But I wanted that money really bad. Dammit, I'd earned it. It was going to take me a little while to shake off the disappointment.

In the parking lot, the midday sun beat down relentlessly from a sickening blue sky. The ocean air smelled like rotting fish. And the sea gulls chortled as they circled above my head like harpies come to carry me away.

As I unlocked the door on the passenger side of my car for Alison, the happy little inheritors caught up to us.

Tia spoke first. "Adam, we're really sorry about the money."

"Hey," I said, forcing a smile and trying to sound glib. "Why should you be sorry? You've got four million scoots. Live long and prosper."

"Yip, yip, yippy. Sticky fingers. Put a helmet on that soldier," Harrison exclaimed.

I had to ask. "Why didn't you guys stick up for me in there?"

They all looked a little ashamed, except for Dottie, who looked sheepish. Harrison explained. "Your investigation uncovered some embarrassing family skeletons."

"Literally," Ernesto added.

"A criminal trial," Harrison continued, "would bring all of that out into public view. My parents, for all their foibles, have always been respected, even revered as pioneers of this region."

"You understand, don't you, Adam?" Tia said.

I tried to climb back onto the high road. "Of course," I said. Oddly, I did understand. I still felt as though someone had reached up my butt, pulled out my large intestine, and danced on it, but I understood.

"Hell, Adam," Whit said. "You can have my share."

Before I could graciously accept, Dottie slapped him on the arm, "Oh, no, you don't, Whit Parkens. That money is for our future."

"Sheep, huh?"

"Not completely," Whit said. "Harrison and I are going to buy the Salmon King plant here in Newport. He knows the business and I know the process. We'll be good partners."

"That's wonderful," Alison said. "But what about the sheep ranch?"

"Don't worry about that," Whit said. "There'll be enough money left over for Dottie to buy all the sheep and mobile homes she can handle."

Tia and Ernesto were holding hands. "You two look like a couple," I said. "What are your plans?"

"We are going on a cruise," Ernesto said. The couple looked lovingly at each other.

"A honeymoon?" Alison asked.

"You got it, hon," Patty Carmen said. "Tiger is going to buy the _Jonah_ and these two love birds are going to help us sail it to Long Beach."

Oil derricks and shipyards. An unusual choice of honeymoon spots, I thought. "Why Long Beach?"

"Tiger's going to spend a little time at the Betty Ford Clinic while Tia and Ernesto stock up on schoolbooks and medical supplies. Then it's off to El Salvador." She snapped her fingers like castanets.

"That's if I don't bump into Liz Taylor," Tiger said. "I hear she's lookin' for another husband."

Patty Carmen gave him a shove. "You old fart."

I looked at Tia and Ernesto. "Isn't El Salvador a little dangerous for you two?"

"It's a new government," she said. "We'll be okay."

Ernesto added, "It is where we can do the greatest good."

"Well," I said, opening the car door for Alison, "it sounds like you've all got your work cut out for you. Drop us a line sometime."

"Yo, ho. Hold my skunk, baby. I feel a song coming on."

Harrison shook his head and said, "What about the sculpture for the Porcelli family plot?"

I was so busy swimming in self-pity that I'd forgotten all about the stone. "I had it trucked down three days ago. It should be in place by now."

"Let's all go have a look," Patty Carmen said. "I'm eager to see if you're as good a sculptor as Alison says."

I tried to beg off. The collective happiness of the heirs was making me ill. But, much like the rest of my life, I had no control. Ten minutes later we were all walking arm in arm through the cemetery.

As we came over the top of a small rise, they caught their first glimpse of the six-foot-by-four-foot slab of pink granite standing on edge at the family plot. We were still too far away to make out the detail in the raised relief carving on its face.

"Wow," Whit exclaimed. "That's big. How'd you finish it so fast, Adam?"

"I was inspired." I decided not to tell them about the eight student assistants from the art school at Portland State University who, under my close supervision, did most of the work.

When we were within ten feet of the stone, Tia began to laugh. Then Patty Carmen joined in.

At first I thought Harrison looked insulted. But his frown transformed into a smile. Soon everybody was howling.

I wasn't exactly sure what part of the sculpture they found more amusing. They might have been laughing at the deeply cut mural of seven monkeys hanging from the branches of a leafy tree, their arms outstretched toward an open chest spilling over with treasure beneath them. But my favorite part was the inscription at the base, from Lavater's *Aphorisms on Man,* "Say not you know another entirely, till you have divided an inheritance with him."

"Adam, it's perfect," Harrison said.

"Wait till you see my bill."